Time Cadets
The Texas Connection

Rich Kerner

02132

This is a work of fiction. Names, characters, businesses, places, events, locales, and incidents are either the products of the author's imagination or used in a fictitious manner. Any resemblance to actual persons, living or dead, or actual events is intentional to provide context for the fiction or purely coincidental.

To Ellen, Liv and George

CONTENTS

ACKNOWLEDGMENTS

Websites:
Mcadams.posc.mu.edu
www.kenrahn.com
jfkassassination.net
www.jfk.org
harveyandlee.net
www.archives.gov
jfklibrary.org

PROLOGUE

Dark clouds were gathering overhead, steadily amassing the rain which, when it finally succumbed to the pull of gravity, would provide the welcome, albeit brief respite to the humidity that had been rising through the summer and had maintained its height unseasonably into the autumn. The breaking of the humidity would bring with it the first signs of the promise of cooler weather. Leaves would begin to turn, waving goodbye to summer and hello to winter as they began the annual separation process with their seasonal host. Whilst the inhabitants welcomed the end to humid, uncomfortable nights, it was tempered with a reluctant acceptance of the inevitable hard winter that lay ahead.

Purposefully the man strode through the sun-bleached grass, faster than seemed sensible in the still searing heat of the day. Fedora perched back on his head and long tailed coat flowing behind him, both giving support to the illusion of speed. His destination was a small shack, isolated in the middle of acres of farmland, surrounded by densely populated trees, indigenous to the locality. Abandoned machinery lay dotted amongst dead wood, discarded by the trees as unwanted limbs, which no longer served any use. The machinery, old and weather beaten, ravaged by years of hard winters and oppressive summers.

The man knocked on the wooden door three times with a sense of urgency. There was no obvious evidence from the surroundings that the property was, or had recently, been occupied. However, a voice emanated from within, delivering a succinct instruction to enter. The man pushed hard on the door and it opened noisily throwing dust up from the floorboards where it had settled over the years undisturbed by the absence of regular footfall. The man didn't need to question how someone could be occupying the space without disturbing or leaving any obvious impression on the surrounding area, because he knew who was inside, and how they got there.

1 TOM

"Just a minute," Tom shouted out in frustration, "I'm just in the middle of something".

"You've got five minutes, and then it is bed. No excuses." his mother responded, exasperated with having the same fight night after night. It wasn't that Tom was a difficult child, in fact, compared to most thirteen-year-old boys, Tom was a veritable angel. There was nothing extraordinary about him either, he was an average child, with average needs and one of those needs was to be left alone when he was preoccupied. "That's it, time's up. Off to bed now."

Tom realised he had pushed his luck far enough and that if he wanted to stand any chance of screen time tomorrow, he would have to log off and get to bed before the sound of his mother's footsteps pounded on the stairs and her shrill voice started to reverberate around his room. A room which Tom regarded as his only sanctuary. A room where the walls were adorned with Sci-Fi posters ripped from magazines which he had saved his meagre pocket money to buy. Barely furnished with just a bed and desk, provided by his parents on the premise of completing homework but which, in reality, he spent most of his time sat at watching videos on YouTube.

Tom logged off and closed the lid of his laptop, Kylo Ren staring back at him. He had an affinity with the Star Wars character, but he was yet to understand why.

Tom wandered off to the bathroom and stood and stared at himself in the mirror. Unremarkable, fair hair cascading around a round face, punctuated with freckles and piercing blue eyes. He hated his appearance. It was unlike anybody else in the family, but of course that was to be expected. He was longing for the summer when he could at least be released from the overbearing restrictions of school policy and style his hair similar to that of his YouTube hero. "May be add a little colour," he thought. Only one day to go and the school could no longer dictate the way he should look. Until then he would have to live with it. He washed up, brushed his teeth, and headed back to his room. Sleep would not come quickly, it never did. There was too much occupying his mind. He was desperate to retain memories of his past whilst trying to accommodate rising concerns in the present and anxiety for his future. All of that and the effects of going through puberty as well. Nonetheless, he made his way to bed, pulled up the covers and closed his eyes in the vain hope of a quick transition in to sleep.

+++

Tom woke with a start. As he did so he reached over to check the time on his phone. It was twelve am. He cursed the fact that he was now awake and would struggle once again to get to sleep. It had taken him an hour and fifteen minutes the first time around. The door to his room was ajar and the landing light was still on, forcing a slither of light in to the room and causing long shadows to form, extending along the room and appearing to congregate in a mass of dark, blackness at the foot of his bed. He had only been asleep for an hour, but it had been enough to make him particularly drowsy and with his imagination peaked it wasn't long before those shadows were starting to take on a life of their own. As Tom began to drift back into a place half way between consciousness and sleep, the shadows slowly began to rise and dance, at first content to satisfy themselves with their own company, swaying, dipping and stretching from the floor to the ceiling. As the movement became more rapid, so the shape and intention of the shadows became more menacing. Swirling, jutting, fighting with each other to gain position in the room. In an instance they stopped, turned, facing Tom as he dozed. Without warning and in a motion of solidarity the shadows threw themselves towards Tom as if to engulf him in their darkness and take him in to their world. A sudden noise brought Tom out of his trance like state and back to reality. It was at this point that he realised he had received a message in his social media group. Tom opened his phone and read the message. As he did so a smile began to cross his face. It was moments like this that reassured him that not all was lost and he was not alone. He rose from his bed with the intention of closing the door, however as he approached it he heard his parents downstairs. It was not unusual for them to be awake at that time of night but it was unusual for them to be talking with raised voices. He knew without hearing that they would be discussing him.

It wasn't the first time and wouldn't be the last. They had done their best to make him feel like one of the family, but he had always known in his heart of hearts that he didn't quite fit in. It wasn't just the fair hair that set him apart, it was the way people reacted to him. Visitors often gave a mere passing acknowledgement; his brother and sister were much closer to each other than they were to him; birthdays were always awkward affairs, as if cheer and joy were being forced on all those present. Tom listened at the door for a few minutes. Enough time to hear that they were worried about him and that they didn't know what was for the best. Tom decided that not hearing anymore was his best option. He closed the door and returned to his bed. The shadows had gone, but so had the smile. Tom rolled over and closed his eyes.

+++

What appeared to be an all too brief sleep was disrupted by the clock radio blaring out the breakfast show, accompanied by the penetrating voice of his mother cutting through the morning bustle like a knife, from the kitchen below shouting instructions to get dressed. Tom rose, wiping the sleep from his eyes. He swung his legs over the side of the bed without energy or purpose, pausing briefly to contemplate the day ahead. Turning off the clock radio which had started to play 'You bring me sunshine' the irony not lost on Tom as outside the rain was lashing against his window. This did nothing to improve his mood nor his outlook on the day ahead. Tom finally left his bed and got ready for his last day at school before the summer holidays.

Tom entered the kitchen, his mother standing with her back to the door, fussing over some sausages sizzling in a pan on the stove. They weren't for him of course, they were undoubtedly for his brother, who apparently was a growing lad. Tom was already taller, even though he was two years younger than his brother. Another sign of the obvious differences between him and his siblings. His mother and father were not particularly tall either. It was not unusual of course, children were often taller than their parents and younger siblings tended to be taller, but there was a stark difference already, and at only thirteen, he expected another few years of growing ahead.

"Hurry up, sit down and eat, you're already running late" his mother exclaimed. Tom wanted to reply sarcastically but he bit his lip, he didn't want to start another day with an argument. It was unfair and he felt deep down his mother knew it as well, but that wouldn't change things and he wanted an easy life. The summer holidays were about to start and, as with previous years, he would spend most days out the house, only returning for meals and bed, so he just needed to get through today. Tom helped himself to cereal and orange juice, packed his bag and left the house for school.

Tom walked down the road toward the bus stop with his coat pulled tightly around him and hood pulled down over his face. Although the rain had eased off, he still needed protection from the elements. As he turned the corner, a shout bellowed out "oi, you look a right muppet in that hood". Although the hood blocked Tom's view of the source of the insult, he recognised the familiar uncompromising voice of his best friend, Jake. Jake lived in the street along from him and met him every morning on the short walk to the school bus. Jake was marginally taller than Tom but vastly thinner, a consequence of malnutrition at a young age and a level of hyperactivity that ensured a continuing absence of weight gain. Deep brown eyes and short brown hair punctuating a pallid face, combined with the slender build, created an appearance of frailty and ill health. However, Jake was physically strong and could hold his own in most situations. A number of which had already tested his mental and physical resolve.

Jake jumped down off the wall and placed a playful punch on Tom's arm. Despite the weather, seeing his friends always lightened his mood and Tom reciprocated by barging Jake towards a bush at the side of the road. Jake stumbled but remained upright and restored himself to Tom's side. "Why you hiding?" Jake asked.

"I'm not, just don't want to get my face wet. It is raining you know".

"I had noticed. Don't bother me though. I like it".

"You're just weird". Both boys laughed as they approached the bus stop.

It was true that Jake was a socially awkward boy, but rather than let it affect him, he often wore it as a badge of honour. Seemed to be pleased to get the attention that was often missing in his home life. He was popular at school, but in a jester kind of way, the class clown as Mrs Hibberd put it. Academically he wasn't going to be in the top class, and he had resigned himself to this restricted ambition, preferring instead to focus on making his class mates laugh. The problem was they were not always laughing with him. With Tom it was different of course, as it was with the rest of their little group. They were as tight as ever and there was no chance any of them feeling conspicuous or self-conscious when they were together. They had built up a strong friendship over the last few years based on mutual feelings of isolation and rejection, which were in some cases baseless to outside observers, but all too real in their own minds. Ironically that sense of not belonging and loneliness had brought them together, like a family they felt they had never had.

The bus drew up to the stop and Tom and Jake got on and took up their usual seats at the front of the bus. The back of the bus was reserved for the older, cooler kids and as year nine kids, Tom and Jake knew their place. "See the football last night?" Tom asked.

"Nah, still don't have Sky and couldn't be bothered to try and stream it. You?"

"Yep, about the only good thing about being at home. Rubbish game though, expect we won't win anything again this year".

The boys stared through the rain-soaked window at the uninspiring view of drab houses, people fighting with umbrellas and cars competing with each other to gain position as they attempted to wriggle their way through the rush-hour traffic, evidently frustrated at the school bus with its numerous stops on the way to the school.

"Tom?"

"Yes" Tom replied.

"What happened to your parents, you never really told me". Jake wasn't usually reserved and was more than happy to pursue a line of enquiry most others would consider sensitive or taboo, but on this topic, he had taken the unusual approach to remain discrete. Until now that is.

"Not much to say really," was Tom's default position on the matter.

Jake had known Tom since primary school and had only discovered the fact that Tom's parents had passed away by accident when they were asked to put together a simple family tree for the end of year presentation in year seven. At the time and in the subsequent two years, the subject had not been raised again, partly because, in a moment of uncharacteristically acute awareness Jake had realised it was something that pained Tom and was therefore a matter best left alone. Again, until now that is! They were both two years older and with the transition to secondary school, had matured sufficiently to broach the subject of death. "So, do you know what happened?" Tom turned and looked at his friend. He had recognised that Jake had respected his privacy over the last couple of years and realised that avoiding the question now would be insensitive to his friend's compassion and patience. He noted the desperate look in his friend's face as if Jake had been bottling the question up for those two years.

"I honestly don't know all the details. Car crash I was told. I had been left with my Aunty who was babysitting me. I think I was one or two. As the story goes, she got worried when they hadn't returned from a meal, the first night out they had arranged since I had been born or something like that. Anyway, she called her parents who must have rang around, including the hospitals. They turned up at the door having found out that there had been

7

a huge pile up on the motorway. They didn't know then, but later found out that a lorry had lost control and ploughed straight in to my parents' car. Died straight away apparently."

"Oh God, sorry mate."

"Not your fault!" Tom smirking, attempted to diffuse the awkward moment.

"No, well, I mean, well sorry anyway."

"To be fair I was too young to really know them, but ever since I found out, I have wondered what they were like and whether I would be happier than I am now."

Tom slouched back in the seat and his mind regressed back to when his parents were alive, striving to extract some sort of memory, other than the events of that fateful night. He was able to conjure up a fuzzy image, one he had been successful in recollecting on a number of previous occasions. Two smiling faces peering over the side of a cot, the female shaking some sort of fluffy toy. The appearances were not always the same, neither the faces nor the toy, but the feeling the memory evoked was always the same. That mixture of joy and sadness.

"I reckon they would want you to be happy."

"Yep I know," responded Tom, trying to hide his annoyance at the obvious observation. "It's not as easy as that. Anyway, what lesson we got first?" Tom knew perfectly well what his lesson plan was, but he needed to divert the conversation. Jake equally welcomed the distraction and opened his bag, ruffling through his belongings until he finally retrieved his lesson plan, which had suffered from being at the bottom of his bag for the whole term, and was barely legible through the creases and food stains.

"After Reg its Maths then after break, English. Didn't Mrs Hibberd say after lunch it was free until home time at three?" Jake added.

"That's right. Last day of term before the summer."

"Can't come quickly enough," Jake commented.

The bus drew up to the school gates and the boys alighted first, one of the benefits of sitting at the front of the bus. As they passed through the front doors, the blue paint fading and pealing at the extremities, their friend Michael joined them. "Alright Michael?" Jake asked. He didn't expect to get much of a response as Michael was not one for idle conversation but persevered anyway. "Looking forward to the summer?"

Michael nodded, "Guess so."

"Any plans?" Jake continued.

"Not since you asked me yesterday!" Michael retorted, clearly irritated by the unwanted attention. Jake laughed, he knew he wouldn't get an answer, so took the opportunity to have a little fun at his friend's expense instead. The bell went signalling the start of registration and the end of Michael's torment, for now at any rate.

"Ding, ding. End of round two," Jake mocked as he sloped off to his class and left Michael and Tom to theirs.

"I don't know why you are still friends with that idiot," came a familiar voice from behind them. Tom and Michael turned in unison and faced Lucy, who looked past them towards Jake as he disappeared around the corner, but not before he had saluted in her direction with a knowing wink.

"Come on, before Miss gets here and we have bigger problems to deal with," Tom strode forward attempting to diffuse another tense encounter.

Throwing his bag down on his desk, Tom took his seat. Lucy placed herself directly behind him, whilst Michael took up his usual seat at the back of the class. Mrs Hibberd entered the room, "Books open, page fifty-six please."

Lucy leant forward and whispered to Tom, "Did you get my message last night?" Tom smiled. Lucy regained her seat, before Mrs Hibberd caught her. Blessed with striking long ginger hair and fair complexion, punctuated with freckles, Lucy was attractive but not in a conventional sense. Reluctant to conform, out of school she would rather wear boy's clothes and hang around with the lads rather than socialise with her female classmates. Whilst she enjoyed school and was academically bright, she despised the restrictions of the school rules and in particular the mandatory uniform requirements which limited her to wearing a navy-blue skirt and jumper, a far cry from her favoured camo trousers and hoodie. School also did not challenge her sufficiently to keep her engaged and as the lesson progressed, Lucy found herself drifting off in to a daydream.

+++

The lessons leading up to lunch had taken an eternity and Tom was convinced that the clock had been moving backwards at one point. The bell had finally gone indicating lunch and Tom vacated his chair, grabbed his bag and together with Lucy and Michael, they made their way to the dining hall. As year nine students they were on the first sitting and Jake was already situated in their usual spot.

"Keeping the space as usual. What took you so long?" Nobody responded and Jake didn't expect one, he was happy revelling in the knowledge that he had beaten them to lunch again, albeit in a race that truth be known, only had one competitor. The three of them took their seats next to and opposite Jake and recovered their lunch boxes from their bags. None of them had what would be considered a gourmet lunch, but cheese and ham sandwiches and packets of crisps were satisfactory enough.

"So, what are we going to do this summer?" Lucy put the question to the group.

"Trip to the Seychelles?" Jake replied.

Lucy rolled her eyes, "Be serious for once will you. I can't bear the thought of starting the holiday without any kind of plan."

"What did you have in mind?" Tom interjected.

"I don't know, some kind of adventure would be great."

"Arctic or Antarctic?" Jake offered.

"Either, as long as you are at the other," Lucy retorted.

"What about checking out the old house on the hill?" Michael volunteered. It was not clear whether it was the suggestion, or the fact that Michael had spoken without being significantly prompted, but there was an uncomfortable silence for several seconds before Jake piped up.

"Awesome."

"That's what you have to say? "Awesome", you do remember the stories, I suppose?" Lucy exclaimed.

"Yep, but that's exactly what they are, just stories," Jake answered.

"Well I for one, do not take them lightly and I am not sure it was the adventure I was hoping for."

Tom appeared to be entertaining the idea, "What was the last one we heard? Something about the ghost of a crazy old man that lived in the house for over a hundred years. Seems unlikely." He continued, "Nobody would hang around this town for that long." Everyone laughed, other than Michael.

"It was just a suggestion," Michael implored.

"Sorry Mike, I was just kidding. It sounds like it could be cool," Tom said trying to appease his friend.

"Whatcha talkin' about?" The friends' conversation was suddenly interrupted. "Well? Anyone gonna fess up?"

"It's got nothing to do with you," Michael responded curtly.

"If youse lot don't tell me, I'll blab to Mum when we get home."

"Say what you want, she's not my Mum anyway and you are not my sister." Michael was clearly irritated by the interruption, especially as it was his adopted sister. Rhianna was not much older but as her birthdate fell in September, she was in the year above the rest of them, and lorded it over Michael, using any opportunity to remind him that she was his elder sister.

"If you don't cut me in, I'll make sure you spend the summer in your room," Rhianna threatened.

"Don't make me laugh, you are about as popular as me at home," Michael said getting increasingly agitated.

"Chill brother, I'm just messing with ya." Rhianna grabbed a crisp from Michael's packet before rustling his hair and wandering off.

Jake's eyes followed her as she walked back to her friends, briskly averting them when she turned to face their table again as she and her friends fell into a bout of giggles reacting to something she shared with them. "Put your tongue back in," Lucy scolded.

"Jealous?" teased Jake.

"No, just bored of you drooling over her, she is way out of your league." Rhianna was undoubtedly attractive, tall, slim with a smooth, dark complexion which contradicted that of her 'brother' who was pasty in comparison. Both incongruous with the rest of their family. Jake had fancied her for a long time and hadn't been afraid to show it. He did accept she was out of his league though.

Tom steered the conversation back to the plan for the summer, "So, when are we going then?"

"No point in delaying. Let's go tomorrow," Jake suggested.

"Fine," Lucy conceded, "but can we make sure we are prepared. We don't know what to expect once we get in."

"We can draw up a list of provisions and sort it out tonight," Tom suggested. "I'll start it and send around on the group chat."

"Hands in," Jake blurted as he extended his arm forward, palms down.

"Got to get back to class."

"Yeah me too."

"Running late."

"Must go." The rest of them muttered in unison as they got up hurriedly to leave, intentionally ignoring Jake's awkward call to arms.

Jake remained seated as the others left, calling out behind them "Hey, guys, don't leave me hanging."

"Laters," Tom shouted back.

+++

The bell sounded for the last time before the summer. Tom immediately rose from his seat, filled with a mixture of relief and excitement. Unfortunately, it was short-lived as Mrs Hibberd reminded the class that the bell was for her not the kids. "But have a lovely summer all," she continued with a broad smile on her face. The smile also came back to Tom's face as he grabbed his bag and joined the mass exodus from the classroom. The summer had officially begun.

The friends met up at the school entrance for one final time as year nine students. Jake stood peering through the gate, his fists clenching and shaking the bars as he mockingly screamed "Let me out of here. So, this is what escaping from prison is like," he added as he re-joined his friends walking towards the bus which would take them away from school and the first step on to the summer holidays and temporary freedom.

2 THE OLD MAN

The first day of summer did not bring with it an uplift in the weather as the rain continued to beat against the outside of the window in Tom's room. The difference was that in comparison to the weather, Tom's disposition was much brighter. Focusing on the break from school and break from his adoptive family, Tom was fully of excitement and anticipation.

The friends had exchanged messages the previous night and had agreed on a course of action which would take them from the mundane to the exotic, or so they hoped. Each had a job to do in preparation, each a cog in the wheel of the master plan. Tom's role was to prepare a plan to gain access to the old building and try and obtain a copy of the property's layout. This would require some research, given the property had stood derelict and abandoned for as long as Tom or his friends could remember. Access would also be challenging as the approach to the house was guarded by a fence which surrounded all sides, and which was seven-foot-tall, topped by barbed wire. Tom had decided that the first step would be to undertake some reconnaissance work. Jake had insisted that he accompany

Tom on this errand, and he had reluctantly agreed on the promise that Jake remain discrete during the entire episode. Of course, Tom was under no illusion that Jake would not break this promise the moment they left the house and he fully expected to be reminding him of the need for discretion as soon as he saw him. At that very moment the doorbell rang and Tom's moment of quiet contemplation was interrupted by Jake's arrival.

Tom made his way down the stairs, rucksack hanging off his shoulder, phone in hand. He acknowledged Jake with the minimum of fanfare, typical for boys of that age. "Alright?"

"Yeah you?" came the response. Formalities over, it was time for business. Tom and Jake left the house without notifying anyone, largely because as far as Tom was concerned, there would be very little interest. He tended to come and go as he pleased. As predicted however, Jake was less than subtle when, not long after closing the door behind them, he blurted "So did you tell anyone we were going to the old place?"

"As discussed, Jake," Tom responded in a rather condescending way, "we should keep it to ourselves and not announce it to the world."

Jake turned around to check that he had closed the door and there was no one overhearing their conversation, before turning back to Tom. "No-one can hear us."

"Yeah, well you never know who is lurking behind curtains."

Jake turned again, paranoia increasing with every word. In his heightened state of awareness, he could have sworn that he saw the curtains of Tom's front room twitch. He almost brought this to Tom's attention but convinced himself that it was just a trick of the light and nobody was watching or listening. Also, he did not want to admit to Tom that he may be right, and that Jake's obvious lack of discretion was putting the whole adventure at risk.

The curtain twitch that Jake had assumed was merely a trick of the light turned in to a more obvious movement seconds later as the curtain pulled back and revealed the face of Tom's mother. Her face stern and determined, unseen, she watched as the boys walked out of view. She did not have a threatening appearance, her blonde hair was pulled back in to a tight ponytail, framing her rounded face which was without any make up but yet showed few obvious signs of her age. She could have passed as Tom's older sister rather than his mother; such was her flattering appearance. Something Jake himself had remarked upon, although in not so respectful terms. On this occasion however, there was a steely edge to her look, which exposed a deeper feature of her personality, one which had not been obvious to Tom, or for that matter the rest of the family. She was harbouring a dark secret, which she sensed was about to be become exposed and which would irreversibly alter the family's future, present and past.

+++

The sun had finally made an appearance for the summer, breaking through the grey clouds which had until recently carried an endless procession of rain. The heat of the sun fought against the damp earth, resulting in a pungent odour emanating from the asphalt and concrete surrounds. The English summer had truly arrived.

Jake had been quiet since leaving the house which had not gone unnoticed. Tom finally broke the silence, "So I was thinking we would take a walk past the house first and see if there was any security today."

The property had previously been subject to a large number of intrusions, largely of a similar nature to the one being proposed by Tom and his friends, and therefore from time to time, external security consultants had been drafted in to secure the property. It was not very often, the cost clearly too high for whoever still owned the property, but it was best to check rather than embarking on the adventure and finding it ending in an early withdrawal, or at worst a trip to the local constabulary. This opportunity for excitement and adventure which rarely presented itself if one remained on the right side of the law, needed careful planning and the avoidance of any schoolboy errors.

"Sounds good," Jake replied. "Shall we take photos on this run or do you want to take a follow up run at it?" he added.

"I think probably leave it to just walking past first, just in case," suggested Tom. "We have plenty of time and nobody is going to be that interested and wonder why we have walked past several times," he continued.

"Affirmative," Jake said suddenly and unexpectedly getting in to some kind of military television character, which caused Tom to screw his face up and slowly shake his head in exasperation. "We could always say we are doing a school project," offered up Jake.

Tom reacted rather too quickly and harshly, "Yes, if we weren't actually on summer holidays." "Oh, good point," Jake acknowledged sheepishly.

They turned the corner and the old structure came in to view. It stood imposing in its surroundings as the rest of the street had long since fallen into disrepair and been demolished, leaving the three-storey house as the solitary building, rising out of a barren land like a lighthouse on a coastal islet. It was the source of much speculation locally as to why the whole area had not been razed and a supermarket or housing estate sprung up in its place, similar to many other parts of the borough. It appeared this lonely, abandoned dwelling was under the protection of a higher force which was preventing it from succumbing to the increasing modernisation of the neighbourhood.

"I wonder who owns it," Tom uttered.

"Council probably," Jake surmised. "Wouldn't be

surprised if some developer gets his hands on it soon though. Can't stay like this forever."

Tom contemplated this further, "It has so far. Been like this for years. Old Mac said it was like it when he was a boy and he must be eighty by now." Old Mac was the current owner of the local corner shop and was the last remaining member of a family which had been resident in the local area for centuries. His family had seen or been part of everything that had happened in the area since seventeen sixty, apparently, or so the multitude of stories Old Mac told, led you to believe.

"I bet Old Mac is the old man that is rumoured to be haunting the house," Jake chortled.

"Maybe his old, old man," Tom joined in. The boys shared a moment of amusement which hid their real feelings of trepidation as they made their way closer to the metal fence obscuring the house to the outside world. "So, keep a close eye and see if you can see anybody on the site," Tom instructed his friend. "Doesn't look like anybody is here but they may be circling round."

Jake tried in vain to remain discrete as instructed but was straining his neck in the direction of the building and its perimeter to identify any disturbance which would suggest an onsite presence. "All clear," he announced as they reached the end of the road.

"Right let's double-back and take some selfies with the house behind us," suggested Tom. Jake duly obliged as the friends posed awkwardly, aiming the camera phone past them towards the property. Jake couldn't help pulling some unflattering faces, but the job was done, and they decided they had enough and headed back home to take a look at the fruits of their labour, but not before taking a short diversion to see Old Mac.

+++

"Morning fellas, school holidays is it? Or are you just

truanting again Jake?" Old Mac pretty much knew everyone in the town, and those that he didn't he knew someone who did, and it never took long for him to become acquainted.

"Yep school holidays," Jake replied. Jake came straight to the point of their visit, "Mac, what do you know about the old house on the hill?"

"What don't I know," came Old Mac's standard response. "When I was at school, not the posh school that you guys go to now of course, but a small schoolhouse down the bottom of the high street, I used to walk past it every day. It belonged to a fairly well-to-do family back then, the sort who have saucers and spoons with their cup of tea." Old Mac had been standing behind the counter attending to customers when the boys had arrived, however he had moved to perch himself on a stool and the boys took this as a sign that they were in for the long haul. "Long row of town houses surrounded it, they've all gone now, after being left abandoned for so many years after the stories started."

Tom's ears pricked up, "Which stories are those?"

"Well, over the years they have changed a bit and rolled into each other as the locals gossip too much." Tom noted the irony, but let it go as he was keen to understand more. "It all started after the War, apparently. The Dad had served in the army but unfortunately hadn't survived. Story goes he came to a nasty end, but the details vary depending on who is telling it. Needless to say, he wasn't in one piece. Anyway, the wife and kids were naturally upset and never really recovered from the grief. The wife in particular died shortly after, they say of a broken heart. The two kids remained in the house and were cared for by what was thought to be their Aunts and Uncles. They continued to be seen out and about, kids went to school, and they all went to church regular as clockwork on a Sunday, but that was it. They kept themselves very much to themselves.

19

Never spoke to anyone outside the family and never came along to neighbourhood gatherings – and there were lots more back then, not like now where people don't tend to get together with their neighbours or the local community anymore. Crying shame if you ask me."

Tom sensed Old Mac may have been about to veer off track, "So what happened at the house?" Tom enquired, endeavouring to steer Old Mac back to the point in hand.

"Well, rumours started of some rather strange goings on. Lots of different 'family members' came and went." Old Mac used his fingers to indicate speech marks, which Tom and Jake took to mean that they were not actually family members. "Reports of bright lights at the upstairs windows and noises, odd noises generating from inside, as if some kind of experiments were being undertaken. But the nail in the coffin for a lot of those living in the adjacent houses was the comings and goings of particular 'family members." He used his fingers again.

"You mean the dead Dad," suggested Jake, uncharacteristically perceptive.

"Yes, indeed, and the departed mother," Old Mac confirmed. "Lots of talk of sightings, at all times of the day and night. Too much for some and slowly the neighbours all left, houses not sold, just up and left, leaving empty properties."

"It all sounds a bit odd," Tom suggested after a moment or two of quiet contemplation.

"Odd goings on indeed," confirmed Old Mac.

"No, I mean why move away, just because of some strange things happening. Didn't anyone try to get to the bottom of it?"

"Well as I said, the family weren't really approachable and at first the neighbours wanted to give them some space to grieve. The longer it went of course the more difficult it became to do anything. Until," Old Mac paused.

"Until what?" Jake interjected.

"Until, a relative of one of the neighbours decided to take it upon himself to investigate."

"What happened?" Tom pushed.

"After he heard the stories from his family, he decided it was all nonsense, and as you say, he decided he wanted to get to the bottom of it. He went over to the house and knocked on the door."

"And", Jake jumped in, impatience growing.

"The door opened, and the gentleman entered."

"Yes", Tom added.

"The door closed behind him.

"And then", Jake becoming exasperated.

"That's it", Old Mac concluded.

"What do you mean that's it?" the boys cried in unison.

"Nothing was ever heard of him again," Old Mac added.

"But didn't his family go looking?" Tom asked.

"Yes, after a couple of hours when he hadn't returned, they ventured over and knocked on the door. The chap who answered said that they had not received any visitors that day, that no-one had come to the house. They tried to get the police involved but there was very little to go on and to be honest, after the war, the police had other things to prioritise rather than missing persons."

"Wow," Jake exclaimed.

"So, you see, there was more to fear than just lights, noises and ghostly images. The locals feared for their lives. That is enough to leave without trying to sell your house. To be fair, given the stories, the prices of the properties had pretty much hit rock bottom anyway."

"Who owns the property now?" probed Tom.

"I heard it was still owned by the family. Put in to Trust for future generations, potentially forever," Old Mac answered hesitantly.

"That would explain why it is still standing then," Jake stated.

"Well I am not sure that helps us much," Tom declared.

21

"Why all the questions anyway?" Old Mac realising there was an ulterior motive for the line of questioning.

"Oh no reason, just interested," Jake proffered.

"I hope you are not considering something foolish like trying to get inside. There is too much which is unknown about what lies within, not to mention it is probably unsafe. Who knows what the state of it is inside, including the floorboards and rotting roof. Could collapse at any moment."

The boys realised that it was time to leave before they aroused any further suspicion. "Of course not. Wouldn't be that stupid," Jake responded nervously. "Must dash, late for lunch!"

The boys exited the shop, the bell located above the door ringing out an appropriately ghoulish ding as they did so.

"So, what d'ya reckon?" Jake asked once they were out of earshot of the old man.

"Well I don't believe any of it," Tom responded with a hint of doubt noticeable in his voice. "I mean I just can't get over why nobody seems to have found out what happened and why. I am sure it is all nonsense," attempting to reassure himself unsuccessfully.

"I agree," stated Jake feebly.

"So, we are still on?" enquired Tom.

"Of course," Jake responded unconvincingly. "Can't wait."

The boys meandered back to Tom's house in silence, pre-occupied with the stories they had heard, their minds wandering and imaginations running wild with possibilities of what might lie behind the closed doors of the old house.

+++

Tom's house was empty when the boys returned from their reconnaissance exercise. Tom imagined that the rest of the family had decided to go for a family day out together given it was the summer holidays. Needless to say, he had not been invited. It didn't really bother him anymore, but it always triggered a sense of wanting, or belonging which he was missing in his life. As best as he tried to hide it, those close to him were acutely aware, even Jake. "Hey, nice one pal, house to ourselves," Jake announced.

"Great, let's get something to eat," Tom replied.

The boys searched the kitchen for sustenance after their emotionally exhausting morning. Deciding on peanut butter and jam sandwiches, they sat down to consider their next steps. Tom gathered up his laptop from his room and placed it on the kitchen table between them as they ate. He hooked up his phone and accessed the pictures they had taken that morning. They scrolled through the pictures one by one trying to ignore the distraction of Jake's appearance which evolved through the various photos culminating in a somewhat unsightly gurning.

"Well looks pretty quiet," Jake observed, drawing no attention to his peculiar faces.

"Yes," Tom agreed. "We need to find the best way through the fencing." The boys continued to look through each photo one by one, focusing on the fencing to identify a possible entry point. Jake was slightly preoccupied with his sandwich but raised his head to view the photo currently appearing on the laptop screen. Tom scrolled to the next one, but Jake spoke up "Hold on, just go back to that one."

Tom hit the back button, "What is it? Have you seen a way in?"

Jake's line of sight had been drawn to the building itself rather than the outer perimeter fencing. "Just zoom in on the house for a minute," he requested.

"What, what is it?" Tom enquired.

"I'm not sure, zoom a bit more."

Tom's heart started to beat faster, he wasn't sure why,

maybe it was the stories he had heard that morning, maybe it was the exciting adventure on the horizon, but something was causing him to become agitated and nervous. "What are you looking at?"

Jake raised his hand toward the screen, "There!" he exclaimed, his finger pointed in the direction of the upper portion of the photo, now blurry from having been zoomed in on several times.

"I don't see anything," Tom admitted.

"There, in the top window, I swear, I swear it is," Jake stuttered, clearly affected by what he had spotted.

At that moment, Tom jumped back almost falling from his stool. As he did so he knocked his plate from the table which had the remains of his sandwich. The plate and sandwich travelled through the air. Everything seemed to move in to slow motion as Tom battled to steady himself on the stool and the plate and sandwich continued on towards the stone floor beneath them. Time itself appeared to slow down. In all this melee, Tom continued to stare at the screen in front of him and in particular on the image which had led to Jake's hysteria. There staring at them from the screen was the figure of an old man.

3 THE OLD HOUSE

"I don't see it," Lucy said, squinting at the blurry imagine in front of her.

"Look there, that is definitely the figure of an old man," Tom pointed out persuasively.

"Could be anything. Trick of the light. Curtains flapping. Who knows?" Lucy was adamant that the boys had let their imaginations get the best of them having spent too long speaking to the crazy old man at the local shop. "Even if it were someone, why do you think it is anything but someone checking out the property, like security?" she continued.

"Well for starters there was no sign that security was there – we checked, and there was also no sign that anyone else had been visiting the property," Jake explained.

"I think you are both nuts. Anyway, does it mean tonight is off?" Lucy enquired, more in hope than expectation.

"Absolutely not," Tom replied. "If anything, this makes it even more interesting."

"If you say so," Lucy responded unconvinced.

Michael had remained quiet to this point, closely

studying the picture on Tom's phone. Tom had attempted to enhance the image and had even inverted the colours to show a negative image, a tip which he had pulled off the internet when researching images of ghosts shortly after the boys had come across their discovery. "I think I can make out something."

"Oh, not you as well, what is it with you boys?" Lucy said rhetorically, exasperated at their desperation to find something which had no basis in reality.

"So, what plan did you come up with to get in then?" Lucy continued, trying to refocus their attention.

"There is a gap in the fencing right next to the gate at the front. It's only small but we think wide enough to get through. The only problem is that there is a quite a bit of open ground from there to the house, which is full of old bricks and stuff from where the other houses used to be. It will be dark, although I checked, and we are expecting a clear night and a full moon so that should provide some light. I don't think we can risk having torches or anything so we will have to go very slowly and carefully and hope nobody is walking past."

"Did I not have to get the torches then?" Lucy questioned.

"We will still need them inside. I doubt there is much light inside. I guess other than the moon shining through," Tom added.

"Sounds creepy," Lucy remarked.

"Of course, the light from the ghosts might help," Jake volunteered somewhat unhelpfully.

Lucy chose to ignore him by diverting attention back to the information the boys had attained from Old Mac. "What did Old Mac say about how the house itself became abandoned? You mentioned the neighbours but I'm still not clear on why this house is not occupied."

"He didn't really get to that and we felt it was time to go before he discovered what we were planning," Tom answered.

Lucy continued "So the image at the window could well be someone living there?"

"Unlikely," Tom suggested. "Whoever owns it feels the need to have security occasionally, so expect no-one is living there, otherwise why bother."

Jake bid to rile Lucy further, given his first attempts were apparently unsuccessful. "I'd be more worried about ghosts."

"Enough already," Lucy blurted.

Jake struggled to conceal a smile but having succeeded in annoying Lucy sufficiently he decided to discontinue any further baiting. Instead he turned to his second love, "Who was on food? I'm starving."

"That was me," Michael confirmed. "But the food is for later, not now. Besides I don't have it with me."

"Great, well I guess it is back home for some tea and then meet up later, once it is dark," Jake suggested.

"Yep, let's all meet at Old Mac's about ten," Tom proposed.

"I'll have to sneak out," Michael declared, "but should be fine."

The friends departed in opposite directions, off to make their final preparations ahead of the night's excitement, which in Jake's case meant filling his stomach.

+++

Tom had spent the last hour checking his watch. He had sat down for dinner with his 'family' who had returned from a day at the theme park. They had, by all accounts, had a lovely day. Tom's absence from this family outing was not discussed, although unusually, his mother had suggested that Tom join them on their next outing. This had come as a surprise to everyone around the table, not least Tom, so much so that there followed several minutes of awkward silence. The mood had changed from one of frivolity and high spirits to one of suspicion and nervousness. There was an added tension in the air which was only broken when Tom announced his plans for the night, well most of them.

"I'm staying round Jake's tonight," he announced.

Tom's mother appeared strangely perturbed by the news. "What for?" she enquired, as if Tom had never before spent nights away from the 'homely comforts' of his family before.

"Jake's mum offered cos Jake had been round here all day," Tom replied slightly flustered by the unexpected attention. The customary response to such an announcement in the past would have been a fleeting gesture of a hand, almost dismissively, acknowledging his approaching absence with little fanfare or obvious unease. This time however Tom was caught by surprise and unprepared for further questioning.

"Do I need to call her to make sure it is ok? I'll call her," his mother insisted before Tom could answer.

"No point," Tom paused buying him a few precious seconds to formulate a convincing argument as to why she shouldn't contact Jake's mother. "She is not there at the moment but said she would call if there were any problems."

Tom's mother was unconvinced but felt she was not in a position to question him further given her discernible lack of interest or concern in the past. However, she knew he was up to something and understood her role in the circumstances. She simply requested he took his phone should she need to contact him and left it at that, for now.

That conversation had taken place earlier and Tom had kept himself to himself, hidden away in his bedroom since, partly to avoid any further uncomfortable conversations about family outings and partly to ensure he did not inadvertently disclose any details of the plans for the night ahead. Any more questions on why he was staying with Jake and the whole plan could come crashing down around him. Not that he was worried about himself, it was more that he would let his friends down. Tom peeked at his watch again, it was nearly time.

At the same time down the road, Jake was spoiling himself with the contents of the fridge. The rest of his family had taken care of themselves which left Jake the freedom of the kitchen. He had learnt to cook for himself at a young age so preparing a dinner of sausages and mash did not provide much of a challenge. Of course, the additional benefit of arranging one's own meals was that he did not have to eat any vegetables. No doubt a source of much jealousy amongst his peers. Having consumed his sausages and mash, Jake was now following this up with a chocolate custard he found in the fridge, washed down with a large glass of orange juice. "Not going to starve tonight," he thought to himself. He had already decided to pack his rucksack with provisions, despite the fact that Michael had earlier confirmed that he had food and drink covered. Jake was taking no chances. For a slight boy, he had a voracious appetite. It was often said he was only able to maintain his slight weight because of his hyperactivity. The only time Jake was still was when he was eating. He finished up just as a message came through on the group chat. "It's time," was all that it read.

Tom didn't bother to announce his departure; the sound of the front door closing would be sufficient notice. Jake had taken the same approach as Tom and had advised his parents that he was staying at Tom's house. As such he left at the same time, provisions stuffed in to his rucksack. His father had commented from the comfort of his sofa that Jake appeared to have enough for a whole week, but Jake had suggested it was mainly his sleeping bag. Lucy on the other hand had not fared so well with her plans to extricate herself from the family home. Her strategy had been to feign illness and take herself off to bed early with a view to climbing out the window and scaling down the drainpipe. It had been successful before but for some reason her parents had been particularly attentive throughout the evening, checking on her every now and then with endless enquiries as to her health and wishes. When the text came, she had been left alone for over an hour. The last time her mother had come to check on her she had pretended to be asleep. She was not certain, but Lucy was confident enough that they would not check on her again before the morning. However, to be safe, she had rolled up several items of clothing into a shape of a human figure placing them on the bed and covered them with her duvet. She had taken some of her hair from her hairbrush and strategically placed it just peeking out from under the top of the duvet. A finishing touch of which she was quite proud. She stepped back to assess her work and concluded that in the dim light of the doorway, her efforts at creating human form would be credible and would avoid any suspicions that she was not present. She checked her phone to make sure there had been no last-minute cancellation, opened the window and made her way out of the house.

Michael grabbed his coat and bag, filled with biscuits, cake bars, crisps and other equally nutritious goods as well as fizzy drinks and water for the health conscious. He had packed extra for Jake, knowing full well he would come under fire if he had failed to provide sufficiently for the group. The assumption was they would be out all night and would not sleep particularly well in the unusual surroundings so they would need to keep their strength up. Michael knew his folks would still be up but was banking on the fact that they would be sufficiently inebriated by that time of the night to slink out of the house unnoticed. He heard some snoring coming from the front room as he crept down the stairs, which validated his expectations. As he reached the door to the lounge which remained ajar, he could see his father slumped in front of the fire, glass of beer almost empty precariously teetering on the side of the armchair in which he was situated. His mother likewise was asleep in the opposite chair, a half-drunk bottle of wine and empty wine glass positioned on the side table next to her. She had clearly fallen asleep whilst sewing as the piece of clothing lay on her lap with needle and thread pointing dangerously upward. Michael did not hold any ill feeling towards his adoptive parents, or begrudge them a drink at night, for they both worked exceedingly hard and the drink was a way of winding down after a long day. Considering they had to deal with the daily grind and the daily traumas from the kids, particularly from Rhianna, Michael thought they did a pretty good job at bringing them up. Michael turned cautiously away from the door, hoping that the beer glass retained its position, that the needle did not slip accidentally pricking his sleeping mother and that both parents remained comatose, unaware of his exit. He was aware of some of the floor boards being predisposed to squeaking, so he made his way carefully and nimbly toward the front door, taking extra care to make as little sound as possible, overtly aware that the only noise he had for cover was the gentle crackling of the fire and the tick-tock of the pendulum of an old grandfather clock. It was at this point that he wished his parents were more avid television viewers. He endeavoured to time his steps in time with the ticking of the clock. The sound of each step seemed to him to reverberate around the hallway like the sound of falling stalactites in a deep cave. He had purposefully left his shoes off until he got free from the house, but he remained overly conscious of each sound as he crept closer to the door. Slowly and quietly he reached the door and raised his hand toward the handle. He gently pulled the handle downwards, attempting to release the latch with as minimal noise as he could. As the internal mechanics started to move, he heard the slightest of chinking as the internal cylinder engaged.

"Just a bit further," he thought as the handle became stiffer, the closer he got to release. Another click. His parents remained undisturbed. The latch released and the door started to open toward him. He manoeuvred himself in to a position that would require the minimalist of openings so as to avoid any unnecessary swish from the door on the carpet as it opened. As he began to slip through the door the silence was broken with an ear-splitting sound that cut through the peace of the night like the shriek of a new-born baby. "Where you goin' at this time of night?"

"Rhianna," Michael sighed. "Keep quiet," he whispered forcefully. "You'll wake them up." Michael nodded toward the lounge.

"I don't think so," Rhianna responded, "they're out like a light as usual."

"Well keep it down anyway," Michael instructed.

"SO, where ya going?" Rhianna repeated emphatically.

"None of your business, just go to bed," Michael replied agitated by the interruption to his plans. Increasingly nervous that his parents could wake at any moment due to the commotion, his mood was darkening with every minute his escape was impeded.

"I'm not going anywhere until you tell me what you are up to, otherwise I'll start screaming and that will wake them up, then you will be in trouble," Rhianna insisted.

"Ok, just be quiet. I'm meeting up with the guys and we are going to camp out," Michael understood he needed to give her something but was not prepared to reveal the entire plans given she could be quite unpredictable, and he was not certain how she might react. His attempts to placate her however appeared to be in vain as she clearly sensed there was more to it and did not let the matter rest.

"Pull the other one," she muttered. "Don't believe ya," she added.

"It's true, just leave it." Michael moved toward the door.

"Well you won't mind me coming with you then, eh?" she proposed. Michael stopped in his tracks, he was not expecting this response and it was clear he did not have any plan to deal with it. He paused, the tick-tock of the clock appearing to increase in volume as each second passed with him standing motionless at a half-opened door.

After what seemed like an eternity, he finally replied with a response that surprised himself. He concluded it could only have been because of the stress of the situation. "Fine, but be quick, I am late now."

Rhianna was surprisingly fleet of foot as she sped back upstairs to her room, grabbed her bag, stuffed it with some additional clothing and returned to meet Michael still standing at the front door.

+++

Lucy was on edge and felt conspicuous hanging around the corner shop at the time of night. She imagined any longer and it would rouse a suspicion with the neighbours, and someone would notify the police. There was a recognisable generation gap which meant a lot of distrust had arisen between the local youth and the senior citizens. It was no longer a class issue. It was considered a result of changing social standards. The older generation came from having lived through the war and post-war years where sacrifice and generosity of spirit meant providing for those who had even less than you. They felt the current generation were all about materiality and a throw-away culture. In essence the older generation felt they owed something to society, whereas the new crop felt society owed them everything. Ironic given the older generation lost more than the younger generation could ever imagine. "It's about time," Lucy shouted out to Michael as he ran in to view. "And what is she doing here?"

"Her fault I'm late," Michael attempted to explain. "She

caught me leaving and wouldn't let me leave without her."

"Well you're here now," Tom said, endeavouring to calm them down. "Let's move."

All of a sudden Jake had another reason to be excited. He was delighted that Rhianna had decided to join their little escapade and could not wait to spend some quality time with her. He sidled up to her. "So has Mikey told you where we are going?"

"No, just said you planned to camp out somewhere. Sounds a bit naff to me, but better than staying in with the oldies," she volunteered.

"It isn't going to be naff," Jake suggested. "We are going to the old house on the hill."

"You are joking," Rhianna shouted in disbelief.

"Straight up." Was Jake's response as he attempted to impress Rhianna with his composure in the face of danger.

"That old place, what for?"

Jake sensed that Rhianna was not as enthralled as he had hoped she would be. His mind had already wandered to visions of having to comfort her inside the old building as she succumbed to the fear and became overwhelmed with anxiety. However, Jake suspected that Lucy was right, and any such thoughts were more likely delusions. Rhianna was clearly not one to be upset by a few ghostly stories.

"Well, er, because," Jake stuttered.

"Fair enough." She replied largely disinterested, retrieving her phone from her pocket instead. "As long as it has good reception."

The rest of the walk was done in virtual silence. Most of the team were preoccupied with thoughts and fears, Rhianna was the exception. She was preoccupied with her Instagram account. As they approached the house, Tom gathered them together and confirmed the plan of action. He pointed to the small opening next to the fence. "That is our entry point."

"Looks like a might have to get on my hands and knees

to get through that," Rhianna expressed incredulously.

"I'll give you a hand," Jake offered, rather too urgently losing any remaining semblance of composure. Lucy was amazed, but at the same time felt a small amount of admiration at Jake's persistence at knocking on a door that was obviously never going to open.

"S'ok," Rhianna replied curtly. She had a predisposition of rolling words into each other and whilst her efficiency might be admired, it often came across quite dismissive. Not that this appeared to perturb Jake's enthusiasm.

"No worries," he answered.

Slowly the group made its way to the small opening and one by one they crept through the hole and on to the other side of the wire fence. Tom stood guard, ensuring that there were no onlookers. Once the last of his friends had made it through, Tom took one last look around. As he peered into the darkness, aided feebly by an old flickering streetlight and the full moon, he thought he observed a movement across the street. There was some chatter from the group which was increasing in volume. Tom called out for them to quieten down. "What is it?" Jake asked through the fence."

"Not sure, thought I saw something," came Tom's reply. As he did so, a cat moved from out of the shadows, where Tom had been staring. The cat stopped and turned its head towards them. The cat's eyes catching the intermittent light from the streetlamp which produced an eerie vision of flashes, similar to a lighthouse through the fog, as the reflections cut through the light mist that was emanating from the warm, still moist ground. Tom hoped this was not a forewarning. With nothing else stirring and the cat continuing on its way, Tom turned and made his own way through the fence, all the time looking back to the dark alleyways. All the friends were now positioned on the other side and Tom made it clear that they needed to be quick to get out of view before they were caught. He added caution given the ground beneath them would be unstable and hazardous. "So quick but be careful," Jake summarised.

Rhianna continued to mutter to herself. Apparently as she had made her way through the fence, in an attempt not to place her knees on the ground, she had snagged the back of her top. Michael had admonished her for making such a big deal about the whole episode, especially as she was not meant to be there in the first place. Jake had jumped in to offer condolences whilst Lucy had felt the whole thing was an extreme reaction to a pulled thread.

The friends commenced their trek across the uneven ground, occasionally tripping on lose bricks and building materials lying around. At one-point Michael took a nasty tumble as he came across a large hole in the ground. His foot slipped from under him and both he, and his overly sized rucksack, plummeted to the ground with a loud thud and a wheeze as the air exhaled from his lungs on impact. "You ok?" Lucy enquired as she moved to help Michael get up.

"More to the point, is the food ok?" Jake asked, sensing that Michael had taken quite a hit and might appreciate a distraction rather than the group obsessing on his plight and adding to his obvious embarrassment. Jake could, on occasions, display a remarkable insight in to the human mindset. This hadn't gone undetected, although not by the one person that he desperately wanted to show some interest in him. She was instead concentrating on plotting a path of her own through the debris using the torch on her phone.

"Turn that off," Tom instructed. "Someone will see us."

"I'm not going to end up like Michael," Rhianna argued.

"No, you'll end up in jail," Lucy suggested.

Rhianna reluctantly switched the phone off, although she had felt it was all a bit of an overreaction. In any case, she had plotted enough of a pathway to make it safely to the house.

She led the way and the others followed. Michael had recovered from his fall and was now more annoyed at Rhianna's presence and the fact that she was clearly upsetting his friends and disrupting their team dynamic.

Having congregated at the house, everyone turned towards Tom in expectation of the next set of instructions. Tom looked back blankly as if temporarily confused about where he was and what he was doing. "So?" Lucy whispered, her arms outstretched seeking clarification of the next steps.

It dawned on Tom that the plan had not extended to penetrating the house. In fact, if he was honest, he hadn't really believed that they would have got this far. He attempted to bluff his way through the moment and suggested Jake wander round to see if he could identify a way in. "Others have done it before so look out for obvious signs of entry," he suggested to Jake. Jake shot back a look which showed the he knew full well Tom had not got a clue but decided to go along with the impromptu plan in any case to prevent his friend's embarrassment and to ensure anarchy did not set in and the whole lot of them end up at her majesty's pleasure.

"Sure thing," he responded as he started to make his way along the outer wall.

Tom was desperately trying to formalise a plan B in Jake's absence, searching the immediate vicinity for an opening, including the possibility of scaling the walls to the windows on the first floor on the assumption that these were likely to be less fortified than the lower ones. Then Rhianna posed the question he was anxious to avoid and the one that he did not have an immediate answer to. "And if he can't find a way in?"

Tom was provided an immediate reprieve from the pressure of answering that question as the group heard movement inside the house. What appeared to be the sound of footsteps interrupted by the occasional dull banging and culminating in the scratching of the inside of the front door set all the friends on edge, even Rhianna. "The place is supposed to be empty. You said it was empty," Lucy whispered frantically in Tom's direction. Tom didn't respond, as with the others he was frozen stiff with fear. The sound continued, finally making way for the sound of a key turning in the lock. The lock itself could barely be seen from where they were positioned, but it was evidently heavy duty, in keeping with the thick oak door in which it was housed. The type of door intended to thwart unwelcome visitors from breaching its borders. Or the kind used to prevent unruly inhabitants from escaping.

Rhianna grabbed Michael's hand. It was not clear whether this was for her own comfort or whether she felt some sisterly responsibility toward her adoptive brother, in any case Michael did not appreciate the gesture and pulled his hand away. As he did so the mechanism clunked violently in to place and the door started to open with an ear-screeching squeal. The friends all gasped and held their breath in unison. "Why would anyone leave a key in the door?" came Jake's voice, shortly before his head appeared around the open door.

"For heaven's sake," blurted Lucy with an intense sense of relief. "Do you have to be such an idiot?"

"Wait, what?" Jake replied, somewhat hurt by the ungrateful welcome he received.

"We were scared stiff," Lucy continued admonishingly.

"Well don't thank me for finding a way in then." Jake was unimpressed by the lack of support for the efforts he had made in the absence of a real plan.

"Look, let's just get in before someone spots us," Tom suggested.

Jake begrudgingly stepped aside to let the others in. Lucy giving him a foul look as she passed.

As Jake closed the door behind them, Rhianna commented on the lack of any real light. "Exactly," Jake retorted sulkily, making a point about how well he had done in the circumstances.

"Right, torches on," Tom instructed. Rhianna turned on her phone again, "I think I might do a live video."

"I wouldn't recommend it. We'll end up with blue lights lighting the way instead of our torches," Michael piped up.

"Alright, keep your hair on," Rhianna voiced disapprovingly.

"So now what?" Lucy asked.

"Let's head upstairs," Michael proposed. "That's where all the stories take place."

The group looked at each other disconcerted by Michael's apparent enthusiasm to rush headlong in to the unknown and a potentially scary situation.

Michael was not waiting for consensus however and before the group had a chance to fully contemplate his proposal, he was already making his way to the staircase. The beam from his torch was hazy from the dust hanging in the air. The light bounced off surfaces as he shone the torch around, illuminating the dust and cobwebs which had been allowed to culminate throughout the property. Undoubtedly nobody had lived in the house for many years, or if they had, they were not keen on domestic cleanliness.

A volley of dust shot up with each step on the carpet as the friends made their way up the spiralling staircase to the upper floors. Audible creaks and groans filled the air as one by one they alighted the stairs, torches and mobile phone lights flickering randomly about the house, like fireflies round a pond. Occasionally a light would land on one of the old oil paintings which adorned the mahogany walls of the stairwell, the faces within the portraits observing the group suspiciously as it ascended. The eyes followed them moving tentatively from step to step, heightening the suspense and trepidation that the friends felt as they moved further in to the old house. There was no talking, each of the new occupants of the house on high alert, listening intently for any signs of life, or as the case may be, the past life. All the signs led to the conclusion that there was no presence other than theirs, yet still they moved with dread of coming across something inexplicable.

They reached the landing on the first floor. All doors were closed. They decided to continue upwards towards the top floor, which had been described as the attic and the reported location of the supernatural encounters. In a period of relative modernisation and incongruous to the rest of the house, this was now a loft conversion, but as with the rest of the deserted house, it reflected the neglect that had passed and felt damp and unloved. The moonlight was well positioned to shine directly through the small cross-barred window, throwing a shard of light across the attic floor. The friends were able to make out a large area which had at least once been occupied as white, dusty sheets covered long abandoned furniture and old boxes were haphazardly stacked at the sides of the room. They had decided that this is where they would make their camp for the night.

"I'll take the bed," Rhianna announced, unilaterally lifting the self-imposed gag that the group had inadvertently introduced as they had made their way through the property. She was the most ill-prepared of the group having been a late addition, and as a result had no sleeping bag.

"Rather you than me," Lucy stated.

"Yeah, you don't know who or what has been there before," Jake remarked. "I'd be happy to join you if you need some company," he added clumsily. "Top and tail of course," he rapidly added as he caught sight of Lucy's disapproving look. Rhianna gave him a look as if to say she would rather take her chances with extra-terrestrial life, than share the same space with him. Jake took the hint and suggested he set up his sleeping bag up elsewhere. Tom chuckled, allowing himself to relax slightly for the first time since entering the building.

The friends organised their things, made up temporary sleeping arrangements and sat together in a circle as a group. They placed the torches together in the centre of the circle, the light shining upward illuminating their faces from below creating ghostly appearances which did nothing to lessen the already unnerving atmosphere of the cold and sinister surroundings. Long shadows shot upwards toward the high ceilings revealing a blanket of cobwebs.

With the clear skies the temperature had dropped, the summer not yet mature enough for warm nights. The friends had largely prepared for this eventuality, huddling in extra jumpers and jackets. However, Lucy continued to shiver, although she could not determine whether it was the result of the chill in the air or the bizarre circumstances in which she found herself. She rose up and searched the room for additional items of warmth. There were no obvious cupboards or drawers worth exploring so Lucy opted to stay close to the group and reached out for one of the sheets that hung over a chair in the corner of the room close to them. As she pulled it toward her she disturbed the years of dust that had accumulated on the surface propelling the particles high in to the air. As the dust fell over the group, the light from the torches created the illusion of a shower of snow descending all around them, the friends gasped in unison ducking beneath whatever could protect them from the onslaught. The dust finally settled and as it did so Rhianna was the first to admonish Lucy for covering them in the mess, jumping up and frantically brushing herself down. "What the hell," she exclaimed. "You've ruined this sweater. Its cashmere y'know."

Lucy went to apologise but before she could respond Michael jumped to her defence. "It's not like she did it on purpose, give her a break." Michael had still not warmed to Rhianna's inclusion and took the opportunity to put her back in her place. "Why don't you just zip it and leave her alone. These are my friends and not yours. Get back to your phone and your phoney friends."

This dose of reality clearly hit a nerve with Rhianna as she sat back down and buried her head into her now dusty sweater.

"Let's all chill a bit," suggested Tom. "We've made it this far without falling out. If we are going to be here all night, we at least need to get on."

"Wise words from somebody so young," a stranger's voice emanated from behind Lucy where the chair was positioned. Rhianna screamed at the introduction of an unfamiliar voice, as the rest of the friends hysterically shuffled on all fours away from the direction of the mysterious voice, the source of which remained blocked by Lucy's figure which remained frozen stiff facing the group.

"Who's that," Lucy squeaked, her entire body trembling with terror.

4 THE STRANGER

Sensing the distress in her voice, the stranger attempted to provide some solace, "Don't worry dear. I'm not going to hurt you. Not sure the old bones are up to it if the truth be known."

These words did nothing to lessen Lucy's anxiety. She wanted to run but her legs were paralysed with fear. The most that she could muster in the circumstances was to move her upper body as she apprehensively started to turn to take a look in the direction of the voice. The torches had been disturbed in the melee and were now left abandoned pointing in all directions creating unusual and sinister shadows across the room. As Lucy was placed between the torches and the uninvited guest behind her, he remained masked in darkness until Lucy had completed a half turn and suddenly the light from the window finally made its way past her and landed squarely on his face. The sudden exposure to the aged features of the man's face, caught Lucy further off guard as she leapt frantically backward and away from him, to the relative safety and comfort of her friends.

"It's not the most flattering of introductions," the man

said, acknowledging the groups reaction to him. "I don't suppose you have some water I could have, do you? The journey always makes me thirsty."

"From the other side?" Jake squealed.

"From downstairs," the man replied somewhat confused. "Tired also, but I am not sure you can help with that."

Tom re-establishing himself as the leader of the group, spoke timidly and almost inaudibly. "Who are you?"

"I really am gasping. And please speak up, I'm quite old you know and not able to hear as well as I once did."

Tom slowly took to his feet and grabbed a bottle of water from the nearest bag. Jake went to intervene as the bag was his and he was not sure he wanted to give up any of his stash so easily, but a hand shot out from Lucy who was starting to compose herself. Her hand remained across Jake's chest as her eyes remained fixed on the old man occupying the armchair in front of them.

Tom moved slowly but steadily forward with the bottle of water. As he came within arm's reach, he raised his hand to the old man and passed him the water. As he did so, he asked again the who the man was with greater certainty in his voice. The old man took the bottle from Tom, unscrewed the top and took a long draught from it. Although only seconds must have past it felt a lifetime to the friends as apart from Tom, they remained huddled together against the far wall.

"Ah that's better. Now, what was it you wanted to know?"

"I was asking who you were," Tom answered becoming more assured as the moments passed and they remained unharmed.

"It's not so much who I am but what I am, to you that is, all of you," the old man responded evasively. "But one thing I can tell you is that you are in my home."

The revelation sent waves of surprise through the group.

They stared at each other trying to comprehend what they had just been told.

Tom spoke up. "But we thought the place was empty. We didn't realise anyone was living here." The revelation slowly dawning upon him that they were now well and truly caught trespassing by the owner of the house, Tom moved to collect his belongings.

"Not leaving so soon are you?" The old man commented. "I am sure you have many more questions and I would very much appreciate some human interaction."

Tom paused, seemingly weighing up his options. The rest of the friends not moving a muscle. "I'm not sure we should be here," he confessed.

"Nonsense. You are more than welcome, although I may have issues with you scuttling around in the dark. Perhaps we could have some lights on? Jake would you mind?"

Jake froze and stared into the old man's eyes. "How…" Jake failed to finish his sentence, stunned in to silence for the first time in his life. His mind whirring with questions. "How did this old man know his name? Certainly, no-one had mentioned it since he had been there, had they? Or had he been there longer than they realised? Perhaps he had been watching them since they entered the house? Did he recollect someone shouting his name when he opened the door?" his thoughts muddled.

"Don't worry yourself with those sorts of questions," the old man remarked as if reading Jake's mind. "If you could just pop the light on then we can have a proper chat."

Jake rose startled and confused, the questions he had still playing on his mind reflected visibly through the expression on his face. He walked in silence preoccupied with his own thoughts towards the door and the switch that operated the light hanging from the ceiling in the centre of the room. As Jake flicked the switch, a short buzz sounded and the lamp above sprang into action, suddenly immersing the room in a bright light which forced the friends to squint and shield their eyes. As their eyes eventually became accustomed to the light, they all turned and focused once again on the old man. In the darkness they had not been able to make out much, relying on moonlight through a window which had been dulled by years of dirt and mould which had been allowed to build up on the panes, and the torches which, since being disturbed, had randomly shed light around the room providing limited clues as to the stranger's appearance. Now however they saw the old man for the first time in all his glory and they were collectively unimpressed with what they saw, for there was nothing extraordinary in what sat before them. The man was elderly, grey and weathered, but with a soft and kind appearance. He would not have been out of place bouncing grandchildren on his knee and offering out Werther's originals. "Disappointed?" The old man enquired, observing the sudden relief on the faces of the friends and increased relaxation in their body language. "Not much of a ghost I know, although the lack of sunshine does have a tendency to make my face somewhat ashen."

Lucy was warming to the old gentleman, but she was still confused about how he came to be in the room and how he seemed so comfortable with a group of strange kids occupying his bedroom. "Doesn't it bother you we are here?" she asked.

"Not at all, it's been a long time since I had a conversation with a group of fine young adults such as yourselves."

"How long exactly?" Jake probed, sensing the old man might be a bit of a recluse, hidden up in the attic of his house.

"Good question, but one which I can only answer after you understand why we are all here."

"Which is?" Tom impatiently searching for some answers.

"Let's start with why you think you are here," the old man suggested.

"Bit of excitement really," Jake replied. "Actually, it was Mikey's idea."

Michael immediately shot him a look of disdain as it appeared to him that Jake was distancing himself from any responsibility and throwing Michael squarely under the bus.

"Ah yes, well Michael may well have made the suggestion, but I suspect that you were all happy to go along with it," The old man coming to Michael's defence.

"To be fair, I did object," Lucy cut in, as the old man twisted his head towards her and gave her a look which suggested that as truthful as that statement might be, her heart had not been in the objection. "A little," she added, becoming aware of the meaning behind the look.

"It wasn't chance that brought you here together. It was destiny. You are on a path, each of you has been chosen. Together you will bring harmony and peace to the universe."

"Isn't that what they said about Luke Skywalker," Jake remarked flippantly.

Ignoring Jake's comment and rather stunned and perplexed by the old man's bizarre revelations, Tom spoke up. "Hang on a minute. Look we are just here to break up the boredom of a long and uneventful summer holiday." He looked around to the rest of the group for confirmation. The response was mostly unanimous with Tom greeted with nods all round, apart from Rhianna who appeared to be in a state of shock as she continued to stare at the old man in disbelief.

"Surely you are joking? Right?" Jake added, realising that the old man might actually be serious, and his friends potentially being taken in by it.

"Not at all. You thought you had become friends and

gravitated toward each other because of your similar backgrounds, but you must know that this is only partly true. You have come together because you are part of something much bigger and more important than the sum of your individual lives. Individually you are nothing, but as a group you have the opportunity to ensure the future existence of the human race and the universe itself."

"Are you crazy?" Rhianna finally plucking up the courage to speak.

"This is just the ramblings of a mad man," Jake suggested.

"I can understand your misgivings. You should know that this is not the first time that I and others have had similar conversations with similar reactions. I remember one time it led to a boy running straight out of the house screaming."

"There are others?" Tom enquired.

"Let me start from the beginning. Well a beginning at least. Bit peckish though – anyone carrying anything to eat?"

The old man was handed a sausage roll by Michael and proceeded to tell the story that he had been told many years ago and one that he had recited many times since. "You may have heard of the parallel universe theory," he began and then looking up from his sausage roll to five blank faces added, "or not." He continued, both with his sausage roll and the story. "Well some scientists, quantum physicists to be precise, suppose that we live in one universe alongside multiple other universes which run side by side through time and space."

"I think I hear Doctor Who coming," Jake quipped quietly to Rhianna, who turned and stared at Jake failing to see the humour in their current situation.

"Thank you, Jake," the old man stated, not looking up from his almost depleted sausage roll. "This concept is known as the parallel universe theory. As a consequence of different decisions, choices or events along the way, each of our selves exists across these multiverses in a different set of circumstances, albeit at the exact same moment in time. A simple example would be that you are here now in this universe, but in a parallel universe you are all tucked up in bed. If you take just the choices you have made today you can see that there may be an infinite number of parallel universes. For example every decision taken since you got up this morning to this point now has led you to this conversation, however you may have made different choices from what you had for breakfast, to what time you left the house," there was an audible murmur amongst the friends as they comprehended the possibility that this old man may have been stalking them. He continued, "which are being played out in alternative universes." The old man bent forward and started to draw lines in the thick dust on the floor which started together, separated, crossed and then tailed off. "I usually find it useful to do a quick drawing. You see you start here with all universes at the same point. No decisions have been made at this point; everything is equal. But soon, as things start to happen, and choices are made the universes go their own way on their own predetermined route."

"But if they are predetermined, surely you are saying that our choices are also predetermined?" Lucy suggested.

"Absolutely. But you see that there may be only two possibilities for the example whether you have toast or cereal for breakfast. These options are predetermined by circumstances and events. Of course, there are considerably more possibilities for other decisions, such as when you leave the house, approximately eight-six thousand if you time it to the second and assume you go out once a day. Although again these are influenced by circumstances and events. It is unlikely that you will never leave the house for example."

"I'm starting to wish we hadn't", Jake chirped, again

falling on unreceptive ears.

"Let me try and show a practical example." The old man rose for the first time and appeared to the friends to be much larger in frame than they expected for a gentleman of his age, making it even more surprising that he had snuck in to the room undetected.

"Tom stand here," the old man placed Tom at the head of a line facing the wall and manoeuvred his friends in to position behind him. "Now all turn around," he instructed. Tom found himself at the point of an inverted triangle. Jake was ahead of him to his left and Lucy ahead to his right.

"Right, now pretend your friends Lucy and Jake are your choices of breakfast. Which one do you choose?"

"You can't start your day without me. It's got to be me," Jake proposed.

Tom chose Jake to quieten him down. He exchanged places with Jake and looked at the old man for an explanation.

The old man elucidated further. "This is the choice you made, but in an alternative universe you are standing where Lucy is standing." He paused before continuing. "Now your next choice has three options, Michael, Rhianna and now Jake." As he manoeuvred Jake into the next row alongside Michael and Rhianna. "Which choice do you make?"

Tom chose Michael who promptly stepped aside.

"Again, in two alternative universes you made a different choice and are standing either where Rhianna or Jake are standing. Now if we look back at your original decision, a second choice would also have followed in your original alternative universe and for the purposes of this example it also had three options. So, you see, in a mere two decisions, with very limited options you are standing in six different positions in six alternate universes."

"I think I understand," said Tom tentatively.

"Well that's good," responded the old man. "Unfortunately, it can be slightly more complicated. If we accept that some decisions have an infinite number of possible outcomes and alternative universes, it is also true that some of those outcomes would also have been reached through different routes."

"Now you have lost me," Jake confessed, although the truth was that he had been lost most of the way.

"Essentially, an outcome or set of circumstances may be the same across different universes. In our drawing here," the old man pointing to the floor where the lines were marked out, "these same outcomes are illustrated by the crossing of the lines, where universes cross. Let's take our practical example. Rhianna's position may have been an option for the second decision you had to take, irrespective of whether your first choice was Jake or Lucy. You may have reached her by following either original decision. These outcomes are the strongest of the predetermined outcomes, and they are the most sacred. Worthy of protecting."

"So, what you are saying is that it doesn't matter what choices I make, I will always end up at the same point?" Tom asked.

"Not necessarily, but there are times when that is the case. There are decisions or choices which are largely irrelevant, such as what you have for breakfast. In those cases, you are more or less likely to come to the same point later that day because of other choices that you make. Of course, here we are using very simple illustrations. Life is not that simple. What if you chose toast and you ended up choking on it and ended up in hospital for the night? You would not be here now."

"That's a cheery thought. And if I had taken two paths which both led here, would there be two of me?" Tom trying to get his head round how the universe applied to him.

51

"No, this is the part that may be somewhat difficult to comprehend," the old man replied.

"Just this part?" Jake asked rhetorically, and again was duly ignored.

"The universes converge, but not in a physical way, more metaphysical. You are at that point because you are at that point, how you get there is largely irrelevant once you are there. You can be in two places at once, but you cannot be in one place twice," the old man tried to explain with little success, noting blank faces looking back at him. "It is rather impossible to explain as you can tell. You could liken it to water running down a window. Two drops moving their own way down until they converge for a while before separating again and moving on. At the point they are together they are one. Have you heard of 'déjà vu?'" The old man paused. The friends nodded half-heartedly. "It is suggested that this happens on convergence. At the point the universes come together you get a sense you have seen the moment before but in reality, it is just a trick of the mind.

Because the event is occurring in two universes concurrently it is a much stronger experience, like the drop of water that becomes larger at convergence. However, the mind struggles to comprehend this phenomenon and rather than the mind processing the event as occurring in multiverses, it processes it instead as having been experienced before. The more universes it occurs in, the stronger the feeling and the stronger the 'déjà vu' appears."

This latter revelation appeared to be a step to far as the friends gawped in silence and the old man decided to leave it there for now. Luckily for him and for the others Lucy also decided it was time for a change in direction. "Ok assuming all this is accepted, what has any of this got to do with why we are all here."

"Your presence here at this time, was predetermined. It is a sacred convergence. In other words, whatever you had for breakfast, you were all going to be here at this time and therefore I needed to be here to let you know of your destiny."

"Which is?" Tom asked apprehensively.

"To be guardians of the past to protect the future. You must protect events in the past that are under threat of a great disturbance. You must ensure that they are not successful and that the past happens exactly as it should," the old man announced.

"Who are 'they'?" Tom asked.

"The disrupters," the old man replied as a matter of fact.

"Oh them," Jake said sarcastically.

The old man continued, "They seek to disrupt the events of the past, hence their name. If the past does not happen as it did then it puts the whole future at risk. Choices are no longer considered and followed, paths are changed, the multiverse becomes unstable and eventually can no longer exist and fails."

"But surely we just carry on in the universes that are not affected," Lucy suggested.

"Unfortunately, they are all affected if one is affected. The whole multiverse is finely balanced and individual universes can only exist in balance with the others. If one disappears because the events and choices are disrupted or taken away at a given point, then it affects all the other universes with their choices and paths," the old man explained.

"And what are we supposed to do about it?" Tom enquired.

"Make sure that the disruptors do not succeed in their efforts," the old man reiterated.

"OK, but if it is happening in the past, how are we supposed to do anything about that?" Tom continued.

"You will travel there," the old man revealed with a level of understatement inappropriate given the size and nature of the revelation.

"Grab your coats, we are getting out of here, he has finally lost the plot," Jake announced as he stood to grab his coat and make his way out of the house.

The old man did not react. He knew that no-one in that room was leaving. They would eventually understand the task at hand and willingly agree to the role they would play in the securing the future for generations to come. "The answer to time travel is to understand that time is not a straight line from beginning to end, rather a string of events that grow and flow within a space. Consider a bowl of spaghetti. Within the bowl of space lies several multiverses which twist and turn around each other, sometimes coming close to each other or touching, but not converging, this is important. At those points the relative times within the multiverses may be different. It is brief, but at these touch points, with the right equipment it is possible to leap across to another multiverse or time in the same universe." Suspecting he was losing them to information fatigue, he drew a close to his revelations.

"Sleep on it," he suggested. "I have given you a considerable amount of information to process and we have a little time to get organised."

Jake turned to look at his friends who had not moved at his behest. "Fine," he said. "But I'm keeping one eye open." Jake proceeded to raise his hand to his face pointing his first and middle finger at his eyes before turning them to point at the old man.

"Unfortunately for you my dear," the old man gesticulated toward the bed whilst speaking directly to Rhianna as he rose from the armchair, "that bed is mine and at my age I can't be giving it up to young folk."

Rhianna was more than happy to give up the bed. She retrieved her possessions and grabbed the cushions from the armchair to create a makeshift mattress for the night. She doubted very much that she would sleep, and it had nothing   to   do   with   the   bedding.

5 THE GOLDEN CIRCLE

The next morning as the first light broke through the window into the room, the old man was already up and had resumed his position on the armchair facing the group of friends who had intentionally grouped together on the floor in solidarity before falling asleep the night before. The lack of cushions had made the seat hard and rigid and uncomfortable to sit on, but it was better than perching awkwardly on the bed. He had never found the bed particularly comfortable either, ever since he had been a young boy occupying the room in its former incarnation as an attic. At that time the bed had not benefitted from a mattress, instead coarse blankets lay between his tired body and the hard-wooden slats beneath. The physical pain had long since evaporated but the mental torture had remained in the memory, to the point that not even the best modern-day quilted mattress could extinguish it.

Of the friends, Tom was the first to stir. As he struggled to open his eyes and wipe away the evidence of very little sleep, the old man spoke softly. "Good morning. Safety in numbers I see. Are you ready for the day ahead?"

Tom adjusted his position and looked up at the old man.

"I'm not sure I am ready for anything," he whispered, hoping not to disturb the others. He welcomed the fact that the old man was awake before the others as he had a number of questions he wanted to ask before they awoke.

"I always thought there was something missing. I don't mean my parents, although I do feel they are part of what I was missing. I mean, it just seemed, well, like there was something that should be in my life. I can't really explain it."

"I understand. I was the same. All those years ago. Very unsettled, feeling there was a deeper purpose to my existence but not knowing what that should be. Until of course my mother sat me and my siblings down, along with my cousins and told us the story that I told you and your friends last night."

"So, you have been in our position?"

"Absolutely, I was the boy who I mentioned ran out of the house! I wasn't running because I was afraid you understand. I was running because I didn't know how else to react. It was all too much to take in."

The old man noticed that Tom was preoccupied with something he had mentioned. "What are you thinking?"

"Did my father and mother know about all this?"

"You should understand Tom that there is still lots you need to hear. I knew your parents. They were good folk. Kind and generous of spirit. Always looking out for those close to them and respectful to strangers. What happened to them was a travesty, a horrible accident."

The old man sensed that although Tom was desperate to get more information on his parents, now was not the right time. If pushed, he would have to lie to Tom for his own protection.

"So, it was just an accident?"

"Yes, it was, just an unfortunate accident."

Tom looked disappointed. The old man guessed that Tom was still looking for an explanation as to why his parents had been taken from him. Had they been caught up in something and sacrificed their lives for a greater good he may have been able to reconcile the loss.

The others started to stir, and it wasn't long before everyone was awake and full of questions. The light of the day was a significant contrast from the ominous dark of the night before and the friends were much more relaxed. The old man tried to answer their questions as best he could but assured them that much would be answered as they embarked on their adventure.

"So, where do we start?" Michael asked, confidence increasing after a good night's sleep.

"The first step is to leave here and go home," the old man instructed. He observed the collective disappointment across their faces. "Don't worry, this is so you can be provided with the tools you need to take your journey together."

"From who?" Lucy asked.

"By your guardians," came the nonchalant response, as if this piece of information should not be a surprise. But a surprise it was, for the friends had no idea that there may be people out there supporting them. They had to this point been under the impression that all they had was each other.

"Guardians?" Jake sought clarification.

"You don't suppose you were accidentally placed with the families you have, do you?" The old man asked rhetorically. "Each family was hand-picked from amongst us, 'the Circle', as it is known. A group that has existed for a thousand years or so. Bound by a common purpose, each member has a defined role to play to meet that purpose."

"How many are there?" Tom asked, a warmth growing within him that the family he had often longed for was starting to present itself in the unlikeliest of ways.

"We are currently tens of thousands," the old man announced.

"What?" Jake exclaimed on behalf of the whole group

which was stunned in to further silence.

"How comes we haven't heard of it before?" Lucy asked.

"It makes no sense for us to reveal who we are, or what we do. There is enough threat from the disrupters without announcing our whereabouts. Furthermore, common knowledge would undoubtedly have consequences for achieving our aims. If everyone was aware of the circumstances in which we operate and our objectives, it is very likely that we would fail to achieve those objectives in protecting the finely balanced multiverse. Some of the questions you have asked, would be the questions asked by millions, who may decide to behave rather erratically in their choices, or be inclined to interrupt the work we do. No, it is much better that we continue to serve the millions by remaining hidden."

"But how have you managed to do so?" Lucy continued.

"Ironically when we are successful, which I should say we have been more often than not to date, then no-one would know. As there has been no disruption to the multiverse and everything and everyone continues as before, then we can go about our business with anonymity. Were we to be unsuccessful, equally we would not be discovered as people would either be in an alternative present, or as anticipated, would cease to exist as the multiverse collapses."

The old man took a breath as he recognised he had once again referred to the ultimate demise of the human race, the world and time itself, in a rather matter-of-fact manner, when it must come as a rather unnerving bombshell to his young audience.

"We do also take steps to prevent our discovery," he continued hoping to deflect the conversation away from the potentially distressful scenario. "For example, no doubt you have heard of the stories surrounding this place." The old man raised his hands and gestured toward the house.

"Yes, part of why we are here today," Michael volunteered.

"The old man in the window? The strange comings and goings? The missing parent?"

The friends were nodding.

"My personal favourite are the reports of curious sounds lights coming from within these walls." The old man tried to lighten the mood by mimicking ghostly sounds. Unfortunately, with the revelations coming thick and fast over the previous hours, the friends were in no mood to appreciate his efforts. He cleared his throat. "Well there really is nothing much to it. If you want to try and prevent unwelcome visitors, then the best way is to create the appearance of danger. Obviously, it doesn't work in all cases. Kids particularly," he looked directly at the faces of the group he was addressing. "Those lights and sounds were rather insignificant in the scheme of things, but over time they have grown in to a life of their own and it helps with our attempts to keep people away," he explained.

"So, what were they?" Michael asked, hoping for some dramatic story of supernatural forces.

"Television," the old man answered rather abruptly. Once again, he was able to reduce the friends to a state of utter confusion. "You see, we were fortunate enough to have one of the earliest black and white sets in the town, not just the street. Those sets were really basic compared to what you kids are used to and were not the most reliable of appliances. The only place in the house we could actually get any reception was up here at the top of the house. Even then the reception was pretty bad, so you had to sit still for fear of losing the picture or sound." The old man smiled to himself as he reminisced to a simpler time. "We had frightful arguments when someone moved mid-programme and we lost reception and didn't see the end. Particularly annoying when watching a whodunnit?"

"A who-what-it?" Jake chirped.

The old man continued to paint the picture of his youth and the amenities they had at the time. By all accounts they were fairly well to do, certainly in the neighbourhood.

"So, you see, the flashing lights and sound emanating from this room were merely the pictures and sound emanating from the television set. But as the neighbours were not familiar with it, they made up all sorts of stories. Partly out of jealousy I fear."

"What about all the other stories?" Michael enquired, clearly disappointed with the first explanation.

"Yes, well there is some truth to the others. My father didn't come back from the war. Died on the beaches of Normandy. A hero by all accounts, but that didn't mean much to me at the time. All I knew was that we had lost him and we were all deeply affected by it. It was true that we, as a family, became slightly reclusive as a result. It was difficult to celebrate with the rest of the town as the end of the war came and we saw lots of other fathers, sons and uncles returning to their families, knowing we would not be able to share in their feelings of joy. Of course, we weren't the only ones in town to have suffered loss, but I guess coming so close to the end of the conflict was even harder to take. Anyway, we had a lot of support from friends and family as you can expect so, lots of visitors to the house."

"We heard a story about a man that visited and was never seen of again?" Tom recollected.

"Ah yes, that was a rather awkward affair," the old man explained. "This was some time after. I was much older by this time. It was probably mid to late 60s and things were a lot different than they were during and after the war. People were a lot more tolerant and err, liberal. Anyway, you must understand that my mother had been alone for some years after the passing of my father."

"OMG," Rhianna piped up. Familiar with the subject matter of many of the stories that filled the magazines she read, she was able to piece together before the others, the events that must have taken place, deducing that the visiting man had run off with the old man's mother.

"Bit of a scandal for us kids who remained in the house.

Not our proudest family moment. Clearly it was an embarrassment for the neighbour who he was visiting, and she invented the story. It suited us not to have the true story come out, even if the times were calling for free love, so we were happy to go along with it."

The old man shuffled in his seat at the awkwardness of retelling the story. Even though the events had taken place several decades before, the friends sensed some residual discomfort. The old man concluded by confirming that all the stories helped keep people away allowing them to get on with what they had to do.

"But that's enough of that for now, you band of young intrepid explorers. Now is the time and the time is now," the old man attempting to stir some action in the group. "Sorry, never been particularly good at motivational speeches. Off home with you," the old man paused to retrieve his pocket watch, which he opened to note the time. The time piece was beautifully engraved, deep gold and adorned with elaborate markings which appeared to be moving as the light bounced off the polished surface. The friends mistakenly assumed that the movement was an optical illusion. It would not be the last time that they made incorrect assumptions.

"You need to be back here by five pm, your window of opportunity will open at six pm and will only stay open for a few minutes. And remember, the disrupters will be around and are hell bent on finding out who you are and will try to distract you, take you off the chosen path."

"Understood," Jake announced, although he didn't really. Out of all the friends of course he was the most likely to let something out of the bag, so it was essential that his friends kept a close eye on him. Tom was charged with this special task, being the closest of his friends.

As the friends left the room and made their way down the stairs, the old man shouted one last instruction. "And don't get seen leaving the house."

"Great. Easier said than done in broad daylight," Jake shouted back.

Tom took the reins once more and slowly opened the front door. It was still fairly early and barring a few early morning dog walkers, the coast was relatively clear. The sun had risen just above the eaves of the old house and the corresponding glare, together with the long shadow created by the house to the front meant that the friends could exit under some cover. Quickly they all exited and made their way back toward the opening in the fence and back on to the street. They reached the street without incident and for the first time in their own company were able to reflect on the events of the last 10 hours. They did so in relative silence, each lost in their own thoughts and experience. Congregated on the corner, looking back at the house, Jake spoke first. "So, what do we do now?"

Tom answered, bullishly, clearly thriving on the purpose that had been handed to him and his friends. "Let's get home and get some more answers and then meet back here this afternoon."

+++

The moment Tom walked through the door to his home he was aware of a radical change in atmosphere. Gone was the anxiety which had plagued him throughout his family life, in its place was a sense of hope and promise. As he passed the door to the living room his name was called out. He turned and walked in to the room to find his adopted parents standing there. Instead of the usual lecture on his attitude, he was greeted with smiling faces, as if a burden had been released from their lives leaving them relaxed and content.

Tom was taken aback by the change. Probably for the

first time in his short life he really looked at them and identified a gentle and welcoming side to their appearance.

Their faces were bright, their eyes wide and smiles broad. It was as if this was the first time Tom had walked in to their lives and they were genuinely pleased to see him and have him join their family. It was at that moment that Tom felt perhaps they weren't all that bad. He wasn't however prepared to let them off the hook easily, having spent his formative years in relative isolation because of them.

"How was it?" His mother asked.

"What?" Tom replied, deciding to remain elusive until they volunteered more of an explanation.

"It's ok Tom, we know you went to the house. We also know you met with George." It was then that Tom realised that he had not thought to ask the old man his name or ask any questions about his background. He had been so wrapped up in what it all had meant for him. He committed to resolve the oversight when he returned to the house later that day.

"And what do you know about it?" Tom asked belligerently.

"We understand your reticence Tom, we do, and we are sorry we haven't been able to provide you with the loving family you so richly deserve, but you see, we were conflicted. Many times, over the years your father and I discussed telling you more, but we were worried it would upset the path we knew you were on. It was paramount that you find your own way and make your own decisions. We honestly tried to act in your best interests."

Tom shrugged his shoulders. He had come to terms with his relationship with his family a long time ago and the opportunity now presenting itself to belong to something much greater made all that pale in to insignificance.

"We have something for you," his mother continued. She handed Tom a box, slightly larger in size than a shoe box and wrapped in a brown cloth with a small insignia embroidered in gold on the front. The insignia comprised a circle, which on closer inspection was several strands entwined, and two hands clasped together. Tom was sure it had a deeper meaning. He wondered whether the strands were meant to represent the multiverse. It was reminiscent of the drawing George had made in the dust at the house.

"It was given to me by the Circle when we were chosen to adopt you, together with strict instructions not to open it, but to give it to you when the time came," Tom's mother explained. "We were put on notice yesterday that the time had come."

Tom moved his eyes back to the package in front of him and started to remove the contents from the cloth. Tom immediately observed an ornate gold artefact of some description. About half a metre in length, with a slight curvature. The centre piece was heavily decorated with a carving of a wolf and the inscription 'Lupus pilum mutat, non mentem'. On either side of the centre piece, the object narrowed to a short length of cylindrical metal which, similar to the insignia, was created from entwined strands and which displayed some wear in the form of four grooves on the top of each side and one on each of the undersides. Each end culminated in a wider piece which appeared to be interlocking joints, like tongue and groove. In addition to the artefact was a piece of parchment. Both sides had writing on it but clearly one side much older than the other as the script was faint and largely ineligible, even if Tom had been able to read Latin. Thankfully it was clear someone had the good sense to translate and the other side had the English equivalent. Tom read it out aloud. "To whom this solely concerns. At one, just a piece, but together the circle. Hand in hand to face the foes, who would our past and destiny depose. The way is lit, that no ordinary men travel. Seek and conquer to maintain order. Responsibility is yours and secrecy dictates, to ensure the

Circle and humanity endures."

He didn't really comprehend what the text meant but he understood the intimation, having spent several hours hearing about their destiny from George. "No pressure then," Tom mumbled.

The note also contained a postscript which was much more recent. It was a sequence of letters, numbers and special characters that resembled some kind of generated password. There was however no sign of how or where this should be used.

Tom's father spoke, "I assume George has given you a full briefing and you understand what is expected of you. We can't add anything as the details are kept to the few and we are not privilege to that information."

"The details are fairly sketchy still," Tom responded. "But hopefully we will get more of an idea later."

"So, you are going back today?" his Mother asked, a hint of disappointment across her face. She felt she had really only just connected with him and now he was leaving.

"Tonight," Tom revealed. "I need some time to take this all in," he declared, before rising and leaving the room. His parents watched him heading up to his room and regretted leaving it so long to engage with their adopted son. They very much hoped he would return safe and sound.

6 DUTY BOUND

Tom had spent the last hour lying on his bed facing the ceiling and contemplating the fundamental changes to his life. He was full of mixed emotions – excitement, anxiety, hope, fear and not a small amount of confusion. As he lay there, he was interrupted by the beep of his phone. He suspected his friends had gone through a similar experience since they had left each other at the old house and were now starting to share their thoughts and many questions on the group chat. Tom reached out and retrieved his phone from his side table. The screen lit up to confirm a message, but it wasn't from one of his friends. It was from an unusual number and certainly not one he was familiar with or one contained in his contact book. In fact, he did not recognise it as being a UK mobile number. The message simply read "download app here". The 'here' was a hyperlink. Under normal circumstances Tom would have been reluctant to click on something which was not from a known reliable source given the risk of malware and other security threats, but this was not in normal circumstances and given the last twenty-four hours he could be forgiven for blindly accepting any instructions without question. He clicked on the link and an application started to download to his phone. The phone chugged through its processing as the application's icon slowly came in to view. It was immediately apparent that the application related to recent events as the icon was a golden circle. After a few seconds the application had completed loading and Tom selected it. As the application opened Tom was presented with a logon box which required a password to proceed. Tom raised himself from the bed and grabbed the parchment from the end of the bed where he had left it on entering his room. He sat on the edge of the bed and entered the sequence at the bottom of the parchment in to his phone. As he selected 'done', he was faced with instructions to change his password before continuing. He was reminded of the warning to retain absolute secrecy so opted for a more complicated password rather than his usual 'Kylo1'. Having selected an appropriate password, the application allowed him to access the contents.

He was presented with a number of options which were highlighted at the bottom of the screen. They read 'Location', 'Resources' and 'Chat'. It was clear that this application was to be used as the primary communication channel when it came to discussing matters of the Circle, both with members of the Circle itself as well as his friends.

He hoped that the other options would provide further assistance and fill in the gaps that remained in his knowledge in relation to the Circle's affairs.

Tom selected 'Location' and was presented with a list of names. At the top was his, followed by Jake, Michael and Rhianna. The only one missing was Lucy, which did not surprise Tom in the slightest. She was after all, the most sensible of the group and had clearly been more cautious in acting on an unusual and unsolicited request to download an application to her phone. Tom switched applications back to the group chat and sent a message to Lucy which read "Just do it. Tom x". Tom switched back and waited.

After several further seconds, Lucy's name finally appeared on the list. Tom decided to select his own name and the app displayed his physical address, time and date. In addition, there were GPS coordinates. There was also an option to find directions, although alongside the usual map, there was a flashing vertical bar below, blinking back at him. Tom returned to the 'Location' front screen and selected Lucy from the list. Her physical location was as expected but included alongside the GPS coordinates was a note that this was in the current universe. A drop down allowed the user to choose what appeared to be different coordinates which Tom deduced were her position in alternative universes. To test his theory, he chose another universe. The note was no longer there and the dot on the map had also moved, although he noted that it remained in the local area. Tom's curiosity was peaked when he caught sight of the option to find directions. Tentatively clicking on the option, the flashing vertical bar clicked in to action. The text started to scroll which provided instructions, not in terms of positional directions, but rather a list of chronological decisions or options he would need to take in order to manoeuvre through the complex web of the multiverse to bring him to the crossroad where he would meet with Lucy in an alternative universe where she had made different decisions and taken different options. Tom's head started to hurt as his mind was blown trying to comprehend it all. As he read the instructions, he visualised the drops of water old George had described and suddenly saw clearly how it all worked. He had no intention of following these instructions, as he knew the path he was on required him to be outside the old house before five pm. Any deviation from this could put an end to everything before it began. However, as he continued to contemplate how it worked, he wondered whether he was actually supposed to follow these instructions. Whether that was the choice he was supposed to take, in order to be outside the old house by five pm. The more he thought about it, the more confused he got. His head started to spin and he quickly put his phone face down to avoid the temptation to look at it, further confusing matters. He laid his head back on the pillow and suddenly realised the enormity of the situation and the conflicts that it presented.

He at once understood the conflict that his adoptive parents had been grappling with, and for the first time in his short life he appreciated the mental struggles that they must have been gone through to preserve his destiny. The question of whether they should or should not tell him. On the face of it, not a difficult decision, but not knowing the repercussions or how it might affect him and his destiny? Not easy. He vowed to at least show them some respect before he left.

His thoughts were broken by the ping of a message on his phone. Tom looked down at the phone and noted the '1' against the chat option, denoting a new message had been received. Tom clicked on the option and the message appeared. It merely advised of "Some background reading" and included links which Tom assumed were to take him to sites on the internet which would include historic details of a point in time which were material to their journey. He proceeded to click on one of the links, but it was soon clear that it was taking him to a private network and not the world wide web. The application on his phone was replaced with the icon of a folder entitled 'Dallas, Texas. 22 November 1963. 32.779903, -96.808427.' Tom opened the folder and several newspaper cuttings came in to view. Tom read through them and realised they reported the events of the assassination of the President of the United States, John F. Kennedy.

+++

Tom had not yet absorbed all the information that he had been exposed to, but he realised that time waited for no man and the clock suggested it was time to leave the house and reunite with his friends. He gathered some of his possessions together, without a clear understanding of what he needed.

He packed his rucksack with some spare items of clothing, a notebook, pen and his phone. He looked down at the charger, contemplating whether where he was going there was even going to be an opportunity to use it. He decided to leave it. He grabbed his coat and left the room, pausing at the door briefly to look round and wonder whether he would see the room again. He closed the door behind him and went downstairs to the kitchen to fill his bag up with provisions. His mother and father were there. They evidently wanted to show support to Tom at this stage of his journey, possibly with a hint of guilt, as they had prepared a bag of food and drink for him. Tom looked in to their eyes and saw something that he had not seen in them before. A combination of pride and sadness, marking this departure from them and the life he had known until now in exchange for the adventure of a lifetime.

Tom was not prepared for this moment and had nothing of real note to say, so instead he thanked them for the food and announced that he was going. There was a moment of silence before his mother wished him good luck, adding that she hoped very much that he would return to see them soon. Tom nodded and turned to leave. As he reached the front door he looked back and saw that their eyes were still on him. He raised his hands and waved at them. As he did so, he noted tears well up in his mother's eyes. He turned and left the house.

+++

The friends reconvened on the corner of the street opposite the old house at the pre-agreed time. Each was brimming with questions, which, in all honesty none of them could answer.

"Why JFK?"

"I didn't even know who he was!"

"What are we supposed to do about the assassination?"

"What are the disrupters planning?"

"How are we meant to stop the disrupters?"

None of them questioned their ability to travel in time and space.

"More importantly, how are we going to get back in there?" Tom was staring at the old house which was now lit up like a beacon in the bright summer afternoon sunshine.

The friends all turned to face the house. "That is a tricky one," Jake helpfully confirmed.

It was close to four in the afternoon on a lovely summer's day, so the streets were particularly busy with passers-by.

"The way I see it," Lucy suggested, "Is we either just brazenly walk up and pass through the fence as though we are supposed to be there and therefore don't raise and suspicions or we create a distraction."

"Did you have any in mind?" Tom asked.

"Not really," Lucy responded dismissively.

"What about a fire?" Michael chirped.

"Great, add arson to breaking and entering," Rhianna scoffed as she rolled her eyes and continued to tap away at her phone. She had a remarkable ability to multitask when one of those things was her phone.

"Any other suggestions?" Tom addressed the group, only to be greeted by blank expressions and shakes of the head. "Well in that case, let's go with the brazen option."

As the group retrieved their bags from the floor and prepared to cross the road, they noted movement at the front of the house. The front door started to open and from it emerged George. Dressed as he had been earlier that day in a full dark suit over a white shirt, interrupted by a flash of colour from a red tie. The only addition was a dark grey fedora which he wore pulled down forward on his head covering his eyes. He paused briefly before heading towards the gate in the fence. His presence attracted some minor attention from those passing, probably locals who were used to seeing the place abandoned. But nobody lingered. George raised his head and looked across the road to where the group were standing. He gesticulated to them to enter. The friends crossed the road and walked through the open gate where George was standing. As they did so, George welcomed them back and suggested they make their way quickly to the house and through the front door.

The moment George closed the front door behind the group he was bombarded with questions from the friends.

The barrage temporarily put George on the back foot. He had expected some questions but did not expect to experience such a vociferous exhibition from the group.

Once he had regained composure, he was struck at how suitable this group of children were for the adventure that awaited them. They had the curiosity and tenacity which were essential attributes for a successful team. He smiled before raising his hand in an attempt to restore order. The friends acquiesced, and George re-established his authority.

"We must move upstairs. I understand you have lots to ask but we must focus on what you need to know, not what you want to know."

George passed amongst them and led them all up the stairs back to the attic room.

"Sit, sit," George instructed as they reached the top of the house. Before he could begin Jake raised his arm, requesting permission to speak. "You are not in school now Jake," George said. "You may speak freely."

"I just wondered why we had to sneak about and not be seen earlier, when you just openly let us all in, in broad daylight."

George smiled. "Well I was being a little naughty.

There is nothing like a little jeopardy to focus the mind. Although I do stand by the view that you lot leaving in the early hours may have raised some unwanted suspicions."

Lucy shook her head, suggesting that they really did not need anything further to focus their minds.

George moved on. "In an hour or so the time will come when you must depart and you need to be as prepared as possible." He produced several packs of documents and distributed them to the friends, each pack had their individual name on the front. "These are your individual instructions," he announced, "each of you have a mission that you must complete. If any of you fail, there is a great risk that the whole mission will fail, and I am sure I don't have to remind you what that might mean for human kind." The friends were constantly reminded so it was very difficult for them to forget, as much as they would have liked to. They opened the packs and proceeded to read their individual instructions.

The pack included an A4 sized black and white photo of someone and on the back of the photo was a biography of the individual. The pack also contained a map and a chronology of movements that the friends concluded was the movements of the individual they were allocated. "These are your targets," George continued. "You will find their expected movements for the time you are there. You must ensure that these movements happen as destined and that nothing or no-one interrupts that.

The friends had only been listening half-heartedly as their attention had been drawn to their information packs. Each of them deliberating on how they were to ensure that the targets would make the movements they were destined to. It seemed like an impossible task, even before they factored in the role the disrupters were meant to play. They had no sense of how or where the disrupters would appear, let alone how they were to identify them in the first place. They saw their chances of succeeding fading with every thought.

After a few minutes of the friends perusing their files, George proceeded to provide them some rules for the road.

"First, you must travel light. Second, keep anything from this universe concealed when you are in another. You are there to prevent disruption, not cause it. When you get there, you will meet a member of the Circle who will help you acclimatise."

Lucy looked up from her pack. "You mean there are people there already? Why don't they just stop the disrupters?" Lucy asked, hopeful that this was the opportunity to forget about the whole thing.

George sensed some apprehension behind the question. "Because they are unable to detect them. They will of course assist you as much as they can but only you will be able to track the disrupters down and prevent them from succeeding in their plans." He didn't like to lie to the group, but it was preferable than telling them the truth, which was that they were somewhat dispensable. There was too big a risk if a member of the Circle was caught and terminated in their own timeline. This event in itself could knock the multiverse sufficiently to cause a destructive chain of events. No, it was much safer for a team to travel from the future to a time where they had not yet even been born. Their disappearance would have a much lighter impact. It was part of the reason that teams of children were much more successful. They had a wider time-band in which to travel.

"How will we spot them?" Lucy continued, clearly in need of reassurance.

"I wish I could help you more with this, but it is different for everyone. It is more of an intuition. You will know when you see them," George could not provide the reassurance Lucy needed and she looked somewhat crestfallen. Tom fortunately noted her change in mood and tried himself to give her some comfort. "Lucy, we are in

74

this together. Don't worry you are not alone."

"Come here, give us a hug," Jake suggested as he moved toward her open armed, only to be immediately rebuffed. "I'm not that desperate," she retorted. This raised smiles all round and lightened the mood, which had begun to be a little tense.

"Good, you must relax and be confident otherwise you may miss something," George advised. "Now take out your artefacts," George instructed. The group retrieved the items they had each been presented with back home and placed them in the middle of the circle in front of them. "You will undoubtedly have noticed that these items join together, and you will also notice that when they do, they form a golden circle. It is no coincidence. This is your gateway to another time and place." The friends looked down at the items. "Pick them up and join them together." The apprehension in the friends was palpable, but slowly they began, one by one to join together. They each grasped their own piece with two hands, placed each side of the centre piece. As they did so, they realised what the indentations were as their fingers and thumbs aligned with the grooves that had been left by countless previous owners. As the last pieces were being put in place, George rose from his seat and moved toward the window. He closed the curtains. This gesture went unnoticed by the group who were fixated on the ornate circle coming together in front of their eyes. With each additional piece in place, the engravings appeared to increase motion, twisting and swirling. Tom realised it had not been an optical illusion after all. Finally, as the last piece clicked in to place, the whole circle became alive with an overwhelming energy.

The circle began to glow and emit a bright light as the entwined strands picked up speed and spun around the circle within the enclosed clench of each of the friends' hands. The energy and movement created a loud rushing wind, but there was unexpectedly an absence of any other sound which the friends would have expected from such violent activity.

George watched over them and was struck with a deep sense of pride tainted with a little envy as he reminisced on his first time. "Hold tight," he called. "When the time is right, you will be transported to the chosen time and place. Good luck."

The friends continued to grasp the circle tight, their knuckles turning white with the effort. Excitement rising within each of them, their hearts beating faster and louder, almost audible in the otherwise serene setting. Shortly after, a bright light encompassed them all and they were finally on their way.

+++

Temporarily blinded, the friends rubbed their eyes and blinked repeatedly to regain their sight and their composure. "So, we are not in Kansas anymore," Jake remarked as he looked around shielding his eyes with his hand from the bright sunshine.

"Where exactly are we?" Lucy asked. The group rose collectively from their seated positions, still holding their golden circle between them. They appeared to be in a field, with a few trees dotted around sporadically. Not far from their position was a river on one side and a road on the other.

In front of them they could see an overpass which appeared to be a busy main road. A few dirt tracks wandered in various directions. The remote location had clearly assisted them in completing their arrival undetected.

Tom suggested they first dismantle the circle and then get their bearings. He hoped they may be able to get some answers from the mobile phone but was conscious that this was no longer the twenty-first century and was not holding out much hope.

Once the circle was once again in its constituent parts, successfully stowed away in their individual bags, Tom retrieved his phone from his pocket and switched it on. The extreme journey appeared to have had no effect on the phone as it bounced in to action as normal, the bright screen marginally affected by the bright sunshine beating down.

Tom held his hand over the phone to produce a shadow which enabled him to read the display. It was working. "It has to be a private network or something, because there is certainly no 4G around here."

Tom selected the map on the application, and confirmed their current position was indeed Dallas, Texas in the United States. The date also confirmed that they had achieved what they deemed impossible; they had travelled in time. The display notifying them that they were currently standing in nineteen-sixty-three. Tom noticed two other things highlighted on the phone's display. Firstly, a message was waiting in the inbox and secondly, there was a countdown in the upper right corner. It currently stood at 3 days, 11 hours, 52 minutes and 54, 53, 52... seconds. Before advising his friends, he decided to read the message. It was from an unknown person who introduced himself as a member of the Circle. A set of directions followed, instructing them to meet him or her on the sixth floor of the Texas School Book Depository building on Dealey Plaza in the next hour. Tom noted the local time was just after noon. He informed his friends. Lucy spoke first, "Do we know how exactly we are supposed to get there without standing out like a sore thumb? We are not exactly dressed for nineteen-sixty-three."

Rhianna piped up, "If you think I am wearing anything other than my own clothes you can forget it." The friends looked themselves up and down. She continued. "In any case, I consider myself a bit of an authority on fashion and believe that my dress is actually in keeping with the fashion of the time." This was undoubtedly correct, but summer had been replaced with the depths of autumn and the temperatures were lower than they were prepared for. The boys were dressed fairly conservatively with shorts and t-shirts which would not have been out of place in the sixties. Jake being the only exception, as his t-shirt advertised the two-thousand and eighteen FIFA World cup which would probably have raised some awkward questions, not least because it was to be hosted in Russia and relations between the two countries at that time were not exactly cordial. Jake agreed to turn his t-shirt inside out. Lucy on the other hand was a different matter altogether. The group considered that a blue cammo top with black skinny jeans was rather more conspicuous for the time that they found themselves in. The friends were all staring at her as she looked down at herself.

"What do you want me to do about it?" She asked, somewhat irritated.

"Where do we start?" Rhianna responded impertinently, sneering as she did so.

Tom suggested they make their way carefully, avoiding unnecessary interaction and hopefully their contact could help.

The group gathered around the phone to view the map and the directions to follow. "So, we are here'" Tom pointed at the screen to the area marked Trinity Overlook Park. "And we need to get here," he pointed to Dealey Plaza which was about a mile away directly east.

"I am not sure that we should go along Commerce Street," Michael suggested pointing up at the overpass ahead of them. "Looks pretty busy. Probably better to go north a bit and head along the railway tracks. We are less likely to be seen that way." He paused as he reflected on the large river to their right. "Good job we are on the right side of the river, otherwise that would have been a bit tricky," he suggested sarcastically. Tom suggested they cross that bridge when they come to it. No pun intended, although it made Jake smile. The friends agreed to start walking north, hopeful that an opportunity to cross would present itself. They gathered their stuff for the short walk to meet their unknown contact.

+++

As the friends trekked through the park north toward the rail tracks that would take them east to their destination, they observed that the country had experienced a long, hot summer. Although the ground revealed evidence of earlier rain, it continued to show signs of a significant period of battering from the intense summer sun. The current temperate weather however, unusually warm for the time of year, made the walk tolerable and they made good time. They passed very few people along the way and those they did were sufficiently distant not to notice their unusual appearance.

As they reached the point where the railway tracks crossed the river, they noted that if they took a short diversion to the left, they could make their way up on to the tracks and follow them across the river. Although they would be rather conspicuous if a train was to pass, it looked fairly quiet and it was worth the risk.

The rail track eventually led them on to a barren piece of land where several tracks converged. They could see their destination across the tracks and were relieved to see that there was a small car park, which was barely populated, between them and the building. The friends took extra care to cross the tracks, avoiding the occasional oncoming freight train. It would not do if one of them was to be killed at this stage of the operation. Once across, a small path took them to the car park behind the book depository. It was mid-afternoon on a weekday and the streets were fairly busy, but not as busy as they would get in the coming days. The building itself was unspectacular. Seven floors of light red brickwork, the front and right side of the building with windows extending the length on each floor, with the exception of the back and left sides which only had three or four windows per floor, with the other areas bricked up. As the friends approached from the rear, they noticed a covered loading dock which extended out from the main structure.

They chose to try and gain entrance through this rather than risk being seen entering the front of the building which was set just off the corner of Elm Street and Houston.

They eased their way through an opening adjacent to the loading bay shutter which led to a short set of stairs which took them on to the main dock. The proceeded alongside the dock and eased open a wooden door which led them in to a vast open storage space which was full of boxes of various sizes, trolleys and lifting equipment, which appeared to be scattered around with reckless abandon. The space was unoccupied, the friends concluding that the workers must be on their lunch break as they heard distant chattering and clinking of glass coming from the floor above. Nonetheless the group moved surreptitiously, using the square pillars as cover which they encountered every few steps. As they made their way further in to the storage space they noticed a set of steps to their right. As they prepared to make their way to the stairs, they suddenly heard voices coming from the opposite corner of the floor to their left. It appeared to be coming from a room right in the corner, past a set of toilets. They all froze, straining to hear what the voices were saying. They were petrified of getting caught. How would they start to explain their appearance or why they were there?

The voices exploded into a cheer and a certain amount of ridicule. They could just about make out that someone announced they were going to make use of the toilet facilities.

From their position in relation to the toilets they would undoubtedly be spotted unless they moved. They each threw themselves behind the nearest stack of boxes to shield themselves from being seen from the direction of the toilets and specifically the individual who was about to occupy them. Michael, who had been the last to react just about concealed himself before the man appeared from the corner room and walked toward the toilets. In his haste Michael had inadvertently knocked his stack of boxes and the top box was now perilously balanced on the box below it. The movement must have caught the attention of the man as his eyes were averted away from the direction of the toilets, to the vicinity of the stack of boxes behind which Michael was taking cover.

There was a pause and then the man changed direction to walk towards the stack. Michael could hear the movement towards him and he held his breath. Michael hoped that the increasingly loud beating of his heart was audible only to him as the man came closer and closer to his position. The man stopped the other side of the stack and gently pushed the top box back in to place. Michael was not breathing, intent not to make any sound that might give away his position. It seemed to Michael that the man was standing there for an age and he wondered how long he could continue to hold his breath before passing out, or worst still audibly gasping and giving the whole game up. Thankfully, as Michael was reaching desperation, the man turned and walked to the toilet. The friends heard the sound of the toilet door opening and closing and as it did so, Michael gasped for air and they all leapt up and ran to the stairs. The entrance to the stairwell was partially hidden by some lifts so they were comfortable they could not be seen unless someone made their way to the middle of the storage area. Consequently, they slowed their movements again as they cautiously made their way up the right-angled staircase to the second floor. As they crept around the corner Tom was at the head of the group and was the first to identify the source of the talking they had heard from the floor below. A wooden door with a square glass window in the upper half stood between the group of friends and the employees on their lunch break. The friends recognised the peril of the transition to the upper floors but understood that it was a necessary risk. They merely had to whisk around the corner and up the next set of stairs. They were confident that once they had overcome this hurdle that it would be plain sailing from then on. There were no obvious signs of occupancy above them.

Tom recognised that the quicker they were, the better, as any longer spent on the stairwell downwards was to expose them to greater risk of being discovered, so he beckoned the rest of the group and indicated that they proceed with speed up the stairs to the next level. Rhianna was the last to turn the corner and as she approached the next flight, she turned toward the door leading to the lunch room. At that moment she caught sight of movement at the door. The door knob started to shift in its position and the door itself began to open inward. Rhianna stopped, immobilised with fear. Her whole world went in to slow motion, transfixed on the door she remained rooted to the spot. Time passed slowly and she felt her anxiety levels grow, the longer she remained in place.

She sensed she was stood there alone for a long time, in full view, as the door opened sufficiently for her to see the figure of a lady exiting. Fortunately for Rhianna, the lady continued her discussion with her colleagues behind her as she was leaving the room, and as such Rhianna had a vital further few seconds to regain her composure and nip around the corner and up the stairs to re-join her friends. It was a scare that focused her mind and convinced her that she did not want to be at the back of the line. She proceeded to push past Michael and Lucy to take up her position in the middle of the group.

As predicted the group ascended the remaining sets of stairs to the sixth floor without incident. As they reached the floor, they peered perilously into the open space in front of them, expecting to be greeted by the author of the message. They were overcome with a mixture of worry, confusion and disappointment as the space appeared to be empty, except for numerous stacks of boxes and the familiar pillars that they had observed on the first floor.

As the rest of the group turned to Tom seeking both reassurance and instructions on how to proceed, footsteps were audible from the adjacent steps leading to the 7th floor. The group were instantly conflicted as to whether they should make a speedy exit or take the risk that the person about to join them on the sixth floor was the contact they had been expecting. They waited in anticipation.

The person reached the bottom step and turned the corner to see the group standing open mouthed, faces blank and fearful. The man was dressed in a dark suit, with white shirt and pencil thin tie. On his head was a jauntily placed fedora which sat on the top of a crop of black greased hair which contrasted with a pale, clean shaven complexion. The man was slim and of average height, with age range estimated at between twenty-five to thirty years old.

"Good afternoon," the man greeted the friends, holding out his hand to Tom as the nearest to his position. Tom responded in kind shaking the man's hand, speedily assessing whether he was indeed the contact they were expecting. He proceeded to introduce himself and his friends. "I know who you are, but you are probably none the wiser as to who I am," he suggested.

"Not really," came Tom's reply.

"Well, you need not trouble yourself with that sort of meaningless information, when you have much more important matters to occupy your minds. But first things, first. Let's change your appearance to make you fit in a bit more." The man proceeded to open a suitcase which was standing up against the wall. From it he produced a number of items of clothing and suggested the friends decide amongst themselves as to who should wear what. The group perused over the clothing for several minutes, even Rhianna taking an interest, albeit somewhat disdainfully. They settled on their new attire. If asked, they were now a school trip to local book depository.

"You now don't look out of place, well not obviously so," the man cheerily announced.

"How did you know we were here? And how did you know what clothes to bring?" Jake asked, still grappling with the concepts.

"We get notified whenever someone from the Circle enters our timeline. I can't explain the science behind it, unfortunately. I leave that to the eggheads. As to the clothes, well quite frankly bit of an educated guess. I saw five had arrived, given travelling teams tend to be kids, I plumped for a range to cover the options."

"And why meet here?" Lucy asked. "Not exactly the easiest place to meet."

The man looked around. "This place factors in the coming days and I thought it might be useful for you to familiarise yourself with the layout."

"Do you have your information packs?" he continued.

"Yes, we do," Tom answered.

"Have you studied them?"

"As much as we could in the time," Tom confessed.

"Any questions?" he asked abruptly.

"I don't think so," Tom answered.

"Not exactly a resounding confirmation, but it will have to do," he said. "I understand you have some sort of device to keep track of time and to take you where you need to go. You should each have the location of your target as well as tracking the whereabouts of your friends.

Don't lose your targets and make sure you are back together before the time runs out. If for any reason you are not all back together at the allotted time, the gateway will close, and with it your ability to get back to your original time."

"So, we will be stuck here?" Rhianna exclaimed, in part dismayed at the thought of having to remain in a technologically repressed time for any longer than absolutely necessary.

"There will be opportunities to return but it is difficult to know when. You are better making sure you are back together on time." The friends were under no illusion as to the sincerity of the man, or indeed the seriousness of missing their slot.

"Ok, so I guess this is it," Tom turned to address the rest of the group. "From now on we are on our own. Stay in touch everyone, don't forget we have the chat on our phones, but I guess try and keep it to a minimum," Tom shot a look in Jake's general direction. "Mobile phones are not common on the streets of 1960's America and we do not want to draw any unwanted attention."

"Before you go, please place your information packs in the suitcase. We can't risk any of you being found with information pertaining to the future."

The friends took one last opportunity to review the files, study the photos and review the movements of their targets before placing the files in to the open suitcase. Once the files were all back in the suitcase the man closed the case, picked it up and addressed the group one last time. "Good luck," he said, then walked past them down the stairs and out of view, leaving the friends alone to embark on the next step of their adventure, possibly the most demanding and dangerous yet.

7 THE DISRUPTERS

The man was standing at the side of the road resting against a lamppost, his eyes down, focused on the newspaper that he had bought from the vending machine a few minutes before. Unassuming and inconspicuous, he maintained his position unnoticed by the passing traffic, glancing up only briefly, periodically to observe the building across the road in front of him. The man was average in height, slim and well-kept with a clean-cut grey suit, white shirt, black tie accessorised by a pair of shiny black laced shoes. All of this was topped off with a neat and well-maintained fedora which he wore pulled down on his head, showing just the slightest lock of fair hair. His eyes were covered by a pair of sunglasses which the casual observer might consider appropriate for shielding the eyes from the autumnal sun, but which were, for the man in question, a necessary tool of his work.

He had seen the group enter the building from the rear, having been provided with instructions to keep the building under surveillance for any signs of unusual activity. He had spent the last few hours periodically moving from the rear to the front of the building, noting nothing of significance, until he had set his eyes on a group of kids skulking around the car park. His attention had been specifically drawn to the way they looked and acted. He doubted very much that they were there by chance given the relative isolation of the car park. Not to mention that they just looked out of place, although he was unable to determine exactly why. Maybe it was what they were wearing. They did not look like all the other kids he had seen. His instructions had been clear, 'observe and do not interact'. It was not for him to question authority and he was happy to spend an hour or two enjoying the late autumn sunshine on what appeared to him to be a rather easy assignment. Had the weather been inclement it may have been another story. He considered how he hated the cold and the rain. Several assignments had led him to spend time in uncomfortable conditions, observing targets whilst the rain lashed against his bare face, clothes drenched through. During this rare moment of reflection, he realised how much he disliked the work he was employed to do.

His train of thought was broken by the sight of his targets exiting the front of the building. He had guessed correctly that whilst they had entered discretely by the back, they would have not wanted to retrace their steps if they were up to no good, instead exiting on to the main street in front of the building and across from his position. He fleetingly considered that they may have been trained for some kind of purpose, given how they were acting, but quickly dismissed the idea, concluding instead that they must have met someone inside who was directing them. He observed that they had a change of clothing and wondered what instructions they had received. There was no indication at this stage, and he had received no further intelligence to enable him to come to any sensible conclusions. His employers had provided a fairly patchy brief. The lack of information had bothered him, and he had almost turned down the opportunity. However, he had weighed up the nature of the assignment with the risks that it presented and decided that on balance he was happy to proceed. It was unlikely he would work for them again however, if that was the way in which they operated. He had stayed alive this long only by being cautious and thoroughly assessing all the risks, which meant having all information possible to hand. He felt very uncomfortable operating with insufficient data. He would carry out his instructions and complete his assignment to the best of his abilities, but once done, he was out of there.

He noticed the friends pause for a few minutes in front of the book depository. They appeared to be discussing their next steps and studying objects that they were holding, but it was difficult to glean anything useful from their strange behaviour. What was clear moments later as the group dispersed in different directions, was that he was not going to be able to continue to observe them all. He would have to make a choice. He chose to follow the one that appeared to him to be the leader of the group. He quickly lost sight of the other four as he remained on the tail of the tall, blonde boy crossing the road at the corner of Houston and Elm.

As he followed the young lad up Elm, seemingly unnoticed, his mind wandered again. He found that, counter-intuitively, letting his mind wander, enabled him to retain his focus on the job at hand. He had followed people in all sorts of situations before and he was proud of the level of skill that he had developed. A key requirement was to remain inconspicuous, which meant not staring intently at the target. A target was less likely to feel they were being followed by someone who was in closer proximity but whose attention was apparently on something else, than a tail which was further away but acting indiscreetly in order to keep their eyes on them. Thus, he could follow at a closer distance without drawing attention to himself.

His thoughts turned toward his current employers and

their objectives. Whilst he was happy to continue to carry out his work in the knowledge that he was being paid, he was uneasy about the engagement. There had been something niggling at him when he had been offered the job. It wasn't the fact that he had not met his employer that bothered him, as this was common practice in his chosen profession, it was more that the target was not clear to him and he had no insight in to the circumstances surrounding them. It was not his place to ask questions of course, other than ones relevant to operational aspects of the assignment, but in this case, he was not convinced of the motivations behind what he was being asked to do and this made him uneasy. He accepted he was no saint and had had carried out many orders in the past which he had felt were potentially morally dubious, but he at least was able to reconcile his actions to a greater good.

There were no such reassurances in this case. He had expected to see professionals. Either organised criminals or security specialists, depending on which side of the coin his employers were on. He had not expected to see a bunch of kids. Surely a less qualified person could undertake this babysitting job. It was also suspicious that he had not received any further contact from his employers since the initial instructions had been provided. They had mentioned something about not being contactable until the time came, which struck him as odd.

As he continued along Elm, still following the young man from out of town, he contemplated abandoning the mission. The risk to his reputation was palpable, on the other hand the type of engagement was equally doing nothing for his standing in the security community.

The clear blue skies were interrupted by grey rain clouds accumulating and it was not long before the heavens opened. It was at this point that the young man boarded a bus which was situated twenty yards from his current position. In a desperate attempt to remain on his tail, he decided to run to catch up with the bus and board before the doors closed.

The only seat available was directly next to his target. It was a risky strategy, but he concluded that it was one worth taking, especially if the intention was to remain on the bus until it terminated. He had observed as he boarded that the destination of the bus was downtown Irving. Forty-five minutes by bus.

+++

"Do you think he will hold his end up?" The gruff-voiced individual situated at the head of the table asked the group in front of him.

"He came highly recommended," came a response from one of the others sitting around the table.

The conversation was taking place in a darkened room. Shutters kept out any light from the outside, whilst a single bulb hung from a bare fitting in the centre of the ceiling emitting a faint light over and across the table. The power of the bulb was sufficient only provide illumination for its immediate proximity; the rest of the room remained in pitch blackness. Not that there was anything to see. Other than the table and chairs, occupied by several drably dressed individuals, the room contained nothing else.

"I am not convinced. I got the impression he was a little sceptical," continued the lead figure.

"We have no choice but to rely on him, until we can make it there ourselves," came a third voice.

There were seven figures in total around the table. The dim light providing few clues as to their physical appearance.

Their features were predominantly masked, only the occasional glimpse revealed as the solitary bulb swung gently from side to side when disturbed. All that would be discerned by a stranger entering the room, should that ever be allowed, would be that they were of differing shapes and sizes, but all equally foreboding.

"When is our window?", the apparent leader enquired.

"Tonight, at seven pm," the individual sat next to him confirmed.

"And he is scheduled to call you then?

"Yes. We calculated that the site of the assassination is likely to be visited by the Circle in the days preceding the event and we have asked him to undertake surveillance at that location. He will let us have details of who we are dealing with."

"We must be ready. This is one of our best opportunities to achieve our objective and we cannot miss it. We must be a hundred percent prepared and absolutely ready to carry out the plan once we travel. The future of the human race is dependent on our success," the leader continued.

"We are ready from our side. Each of us has a clear mandate. Our assessment is that we can still achieve our aim with only a partial success, w-"

"Less than complete success is not acceptable," the leader aggressively interrupted his subordinate. "You must each successfully carry out your brief or there will be repercussions. This stinking race must be wiped from the face of the planet. It is pure evil and we have no other choice but to ensure its absolute desolation. The multiverse will have an opportunity to re-establish itself in peace and harmony. A new creation, a new genesis." He stood ready to address the group in more consolatory terms. "We have seen centuries of pain and suffering, of devastation and the annihilation of all that is good. The planets and universes lived in comparative harmony before the human race entered the scene and embarked on their ruinous journey. Ours may be seen as an equally evil task, but our resolve must not falter.

We have an obligation to a higher power that is good,

and we must remind ourselves of this whenever we doubt our intentions." At this he regained his seat and looked around the room at the heavily cloaked occupants. He felt no remorse for the actions that those in front of him would have to undertake in the coming hours and days. For his part he was utterly determined to force the extinction of the human race. The rewards guaranteed in the afterlife.

"Let's get to work," he continued. "We will go through the plan to make sure nothing is left to chance. First, the lead proposition, the one with the most disruptive impact."

The man to his side took up the narrative. "That would be me. Our target is a man named Lee Harvey Oswald. He is instrumental in the sequence of events in the timeline of the universe that we are looking to disrupt. Our estimates are that our success in this element of the plan will create the largest impact. Should we…" the man hesitated as he caught sight of the glare from the leader. "Apologies, our success is calculated as a 90% certainty that the universe will be irreversibly damaged. Our approach therefore is to apply additional resources to this endeavour. My colleague here," the man gestured to the figure to his left, "will assist me. Our focus will be to prevent the target from making it to his destination of the sniper's nest on the twenty-second of November 1963. We have identified a number of opportunities along his timeline which we can exploit in order to achieve this. The absence of the target at the expected time and place will result in a cataclysmic disturbance to the recorded history of the event which will preclude the universe from continuing on its path leading to its insurmountable destruction, and in turn knocking the multiverse balance sufficiently to create a domino effect leading to the ultimate demolition of everything we know." It was a rousing dialogue, if somewhat unnecessary, intended to please his leader and place him in favour within the group. It had the desired effect. "Excellent work," the leader expressing his utmost gratitude for the effort. Who is next?"

"My mission," said a quietly spoken man at the end of the table, "is to disrupt the assassination itself. Our intelligence is that there are others involved in the final stages of the assassination and my attention will be focused on one individual who we consider is key in the conspirators' plan." The unassuming confidence of the man was unnerving to those around him, but it was apparent to the leader that here was someone he could trust to get the job done. "Very good. Next," the leader commanded.

A less eloquent and insecure man was next to speak. "I will be covering the plaza and trying to get the police to focus on events leading up to, and individuals involved in, the assassination."

A short pause ensued as a consequence of the abrupt conclusion to the disrupter's description of his part of the plan. The leader did not comment but instead turned his head to the next along the line. The man looked up feeling the intense stare of the leader boring in to him. "The plans for the route of the motorcade have been published. Our analysis is that the route should remain untouched, so as not to alert the assassins who may be able to change their plans and complete their objective. Instead I will be taking steps during the journey from Love Field to Dealey Plaza to move the motorcade away from the kill zone."

"Do you have further details of your plans?" The leader pressing for more information to give him comfort regarding the prospects of success.

"My intention is to create some crowd trouble along the route, or to introduce a traffic incident."

"And you think that will be sufficient?" The leader enquired.

"Depending on who is involved in the conspiracy, there may be very little appetite for a change in the route even if there is deemed to be a security risk or obstruction, however we must assume that those in control on the ground will not be conspirators and will make decisions in our favour."

"Good. And finally?"

"My role is one of a fail-safe, sir," a deep, raspy voice piped up. "In the unlikely event that we are unsuccessful in preventing the assassination, we have a secondary event which is likely to prove successful in our overall objective, if we can ensure its disruption. On the twenty-fourth of November, Lee Harvey Oswald will be assassinated by Jack Ruby. With his death, the real story of his involvement in the events of the twenty-second of November will die. If we keep him alive, it will significantly disrupt the universe's timeline in that the true events of the day will be revealed, and thousands of people's lives will be irrevocably changed.

All those who had or have an interest in the day's events, conspiracy theorists, governments, casual observers will all be impacted. The universe itself will be unable to maintain its stability with the fundamental changes to all these people's lives. It will collapse under the pressure."

"I am satisfied that our plans are sufficiently robust to achieve what we need to. It is time to put it into action."

And with that the group rose and left the room in silence.

+++

"Two hours. Two hours sitting here watching a boy, watching a house, in the rain," he mumbled under his breath.

He was losing interest in the engagement, particularly as the pleasant autumnal sunshine of earlier was now just a distant memory. He checked his watch and noted the time was just before six in the early evening. Since alighting the bus and walking the short route from Oakview Park along West Fifth street, the boy had not moved. He had positioned himself just by a collection of oak trees on the south side of the road looking directly across at an unimposing property.

A Ranch style tract house, typical of those constructed in the last decade or so. Single-storeyed side-gabled house with a front-facing hip-roof forming part of a single-car garage.

Leading up to the house was a concrete drive with a concrete drainage ditch running alongside. Whatever interest this house had for the boy it had kept him occupied for a long time. Other than cars passing by, nothing had happened during that time. The man was struggling to decipher what interest his employers had with this boy. Nothing of note had occurred since he had started to observe the group earlier that morning and he was at a loss as to what he was expected to report back to his employers. He reminded himself however that he was a professional and would report just what he had seen. He was not being paid to make any assumptions or come to any conclusions.

He had passed by on the other side of the road shortly after the boy had arrived, having followed him at a discrete distance from the bus stop. He was positioned with a view of the boy but sufficiently out of sight so not to be noticed either by the boy himself or any neighbours prone to peeking out of their front windows for a chance of some neighbourhood gossip. It was probably strange enough for the neighbours to see a boy stood static in the same place for such time without also seeing a grown man observing him, no matter how inconspicuous he could make himself. His position however on the corner with Lilac Lane was enough not to rouse suspicion. He lit a cigarette and assumed a position which suggested he was outside his house to enjoy a smoke.

Shortly after and before he had finished the cigarette, he noted the boy change the direction of his gaze. The boy was now looking east down the road. From his position on

Lilac he could not make out what he boy was looking at, but it was certainly something of interest as his eyes remained transfixed. He noted the boy shifting his position moving further in to the trees blocking the view of him from the road. He deduced that the boy had his eyes on a moving object coming up the road toward their positions. He considered moving to get a better view of the object but calculated that the risk of being noticed was too great.

Instead he would bide his time and wait to see if the object of the boy's fascination came in to view. At that moment however, the boy edged back forward, suggesting to him that the vehicle had come to a stop or turned direction. His training kicked in and his quick assessment of the information available to him and the relative risks supported the conclusion that he needed to move to take a look before the object disappeared out of view. In his favour the corner of Lilac and Fifth culminated in a wide turning circle which was surrounded with deciduous trees and bushes which retained their leaves and foliage at this time of year, providing a sufficient amount of cover. With the boy also occupied with the vehicle further down the road he was able to cross over with reasonable confidence of not being observed. He arrived on the opposite side of the road just in time to see a black 1954 Chevrolet Bel Air turn right in to Westbrook Drive. As it did so, it immediately came to a stop, the red brake lights lighting up the intersection in the fading light of the evening. The passenger door opened, and a man stepped out. The man appeared to be of modest height, he estimated about five foot nine, slim, maybe a hundred and forty pounds and short cropped hair. It was difficult to ascertain the clothing he was wearing, but it appeared the man was a labourer of some sort. The man closed the car door and headed along the road toward them. Having seen enough he decided to return to his position of relative safe harbour back across the road. He could no longer see the man who exited the car, but the boy remained in view. Instead of focusing on the man, the boy was now nervously looking up and down the street, as if surveying, looking for some other activity. As far as he could make out there was none, and the boy resumed his sights on the house opposite. He remained in place for the next hour, occasionally adjusting his position as neighbours returned from their daily commute or departed for an evening out.

+++

Unlike members of the Golden Circle, the disrupters were not constrained by travelling in a group. Smaller in numbers than the Golden Circle they had needed to find a way to develop the ability to move between universes individually so that they could be more effective. In direct comparison, the Golden Circle, who had many more members and a philosophy of working together continued to use the original method of time travel which had been developed far in the future.

The development of time travel had been with noble intentions. The Earth had been in decline for centuries and was at risk of dying. The atmosphere had depleted, the polar ice caps melted, land either under water or scorched by the increasing temperatures. Crops no longer grew and more and more species became extinct. Only the humans survived, by adapting to the deteriorating conditions. Ironic given they were the cause. A group of scientists and other forward-thinkers had embarked on a crusade to reverse the impact of climate change and to prevent the ultimate decimation of the Earth. They had devised a plan. They would work towards developing the ability for time travel and go back in time to a point where they could encourage the human race to make better decisions for the sake of the Earth's future. They felt that if they were able to influence behaviour early enough, only small steps would be required to make a significant difference.

It quickly became apparent however that their attempts were largely futile. Small successes were recorded but too little, too late was being done to halt the juggernaut of ruin.

Frustrated by the lack of progress, a small group began to meet in secret, discussing more radical steps to take. They eventually concluded that the only option open to them was total destruction. Their faith placed in the hope that the multiverse would re-establish itself and regenerate, loosely described by them as the 're-bang'. A splinter group was formed, dubbed 'The Disrupters'.

The Golden Circle retained their faith that the human race would eventually come through and continued to take the small steps to encourage acquiescence. However, with the growing threat from the Disrupters, their mandate increasingly became about preventing the Disrupters from achieving their aim. Each generation of the Golden Circle throughout the ages, assisted by future technology, tracked the comings and goings of the Disrupters. Analysts mapped these historic movements and were able to identify significant events. These were reported to the elders who arranged for teams to travel ahead of time to thwart the Disrupter's intentions.

The Disrupters were aware that as soon as they entered another time and place, they were immediately discoverable. They were aware that the Circle kept them under constant surveillance once they appeared, determined to protect the human race and foil the Disrupters' plans. They considered it therefore of paramount importance to travel as close to the impact time as possible. But preparations were required and those with the largest amount to do, were about to start their journey.

It was a constant source of perplexity to the Disrupters as to why the Circle was so adamant in protecting a race that was itself hellbent on self-destruction. It was clear to them that the human race was fundamentally flawed with an inherent propensity to evil. The Disrupters saw themselves as saviours, merely facilitating the early, inevitable demise of the human race and providing an opportunity for a new birth before it was too late and the damage to a prospective multiverse irreversible.

The leader deliberated on this as he braced himself for the end of civilisation as each Disrupter disappeared in to the past. He allowed himself a few moments of regret at not being on the front line during this historical sequence of events. He had done enough previously to justify his position as leader and, irrespective of whether he was able to physically participate or not, remain absent should he choose to do so. There was no criticism from any quarter, however he felt personally inadequate in the circumstances. The pain running the course of his leg gave him a timely reminder of his incapacity. Despite this, he remained self-critical.

+++

Darkness had taking hold and the temperature dropped as the flash of light lit up Greenwood cemetery. The dark figure that emanated from the centre of the light had a disturbing aura which was harmonious with the eerie surroundings of tombstones and crypts, home to the dead.

The rain clouds which had gathered overhead prevented any natural light from illuminating the cemetery. Instead dim lights from the surrounding streets overcame their struggle to shine through the branches of the cedar trees, intermittently bouncing off the tombstones and statues bringing them to life. A casual observer out for an evening stroll would consider the atmosphere somewhat menacing, but not the visitor on this occasion. Bold and confident the man, dressed in a long, dark overcoat and wide brimmed hat, forced his way through the dank and gloomy night in the direction of the documented motorcade route. His purpose to walk the route to identify the best opportunities to set up possible distraction points, to divert the motorcade away from the published route and the killing zone along Elm.

He calculated that the greatest likelihood of success would be found close to Dealey Plaza as an earlier obstruction could easily be diverted without significant change to the published route through the centre of downtown and back to the killing zone. However too late in the route and it was likely the motorcade would merely take a short diversion of a block or two to get back on to the proposed route, which would not have the desired effect. If he could create a significant enough delay, then the motorcade would undoubtedly cut the route short in order to keep the president to his itinerary and thus avoid the assassination attempt.

Cursing the weather as the rain continued to fall with an incessant heaviness which soaked him from head to foot, he increased his speed until he reached Cedar Springs Road, which had been advertised as a section on the motorcade route. Whilst the conditions and the darkness undoubtedly assisted in keeping him inconspicuous, he was keen to complete his reconnaissance as quickly as possible. It was about five hundred metres along Cedar Springs Road when he saw an opportunity.

There was a major intersection which he judged would make the perfect setting for a traffic incident, causing a substantial blockage to the motorcade. The planned route had the motorcade continuing across the intersection along Cedar Springs Road before turning left onto North Harwood. If he could create enough of a disturbance before the intersection, he considered that the motorcade would be significantly delayed and ultimately forced east on to McKinnon Street. This would divert the motorcade away from downtown Dallas but more importantly was a route out to the Trade Mart. He calculated that the secret service was unlikely to risk staying on an unauthorised route for too long, so once diverted he was banking on them taking the shortest route to the Trade Mart where the president was due to speak at a lunch. He was satisfied that this was the best chance he would get and given the conditions was happy to bring a halt to his exploration. He decided instead to seek shelter, a warm meal and some privacy to plot the rest of his plan.

+++

Suffering from exhaustion and the ill-effects of the now sodden clothes he was wearing, Tom was doubting whether he had the metal to complete the mission he had been handed. It was either the time travel or the fact that the last few hours had been intensive and quite a strain, but he was feeling unusually tired. It was at that point that he realised that he hadn't eaten since arriving. The events of the day had so far distracted him sufficiently that he had not thought of food, but it was beginning to take its toll and his stomach was calling out for sustenance. As he plundered his bag for something to eat, his thoughts moved to his friends, Jake particularly who must by now have consumed the entirety of his backpack. He understood the role he had to play over the coming days but was less familiar with their tasks. He had every faith in them of course, more so than himself, but then he had always suffered from an unhealthy measure of self-doubt. The rain continued to beat down with no indication of any imminent respite. He chose to hunker down and pull his jacket up around his neck to close out the damp getting through. He devoured the contents of his lunch bag and finished his water. He then turned his mind to the night and the thought of replenishing his supplies. He had no plan for this and was certain that if he didn't come up with one it could have a disastrous effect on the success of the mission. However, he didn't have long to worry about this as his phone vibrated in his pocket. He removed it from his inside pocket and clicked on the message icon which was flashing. It showed a number of messages which he had obviously missed earlier. His emotions buoyed by seeing that a number of messages were from his friends, he scrolled to the latest message first as this appeared to be from the Circle.

He opened it and fear immediately rose within him. Had he not just have eaten he might have confused the feelings with hunger pains, instead he felt like throwing up. The message informed him that the first of the Disrupters had arrived and that the Circle were tracking his movements which remained in downtown Dallas at this moment. His heart sank at the next line. Michael had been dispatched to locate and monitor the Disrupter for further intelligence on his plans. Their assessment was that there was unlikely to be any further arrivals until the early morning as the risk was too great for them, but that Tom should stay alert to further messages, in particular if an arrival appeared close to him. He was advised to find somewhere to rest for the night and be back at his position by five am. Tom noted the time was now thirteen minutes past eight. He had hoped for a little more assistance from the Circle, 'find somewhere to rest for the night' he muttered audibly under his breath, with a tone which conveyed a not insignificant level of frustration.

"Where exactly?" he said, to himself as he surveyed the locality. He saw a man standing down the end of the road enjoying a cigarette, clearly unable to do so within the confines of his own house, as no-one would choose to stand out in this weather without good cause. He could go and ask him, but what would he say. He checked the map on his phone but that was reasonably unhelpful. He had noted a couple of signs for boarding rooms on his walk from the bus stop, so decided to retrace his steps and see if he could find a vacancy for an out-of-town eleven-year-old boy.

+++

He observed the boy gather his stuff and head back down the road that they had previously traversed. He checked his watch and noted the time. His instructions had been to call a number after seven in the evening for a debrief. It was now after nine. He suspected his employers would be unsatisfied with the level of information he could impart to them, but instructions were instructions and he had never failed on an engagement before and he was not going to start now. There was an irritating concern that give the lack of information he would not be paid for the work he had done, and it was not like he could easily track them down for payment either. But he decided to put those thoughts to the back of his mind and address it should the issue arise. His first objective was to locate a payphone and get out of the irksome rain.

Rather than follow the boy, he chose to explore the roads parallel to the one he was on in search of a public phone. He was fairly certain he hadn't been seen by the boy but having tailed him for the best part of the day, he felt the risk of continuing to shadow him further at this time of night, when there were fewer people around just didn't make sense and he would gain very little additional intelligence in any event.

Eventually he came across a payphone which was relatively isolated and given the weather he was confident that he would not be overheard by some errant passer-by.

Nonetheless he remained cautious, a product of years of training in the secret services followed by several more as, what some unfairly labelled, a mercenary, a term he did not much care for himself. He preferred self-employed security specialist. After all it wasn't all about the money, although he did have to acknowledge that private practice was much more rewarding in that sense than his years in the forces and as a private protection officer had been.

He raised the ear piece and dropped the coins in to the slot on the phone. He waited for a dial tone to initiate, and then punched in the numbers he had been given at the beginning of the operation. The line emitted several short beeps during which he played out in his mind what he was going to report. He checked his watch to confirm the time again and realised that he was a little early. He moved to hang up but just at that moment there was a crackle on the line as it jumped in to life. A sombre voice spoke. "Tell me what you have learnt."

He had endured plenty of sinister situations which would normally have ensured he was prepared for the occasion, but something was unnerving him this time. He was full of anxiety but was heavily relying on his training and adrenaline to get him through. "I followed your instructions and kept the building under surveillance. Nothing of significance was observed until just after twelve-thirty, eastern standard time. There was a group of five children, I would say no older than twelve or thirteen. Their appearance was somewhat unusual, although I cannot confirm exactly in what respect, but they were, in my view not local kids. My assessment was that they were likely to be from out of town maybe from the west coast or some other hippy enclave." He paused, conscious that he was relaying his own opinions rather than facts, which he suspected would be of no interest to his employers. He continued, "They approached the building from the east,"

"They would have needed somewhere isolated," the Disrupter mumbled, commenting to himself.

The man was not sure of the relevance of the comment but was aware of Trinity Overlook park to the east of downtown which would have been an isolated environment and wondered if he was making reference to that location. He did not mention it. Instead he continued with his report. "They remained inside the Texas School Book Depository on Elm for approximately forty, four-oh, minutes before exiting on to Elm through the building's front entrance. I observed that they had a change of clothing, which enabled them to better blend in." The man on the other end of the line interjected, "We will need to know details of their appearance, but for the moment proceed with what happened."

"I observed them communicating on the steps of the book depository and viewing some handheld devices. From my position I was unable to ascertain the nature of the devices or the matter to which their interest was focused.

After a further five minutes they advanced in different directions. I assessed that the leader of the group was a young man, approximately one hundred and twenty-five centimetres in height, slim with blonde hair. I made the decision to choose him as the subject to tail." He continued to describe the journey he had taken following the boy out to Irving where he had remained transfixed on the house on West Fifth street. As he was getting closer to the end of his narrative his anxiety was growing. There had been no feedback from the voice at the end of the phone and he was none the wiser as to whether the information he was relaying was of interest or use to them. He had no idea of their expectations and he was in the dark as to what would happen if they were dissatisfied with his report. A feeling of dread rose in him as he considered their options, which could be far more ominous than a matter of non-payment. "The boy then retraced his steps along West Fifth, I determined, looking for shelter from the rain. That concludes my report." As the words left his mouth, he caught himself gripping the receiver tightly, his knuckles white.

"Thank you," came the response which suddenly filled him with a great sense of relief. He relaxed but said nothing. The voice continued, "please describe the children in more detail so that our team can identify them." The words in themselves fairly innocuous, but the suggestion was plain and the manner in which it was delivered sent his anxiety level back up the scale. He was bemused by the reaction he was having to these individuals. He had dealt with drug smugglers and hired killers with no sense of trepidation, yet here before him were apparently far less dangerous individuals sending him in to a state of unforced panic. As much as he abhorred any harm coming to children, and animals for that matter, and had always set a line that he would not cross when it came to accepting engagements, he sensed that if he refused, his own life would be in danger. He could of course be wrong and maybe they would not harm the kids. He tried to convince himself of this, despite his instincts shouting otherwise. Nonetheless, despite his reservations, he continued to describe each of the children in detail.

"Thank you for your services. Payment will be made as agreed. I assume I do not have to remind you of the confidential nature of your engagement?"

He couldn't help feel that the last question was rhetorical in nature and a far from gentle warning to keep his mouth shout, but he answered anyway, "Of course, my reputation, as you are aware, is built on absolute discretion." It was a bit of a rebuff and he surprised himself with his own boldness, but he had come to somewhat despise these people and with the engagement at an end knew he had nothing to lose. He certainly would not be working for them again. The line went dead.

Conflicted, he had a decision to make. His head was telling him to walk away, pick up his money from the agreed drop off point and leave town, but his heart was telling him to hang around and see what played out. He rarely felt remorse for any actions he had taken but, on this occasion, he felt that he may have some responsibility for these kids, especially now that he had put them in the way of imminent danger. Furthermore, the overwhelming desire to get one over on these arrogant creatures meant that his heart overruled his head and he decided he would stick around.

He was not sure whether this was out of a misguided sense of duty or mere curiosity. In any event he convinced himself that on balance it was the right thing to do, so he followed the road back towards Fifth to see if he could track down the boy.

8 THE CALM BEFORE THE STORM

Tom removed the remaining rain-soaked clothes and hung them on the end of the bed. He felt particularly vulnerable sitting on the bed in just his under-garments, but he did not have a spare set of clothes, his original set have been taken by the member of the Circle whom they met at the book depository. He hoped he would get them back. He didn't have much in this world and could not afford to lose the precious little he had. As he sat there, exposed, he had the first opportunity to truly reflect on his situation. Were it not happening to him first hand he would not have believed it. He summarised the events of the day in his mind. He had travelled through time and space, met a stranger in a strange place who gave him instructions to follow a man who in the next twenty-four hours would be arrested for the assassination of a US president. And it was his job to make sure that it happened. He recognised the absurdity of it and couldn't help but feel aggrieved that the history books of the future would not record the role that he and his friends will have played. Although perhaps that was for the best when, on further consideration, it struck him that there may be significant implications if they were identified as being involved in the events that were soon to follow. For example, how the hell would they get back home if incarcerated in a US jail in the nineteen-sixties. Now whilst there was nothing special at home to tempt him back, he would rather take that than rot away in a foreign prison, or worse still, face death row. Perhaps it was better that their efforts go unrewarded. At this point his attention was drawn back to his phone and the messages he had received from his friends. He retrieved the phone from his jacket pocket, where he had stored it away from the rain. He opened up the app and made his way through the messages.

The first was unsurprisingly from Lucy. She and Rhianna had stayed together and had spent the rest of the afternoon looking around Dealey Plaza. It had remained uneventful. She explained that the time for them to get involved would be when the crowds gathered in the morning, therefore they had decided it was much more sensible to focus their efforts on finding somewhere to stay out of the rain. It didn't take much for Tom to realise that Rhianna must have been getting on Lucy's nerves. Lucy went on to give further details on their day together and Tom was reading between the lines.

The reference to frizzy hair was particularly telling. Tom began to forget about his situation as he chuckled to himself picturing how the day had probably gone for them. He was mightily relieved to hear that they were safe, even if Lucy had been tormented for the day. According to Lucy's account, they had been successful in blagging a room at the Adolphus Hotel on Commerce Street, a few blocks from Dealey Plaza. Lucy described how they had wandered aimlessly for a while following their reconnaissance of Dealey Plaza. Rhianna had started to complain that her feet hurt, and that she was soaked through when they had come across the entrance to the hotel. They had glanced up at the ornate façade and immediately concluded that it was beyond their budget, but they agreed to try their luck anyway. At the very least they would get out of the rain. She described the interior as elegant with crystal chandeliers, velvet furniture and dark wood panelling, comparing it to something out of a nineteen-twenties Hollywood movie. Their attempts to get a room however had not started well with an overly officious receptionist insisting on calling the General Manager when they confirmed that they were not currently guests of the establishment and had no money for a room. Their fortunes changed however when they did a remarkable job in pulling on the General Manager's heart strings with a sorry tale of having all their bags stolen and having to wait until their parents could arrive the following day to retrieve them and take them home. The manager, Mr Anderson, had instructed them to call him Andy and to ask of any of his staff should they require any assistance at all. Apparently, he had two young daughters himself and hoped that should they ever be found in such a desperate state that someone would be generous enough to come to their assistance. They expressed their gratitude and suggested that just a warm meal and a bed for the night would be sufficient. By all accounts Rhianna's acting abilities was second to none and her American accent was so accurate that the manager had guessed they were from somewhere on the west coast. Thankfully Lucy had paid attention during a fairly loathsome geography lesson in school and was at able to provide confirmation that they were indeed from Los Angeles, California. The lack of further detail was explained away by a sudden acknowledgement that they were still rather in a state of shock from the mugging, and very tired and would very much appreciate being shown to their room. The receptionist, showing a remarkable turnaround in attitude, explained that they usually had some free rooms on the nineteenth floor even during busy periods such as this, given the rumours. Observing the apparent confusion crossing the girls' faces as they looked at each other, the receptionist had gone on to explain that there were rumours that the floor was haunted although she had never experienced anything supernatural herself. Apparently, a bride-to-be had taken her own life when her fiancé had not turned up for the wedding.

She curtailed her storytelling when she caught sight of the glare from the General Manager. They had been shown to a room on the nineteenth floor and were thrilled when they were presented with the luxurious space containing a large soft bed and adorned with soft furnishings, including heavy drapes over the windows. The porter who had showed them to the room did not speak much English but apologised that there was just the one bed. The girls waived his apology away suggesting they were more than happy to share, given their predicament and the fact that they were exhausted and could sleep anywhere.

Tom mulled over the experience the girls had had as he looked around his own room. In comparison he could only describe it as a box with a window. The carpet on the floor had seen better days and it was not just the style that was out of date. He was pretty sure he could identify several stains which had made themselves at home within the pile. His experience in blagging the room was also not as smooth. He had noted the sign in the front window of a room to rent and had approached whilst formulating his back story. When the door opened, he found himself facing what he could only describe as a gentleman of limited means. The man was half dressed, sporting a dirty white vest top and oversized jeans.

He had a cigarette protruding from his lips, which wiggled as he spoke. "Can I 'elp you?" he had enquired rather unconvincingly. Tom had regained his composure sufficiently to impart his story to this unfortunate man, well the story he had invented at any rate. He had described in great detail his predicament of having arrived to stay with relatives only to be surprised to find that they were not at home and advised by the neighbours that they were not due back until the following day. However, Tom had decided not to follow his original plan of playing to the homeowner's sympathy, as he suspected it would fall on deaf ears. Instead he decided the best plan of attack was to show he could pay.

The man was clearly in need of money. The man had looked pretty indifferent and Tom had expected the door to close on him any moment, but when Tom took out the roll of notes that he had been provided by the contact at the book depository, the man's demeanour had instantly changed and he had shrugged as he moved aside to let Tom in to the house. "Ten bucks a night," the man had growled as he shut the door, closing off any potential escape route. "Fine," Tom had spluttered in response.

"Up front," the man continued, clearly not trusting his new tenant. Tom paid for two nights to be on the safe side and the man showed him the way to the room. A room, which he was now occupying and appraising and which it must be said, was not worth ten dollars a night.

Tom laid back on his bed, trying not to think about the other guests that might be occupying it. He looked back at his phone to go through the other messages. He scrolled to a message from Michael. Tom hesitated, knowing that Michael was the first to be engaging with the Disrupters. He was reluctant to open the message in case it was bad news.

The message appeared to grow in size on the display the longer and harder that Tom stared at it. Finally, he plucked up the courage and selected the message. Squinting as the display changed to reveal the content of the message.

Immediately Tom was filled with a sense of relief.

Michael in his wisdom had commenced the message with an underlined sentence "I am fine." Simple but effective and Tom was super grateful. He was, according to the message, tucked up in bed at a hostel. Michael had quickly got to the chase, describing the details of his encounter. On the face of it, an apparent straight forward affair. However, Michael had intentionally decided to omit some elements of the story so as not to worry his friends.

Having received his instructions to monitor the movements of the Disrupter, Michael caught a bus taking him north in the direction of the Disrupter's arrival point.

He had calculated that the Disrupter would have already left this location and would likely be scouting the planned motorcade route. As such he had made his way to the nearest point where the bus would cross the planned motorcade route and alighted there. It was not long before he observed some shadowy figure in the distance coming toward him. There were very few people out and about given the terrible conditions, which he considered to be both a blessing and a hindrance. Michael was able to easily identify the possible target, but he was also more easily detectable unless he took appropriate measures. He remained at a safe distance, hiding in the shadows of the buildings along the street. He ducked down an alley way as the Disrupter passed him along the route. He managed a momentary glimpse of the Disrupter as he passed by and what he saw sent a chill down his spine.

The figure was ominously dressed in black and sporting a hat reminiscent of the evil clerics of the Spanish inquisition. However, Michael observed much more than the individual's attire in those brief seconds, he saw pure evil. Even at his tender years he could spot it. The feelings and memories of a past that he had long suppressed resurrected from his deep subconscious. Michael continued to stand, with his back pressed against the brick wall, staring up at the rain as it poured down hitting him square in the face. Michael needed some inner strength and he was desperately looking to the heavens to find the inspiration. The few seconds that he remained there, his legs immovable, seemed like minutes. It was the bright lights of a car's headlights lighting up the rain like an exploding firework that refocused him. Nervously he stepped back toward the main street and peered around the corner in the direction of the Disrupter. Sufficient time had passed for the individual to be some way in the distance cloaked by the dark, only temporarily and briefly visible as a silhouette against the lights from the oncoming traffic.

Michael stepped out and followed, squinting from the bright glare from the cars that passed and the rain lashing against his face. He was just able to keep the figure within view and make a mental note of his actions. As the individual came to a stop, so did Michael. He did not want to take any unnecessary risks. He stared as the individual appeared to survey the surrounding area before, to Michael's absolute horror, turned and made his way back in Michael's direction. Michael froze momentarily as he recalled the ashen features that had paralysed him with fear minutes before and to which he was now about to be reintroduced.

He understood however that the Disrupters were undoubtedly now aware of who had been sent to stop them and he had no choice but to make himself scarce or risk being caught and suffer whatever evil they would inflict on him. Michael did the only thing he could think of at that moment, he turned and ran.

+++

Tom had left Jake's message to last. He had no idea what to expect as his best friend could be unpredictable at the best of times. At the very least he expected him to mention food at some point. Tom selected the message and then smiled as he read the opening sentences which announced that Jake was "starving". Jake had blagged a room at the family house of a local minister. After having left the group, his priority had been to search for food before anything else. He knew the little provisions he had left would not last for long.

However, as the heavens had opened, he had sought refuge in a local hall, which it turned out was the meeting place for the local Christian community. As he had entered the building he had been met by a young lady. Tom imagined Lucy rolling her eyes at this point as Jake went on to describe the girl in a great deal of detail. Jake had told the young lady a story of domestic abuse, which unfortunately was more relevant than Jake wished to remember, he had explained how he was homeless and looking for shelter. The girl had allegedly immediately conveyed the message to her father who was the local minister. After significant persuasion, he had agreed to put Jake up for the night. It was not long before Jake brought the story back to his stomach, as he revealed how he had just eaten the best home cooked meal he had ever had. He confessed that it had come at a price as he had had a rather awkward moment when he tucked straight into the food whilst his hosts stared at him.

Realising his error, he had sheepishly returned his cutlery to the side of his plate as they took each other's hands. His gracious hosts had not made a big deal about it but had invited him to join them. They proceeded to close their eyes and the minister led them in saying grace. There was however always an upside and Jake was delighted that he got to hold hands with the lovely Hope, whom he suggested may have a crush on him. "Cue more rolling eyes from Lucy," Tom thought.

Satisfied that his friends were safe, at least for now, Tom replied to all. First apologising for leaving it so late, he gave a quick account of his day, which he felt had been somewhat uneventful. He wished them all good luck for tomorrow and suggested they conserve their energy and get some sleep; he expected a busy time ahead. His last instructions were to ensure they kept their phones close.

As he lay there, his thoughts turned to what might be in store for him the following day. Although he understood what needed to be done and why, he was none the wiser about what would happen once he stepped out of the relative safety of his room. He felt very ill-prepared and the voice of Mrs Hibberd suddenly reverberated in his head, "Fail to prepare, prepare to fail." He was a long way from school and home now and the intense nature of his present circumstances reminded him how, perhaps, he did not have it all that bad back home. He would certainly be happy to swap places right then if he could. His stomach turned, and he moved his tired body to assume the foetal position, hoping to gain some comfort and get some sleep before the events of the next day.

If Tom was hoping for an easy transition in to sleep, he would be sorely disappointed. He tossed and turned for a considerable time. The condition of the bed did not help, but Tom was fully aware that his inability to get to sleep was nothing to do with the inferior quality of his mattress and more to do with the worry that filled his thoughts and made his entire body ache. In a perverse way he longed for his own bed despite the dark shadows that loomed over him night after night causing him to have the nightmares he had lived with as long as he could remember. Now he was presented with real fears and real danger. Something he was finding less easy to reconcile. Eventually Tom fell in to a fitful sleep, exhaustion overcoming his whirring mind.

+++

It was early when Tom was awoken abruptly, disturbed by the vibrations coming from his phone. He immediately knew what to expect – the rest of the disrupters had arrived.

9 THE PATSY

Tom had thrown his clothes on and grabbed his bag before exiting his room. He had hoped not to bump in to his temporary landlord as he made his way to the front door, but he was out of luck. The man was standing in the corridor outside his room, dressed identically to the day before. Tom suspected he may not have changed his clothes, although he couldn't be sure that the stains which stood out on this vest were the same as those that he had noticed the day before.

Clearly Tom was cognisant of the fact that he had no grounds on which to criticise given he was also wearing the same outfit two days running. Tom was not interested in engaging in a conversation and he desperately hoped that the feeling was mutual. However, the man was blocking his exit.

Tom wondered whether the man had been outside his room all night, perhaps concerned that this young stranger would steal from him, although it was not obvious that there was anything of value worth stealing. Tom gave the man a gentle nod as he approached and was delighted when the man stepped aside with no need to converse.

Tom opened the front door and peered out in to the breaking dawn. There was still a light drizzle in the air, but the heavy rain of the previous day had at least abated.

Tom made his way back to the house on West Fifth. He noted the time and was aware that in a few minutes he would observe the man he saw the previous evening exit the house and make his way down toward the turning with Westbrook Drive. His notes had dubbed this man 'the patsy' and his schedule suggested he was making his way to get his usual lift to work. Tom was on high alert. He knew he had to avoid being seen by the patsy, but also was aware that he needed to keep one eye on possible Disrupter activity. What that might be however, he was none the wiser. Tom remained on edge as the time came and the front door of the house opened, and the patsy exited. Tom was well out of sight and had a good view down the road. He was confident that there was nothing untoward. He followed the patsy, crossing the road as he approached the turning to get a better view. Still nothing. Tom acutely felt all of his senses peaked. His heart was beating faster, and his mouth felt dry. The street was quiet, despite the time of day and Tom almost felt his heart leap out of his body when a startled bird flew out of the nearby tree squawking loudly like an alarm, as if warning Tom of the dangers ahead. This had not gone unnoticed by the patsy either who had turned back to look for the source of the noise. Tom had averted his gaze. As he had done so he thought he spotted someone two hundred yards ahead of him, perched behind a tree at the intersection with Story road. In his heightened state he was unsure whether his brain was playing tricks on him but decided to keep checking just in case. He looked back in the direction of the patsy and saw him turn the corner in to the driveway behind a house. He caught sight of him putting the package he was carrying on to the back seat of the black 1954 Chevrolet Bel Air before closing the car door and walking to the back of the house.

118

Tom lost sight of him at that point and returned his scrutiny to the man behind the tree. He was no longer there.

Suspecting he may have imagined him; Tom focused his intention back on the patsy. Several minutes passed before he returned back in to view, shortly followed by another man.

They both got into the car and the brake lights illuminated as the engine started and the car moved back from the drive on to the road. The car drove towards Tom's position opposite the junction before pausing and eventually turning left on to West Fifth. Tom put his head down in order not to draw attention to himself and crossed the road opposite their position. At that moment, Tom became acutely aware of the noise of a revving engine coming from behind him further down the road. Turning, concern rising within him, Tom spotted a bright red Ford Mustang picking up speed and travelling in his direction. The overcast conditions ensured that there was no glare on the windscreen and only the few drops of rain that had started to fall prevented him from getting a clear view of the driver, until the car was approximately a hundred and fifty yards away. At that point, Tom's worst fears were realised. As the Mustang picked up speed, much too great for the suburban limits in place, Tom saw the profile of the driver and he suddenly felt sick to the core. He had no doubt that what he was looking at was a Disrupter. The pale, gaunt face that was staring out of the front of the car, intent on destruction, shocked Tom. There was no compassion behind the dark eyes which were fixed on the road ahead. Tom found himself in a state of disbelief, unable to comprehend the situation, dangerously delaying necessary action. As the car got closer, the revving of the car's engine became deafening. It was clear, the Disrupter intended to cause a collision with the Chevrolet. Tom knew the moment had arrived. The destiny that he had been forced to accept was in front of him. Time appeared to slow down, each second feeling like a minute. Tom continued to stare at the Mustang, his heart beating ever faster, his body stiffening, his legs weakening. It was increasingly apparent that if he did not act now, and quickly then he would fail, the Disrupters would win and the end of the world as he knew it would be on him. His gut instinct took over and he started to move from the safety of the curb to the danger of the road.

His plan, which had been speedily and crudely formed as he had stood staring at the oncoming car was to step into the road and cause the car to change its direction away from its target. He took several small but urgent steps in to the middle of the road as the car progressed at speed toward his position. Everything appeared to be moving in slow motion and although Tom was putting himself right in the path of danger, oddly he started to be filled with confidence and serenity. Could this be the calm experienced before imminent death or was he just full of adrenaline. He wasn't to know which, but what he was certain of was that it was his duty to stop the car reaching the Chevrolet. One further step and it was now just him between the Mustang and the Chevrolet and the imminent multi-universal destruction. Tom only had hope to hold on to as he stared directly at the Disrupter through the windscreen of the Mustang bearing down on him. The car must have only been a hundred yards away. The driver must have seen him. But it was not slowing down, not stopping or turning. His eyes momentarily met those of the Disrupter, and it dawned on Tom that impact was inevitable. He judged he had mere seconds left before the car reached his position.

+++

The Disrupter had spent considerable time studying the reported movements of the target. He was adamant not to leave any stone unturned in his ambition to be the one who brought success to their organisation and who gave hope to future generations. He selfishly wondered if they would honour him in some way. He wanted a legacy. He returned his thoughts to his plans, going over them in his head time and again. His plans were based on what he felt was the best opportunity for an early intervention, closer to the Randle residence at the start of the target's commute in to work. As soon as the car got on to the Stemmons freeway and the busy rush hour traffic he calculated he would be unlikely to stop the car before it reached downtown Dallas. The later he left it, the greater the risk of failure. He was not going to be the first one to be blamed for failure of the task. No, that could not happen. He would be ostracised. Getting in an earlier attempt also increased his odds of overall success as he may be able to rely on later opportunities to fall back on, if his first attempt proved to be unsuccessful.

He had arranged the hire of a car and decided that a car accident was the best way to prevent Lee Harvey Oswald reaching the book depository that morning. He took a moment to imagine the look on the faces of those who were expecting him to be there to assist them. He evaluated that this episode in itself would be sufficient to create the devastating chain of events that they were hoping for and his own personal glory. The moment was abruptly disturbed by a rasp on the car door window. He wound down the window and a figure outside crouched down to speak to him through the gap. "Nice car," it was his colleague. "Not exactly discrete though."

"It will do the job," he responded, his tone evidently asserting his authority. "Get in and we can get going." His colleague entered the passenger seat. "I'll drop you off on the way. I need to get to Irving before seven am." His colleague was fully aware of the plans but apparently not a part of the initial stage. "If I am not successful, you will

121

need to follow plan B from downtown. As you know we are not a hundred percent sure which way they will walk once they get to the parking lot, so I suggest you wait there and observe.

If I am able, I will get to you as soon as possible, but if you see the chance take it," the man looked to his colleague for assurances that the instructions had been understood. When no obvious acknowledgement was received, he pressed the matter, "OK?"

"Yes, OK. Understood," came the curt reply. There was a palpable amount of resentment between the two of them.

They drove the rest of the journey in silence until coming to a stop at the parking lot two or three blocks away from the book depository. Once his colleague exited and closed the door, he drove off without further discussion. He drove toward Irving to complete Plan A which he regarded as the only plan.

+++

The noise of the car's engine reached fever pitch. The Disrupter's hands clenched the steering wheel, knuckles white. Tom closed his eyes tightly, his whole body preparing itself for impact. As the Disrupter got closer and closer all his focus was on the glory of the mission. It would unquestionably be he and he alone who was responsible for its success. But slowly, as he stared at the young boy, the only thing between him and glory, he was overcome with a deep sense of doubt, like a dark cloak descending on him.

His customary self-belief was beginning to abandon him at the most critical of times. His mind had allowed itself to compute the different variables and possible outcomes from his actions. The conflict arising in him as he considered whether dispensing with this young member of the Circle was the best option. There was a possibility that by running down this boy he may miss the primary target. This was a risk, no matter how remote, that he was not prepared to take.

Suddenly he was faced with an unfamiliar feeling of panic, his self-assuredness draining from him. The glory that he had envisioned and which he had been revelling in only moments ago, was slowly dissipating. Had he left it too late, however? It appeared he had. Collision inevitable, he would have to take the risk.

As he accepted his fate and the fate of the young boy ahead of him, he became momentarily distracted by movement in his peripheral vision. He impulsively moved his eyes to look at the source of the distraction and watched as it rushed ahead of him and connected with the boy, knocking the by out of the way of the car, just before the moment of impact. At full throttle he passed by, twisting his head left to view the two bodies entwined and rolling together at the side of the road. As he did so he had inadvertently pulled down slightly on the steering wheel.

Regaining his composure and turning back to re-establish his sights on the intended target he realised he had taken the car off course and was headed for the pavement. He desperately attempted to rectify his error and pulled down on the steering wheel, but the front wheel clipped the curb and sent the car veering off in the opposite direction. The car was now completely out of control and despite the vain attempts by the Disrupter to get the car back on an even keel, the car uncontrollably shifted from side to side as it continued at a pace down the road. Finally, the Disrupter slammed his foot hard down on to the brakes, but it did not have the desired effect. Instead of coming to a halt, the car entered in to a dangerous spin, catching on the slippery surface from the damp conditions. The car continued to spin forward towards the junction. The Mustang flew through the junction coming to a standstill across Story Road. The Disrupter looked up and glared through the driver's side window, attempting to make out the position of the Chevrolet through the greyish smoke emanating from the tyres and steam rushing from the radiator of his car. The Disrupter noted the disappearance of the Chevrolet and with it his opportunity for personal glory. Disappointed and deflated he continued to stare out of the driver's side window. Had he chosen to look out of the passenger window instead however he would have seen the five tonne Peterbilt 281 eighteen wheeled truck bearing down on his position, like a bull charging a matador.

Tom, and the man that had saved him from imminent death, had come to a rest and sat up at the side of the road just in time to witness the truck careering in to the red Mustang that had been hell-bent on mowing him down seconds before. Although they were at a safe distance from the site of the crash, the sound of the screeching tyres followed by the thunderous crunch of metal on metal forced them both to instinctively take cover. When they resumed their positions, there was no sign of either vehicle. The momentum of the truck had ploughed at speed into the Mustang, forcing it into a cannon-roll down Story road.

Tom and the man jumped up and ran to the junction to view the carnage. When they reached the intersection, they saw first-hand the devastating aftermath of the crash. The Mustang was unrecognisable from the car that he had seen speeding towards him, the crumpled remains of the bodywork lying listlessly in the middle of the road like roadkill. The road was littered with metal fragments, smoke was bellowing from the wreckage and a puddle of liquid was forming alongside the remains of the Mustang. Traffic was backing up behind the truck, which now stood at the head of the queue of passive spectators. Screams and shouts went out, not in pain but as a warning. The truck driver leapt from his cab and raced away from the scene. Tom was initially confused by what he was seeing until he realised that a fire had ignited under the remains of the vehicle. Drips of fuel from the broken fuel tank were feeding the fire until the puddle of fuel and subsequently the fuel tank exploded in a vicious ball of flames and black acrid smoke. Spectators in the vicinity, including Tom, dived for cover, protecting themselves from the falling debris. Others, in the relative sanctuary of their vehicles looked on in disbelief as the fire continued to rage, lighting up the line of fuel that had been sprayed in all directions in the wake of the car as it had been forced reluctantly down the road. Drivers and passengers scrambled to get out of their cars seeking safe harbour as the line of fire travelled towards them.

"Hey kid, you're lucky to be alive," the man spoke as Tom continued to stare at the carnage in front of him through the haze of the heat being produced by the inferno. Tom turned, still in a state of shock and looked himself up and down, reassuring himself that all body parts were accounted for.

"Thanks to you I guess?" The man did not take offence at Tom's seemingly ungrateful response, putting it down to his state of shock. Tom was not predisposed to rudeness and realising how he must have sounded sought to quickly remedy the situation. "I mean sorry, what I meant to say is, thank you very much. I owe you my life."

"Don't mention it," replied the man, a smile appearing on his face, oddly juxtaposed to the surrounding pandemonium.

"So why did he want you dead?" the man asked.

"What, sorry?" Tom buying himself some time to respond to what was a particularly difficult question to answer.

"I noted he was not exactly slowing down when he noticed you in the road," the man was pressing for some answers. He had been correct is his suspicions that his former employers were intent on bringing harm to this group of kids and now he needed to understand why.

"Yes, it looked that way didn't it. I, er, I," Tom was struggling to find a reasonable explanation, so he decided ignorance was the best option. "No idea," he unconvincingly offered.

"Well at least no harm came of it," he paused reflecting on the flames lapping against the misshapen bodywork of the Mustang. "Well not to you anyway."

The faint hint of sirens could just be made out over the crackling of the fire, car horns and other commotion going on around them. "I suspect it may be better if you and I were not around when the cops get here," the man suggested.

Tom looked at him, not knowing whether he was someone who could be trusted. It surprised him that this stranger was proposing they leave the scene of a crime, but he couldn't find fault with the suggestion. Although he was unsure whether he trusted him, at the very least the man had saved his life so he should give him the benefit of the doubt.

He was also currently feeling very alone and vulnerable and an ally was welcomed. The man sensed some hesitation and realised how it must look to this boy who was being invited by a stranger to leave the scene of an accident in order to avoid the police. "I have an important meeting to go to and once the police get here, sorting this mess out could go on for hours," he lied. "It's up to you but I am happy to give you a lift in to town if you don't fancy hanging around."

Tom recognised that this man, whoever he was, suspected something, but it was an offer to get back to his friends and therefore a risk worth taking. "Thanks, that would be great. What's your name?"

"John," he lied, a tad too quickly he felt. He had been using aliases for years, so it came naturally for him to use one at the drop of a hat. This one was not particularly imaginative, but it would do the trick in the circumstances.

"I'm Tom," Tom said, holding out his hand.

"Pleased to make your acquaintance Tom," John said as he shook his hand. "We had better be going. My car is down here." They set off, leaving the incident behind them.

+++

The Chevrolet which, unknown to the occupants had had a lucky escape, pulled in to the warehouse car park off Munger Street. As instructed, the Disrupter who had been assigned to instigate plan B was observing from a distance.

The target got out the car and retrieved a package from the rear seat. The driver remained in the car as the passenger walked down Munger toward Houston. The Disrupter hoped that the target would continue the walk alone and an opportunity would present itself to intercept him before he reached the book depository. However, it was only a few minutes before the driver turned the engine off and followed his colleague. The Disrupter cursed but did not give up hope of completing the task before they reached the building. It would be considerably harder to implement the plan once they were inside. The Disrupter followed at a discrete distance but close enough to jump into action should the opportunity arrive.

+++

The journey had so far been uneventful, each of the passengers reflecting on the morning's events and assessing their position, keeping their cards close to their chests. Reluctant to give the appearance of being as mad as a box of frogs, Tom had decided brevity in his answers was the best policy. John had asked him several questions about his background including where he came from and why he was in Dallas. Tom had kept to his story of visiting family who were out of town. "So, are they English too? Your family," John had asked, picking up on Tom's accent.

"My Aunt is," Tom suggested. "Came over in the 60s and met an American, who she married."

Tom noticed a quizzical look from John as they continued along the Stemmons highway toward downtown Dallas. Tom realised his mistake but attempted to cover his tracks.

"I meant came over in '60. Got married very recently."

"First time out to see them?" John asked.

"Yes. First time out of the UK. We don't have a lot of money and it is quite costly to fly over." Tom felt he was doing ok, but the questions kept coming thick and fast and he was not sure he would be able to continue this level of deceit without slipping up worse than he had already.

"So where are they now?"

"What do you mean?" Tom stuttered, trying to recall what excuse he had given for being on his own.

"Well, you mentioned they were out of town. I was wondering where they were, given they knew you were coming out," John explained.

"Ah well, away on business. My uncle works away, and my aunt doesn't like to be home alone as she does not know too many people yet. I guess they just got the dates mixed up." Tom recognised he was flapping, but it was at least more plausible than travelling from another time and place in order to combat an evil society who wanted to bring an end to civilisation.

John reflected on how well the boy was doing in the circumstances. He was not sure he would have been so imaginative at his age. Still he thought he would have a little fun at his expense nonetheless. "So, what does he do, your uncle?"

"Salesman," Tom blurted.

"Oh really, me too. What does he sell?"

"Not really sure," Tom looked out the window for

inspiration and noted a billboard advertising electrical goods.

"Electrical goods, I think."

"No way, me too," John smirked.

Tom suspected he had been rumbled but was not going to concede unless he absolutely had to.

"What company, I might know him." John was enjoying teasing the boy. Meanwhile Tom was becoming increasingly uncomfortable.

"Not sure of the name."

"What is your uncle's name?"

"I'd rather not say," Tom said, desperately. There was a silence which followed which Tom struggled to deal with.

He was not a great talker, but he hated silences. It reminded him of too many occasions around the dinner table back home when the rest of the family fell silent discussing family matters recognising that Tom was not a real part of the family.

"Ok, look I can't tell you everything, because, well you just wouldn't understand," Tom broke the silence. "There is a group of people who are looking to cause a lot of problems, and me and my friends are here to stop them."

Knowing what he did about his former employers, John recognised that there was truth in what he was hearing, but he knew he would need to react surprised if he was to keep up the pretence of being a stranger with no knowledge of the affair. "Oh really," John feigned a sarcastic tone. "How exactly do you intend to stop them?"

Tom failed to pick up on the signs and mistakenly thought that John was accepting his story. Buoyed by this, he decided to open up a little. "We know what they are trying to do, so we just have to do something which stops them carrying it out."

"I see, like stepping in front of a car?" John said incredulously.

"I was kinda hoping he would swerve out the way,"

Tom accepted that it had been a dangerous assumption and for the first time since he had faced death headlong, he suddenly felt a sickness in his stomach. The adrenaline had left his body and he was coming down from the high.

John noticed the colour drain from Tom's face and sensed that Tom was looking for someone to talk to. It had been a traumatic few hours and he predicted that Tom was not a veteran of such situations. "As you are being so open, I should say that I am not currently employed as a salesman.

It is enough for me to say that I am self-employed and work in security. I have a certain set of skills that is well remunerated. Perhaps I can help." John hoped that these words would provide some comfort to Tom. John had been uneasy about his role to date and he was excited by the prospect of perhaps utilising his skills for the benefit of this young group of protagonists, especially given his dislike of his former employers. He was not expecting to be paid, but maybe he just needed to feel better about himself.

Tom looked at John. He trusted his instincts and felt an inner comfort in the words being spoken to him, especially given the events that had already transpired that morning.

Tom checked his phone discretely. The time was just after eight. He expected his friends to be gathering around Dealey Plaza and his intention was to meet them there.

"What is that?" John was nodding towards the phone which Tom had been unsuccessfully attempting to conceal. Tom looked down at his lap. He had no answer to that question, and he suspected the truth would not be palatable. He chose to be creative with his answer.

"It is a just a radio."

John was not convinced but would let it go for now. "Where are we off to?"

"Dealey Plaza please. I need to meet up with my friends. I think I have successfully done my part, but we still have lots of work to do," Tom hesitated before continuing. "I think we could do with your help."

"I am happy to help, but you are going to have to give me more. I need to understand what I am getting in to," John replied.

Tom was nervous about revealing too much but recognised his new friend's need for some assurances. "Fair enough." Tom decided to provide John with the details of his mission, careful not to disclose that the United States president would be killed or that he and his friends had travelled through time to ensure it happens. He felt to divulge these details may well result in loss of the much-needed support.

During the rest of the journey they engaged in a cat and mouse conversation. Tom endeavouring to avoid disclosing contentious details, John pushing hard for as much intelligence as he could.

+++

The target was walking at quite a pace and looked, to any casual observer, to be on a mission of his own. The Disrupter continued to follow, closing in on the target's position, the driver of the Chevrolet having dropped a fair distance behind and now considered to be out of the picture.

The streets were busy with workers making their way to their respective employments, single-minded in their focus and taking no notice of the Disrupter. The Disrupter reducing the distance to the target, suddenly saw an ideal opportunity to complete the objective. It would cause some commotion, but the Disrupter could disappear in the resulting throng. There was little time left however as the target was almost at the ideal position. The Disrupter broke in to a run, speeding toward the back of the target, intent on colliding with him and pushing him forward on to the railroad tracks that crossed with Houston. Barging past oncoming pedestrians sending them hurtling, ignoring the disgruntled looks and shouts of objections, the Disrupter could see the long train approaching from the right side and was moments from connecting with the target. Arms rising to extend out towards the target's back, as the disrupter reached top speed making every effort to reach the target before the train. Out of nowhere the Disrupter was rammed sideways away from the target, and ended sprawled, face-down on the pavement. The opportunity lost and the Disrupter peered back from the position on the floor to see the target move forward on to the back steps of the school book depository. "Are you ok ma'am?" a voice enquired from the ensuing crowd, reaching out a hand to assist the woman he had just laid flat. The Disrupter ignored the outreached hand, rising from her position to regain her feet, she dusted herself down and walked off toward the book depositary. As she moved, she mumbled under her breath that she would now have to do it the hard way, the man who had knocked her over, turned and spoke to a young man beside him, "Just in time, eh kid".

"How did you know it was her?" Tom asked.

"In my line of work, you can spot evil quite easily," John responded, as they both followed the woman with their eyes.

"I thought I had completed my part but looks like I have another problem to deal with and she is headed for our guy so we need to keep up and make sure we stop her," Tom suggested. "My friends will have to wait."

They watched as she continued down Houston, glancing up at the book depository as she passed. "It appears she is not an immediate threat," John suggested as they saw her pass by and not follow their man in to the building.

"We need to find out what her plans are," Tom advocated as he set off to follow, John in tow.

10 THE MOTORCADE

Michael woke from a restless night with very little sleep. Every time he had closed his eyes he had been confronted with the gaunt, ashen features of the Disrupter. Deep-set black eyes staring back at him, filled with anger and darkness. The feelings that had risen up inside of him and reminded him of darker days occupied his thoughts throughout the night. He had underestimated the enormity of the task at hand and the impact that it would have on him. He knew it would be no walk in the park, but here he was, scared witless, frightened to leave the safety of the hostel he found himself in. But despite his quiet demeanour and apparent sensitivity, he had an inner strength which he was able to call upon. The abuse he had once suffered was a double-edged sword in circumstances such as this. On the one hand it resurfaced like an unwanted relative at Christmas, but on the other hand it reminded him of what he was able to overcome. As a consequence, Michael did not stay scared for long. He gave himself a pep talk, grabbed his jacket and stormed out of the room with a steely determination not to let himself or his friends down.

Michael made his way from the hostel on Maple Avenue across to Cedar Springs Road and then on to the junction where he noted the Disrupter had paused the night before.

Rush hour was in full swing, the roads were busy with traffic but there were no obvious signs that in the next couple of hours, the president of the United States would be travelling along them. Michael was surprised that there were no police cordons or roads closed in anticipation. He was filled with a sense of foreboding. At that moment he understood that he was unlikely to receive any third-party assistance in completing what he had to do, it would be up to him alone to stop the Disrupter.

He calculated that he had some time to examine the area and assess where the key dangers lay. Ultimately however he would have to keep his wits about him and keep his eye out for the menacing figure that he had seen the night before.

Michael checked his watch. It was ten thirty-five and the scheduled time for the motorcade to pass by the junction between Cedar Springs Road and Pearl Street was just after twelve. He had no idea what the Disrupter's plan was. He suspected it would have to be something major in order to divert the motorcade away from its planned route but other than that, there was no other intelligence that he could rely on. He had checked his mobile several times that morning but other than messages from his friends all confirming that they were safe, there was nothing new to assist him with his task. He started to think through the possible ways in which the motorcade could be affected. It soon became clear that he would need to narrow those eventualities down if he had any chance of being ready when the time came. He had understood that the Disrupters were seeking to keep the president alive so assumed that any plan must involve moving the president away from any danger rather than putting him in further danger, otherwise they could not guarantee the outcome they desired. Furthermore, it must be a plan which would not necessitate the intervention of law enforcement officers, as this would undoubtedly raise an early alarm and give time for the security services to plan an alternate route to Dealey Plaza. Michael concluded that the easiest way would be to block the road somehow requiring the motorcade to change route at the last minute and with so much doubt in the mind of the security services they would likely move the president immediately to a safe destination.

He was pretty sure he knew what was going to happen and where. Now he just needed to find the Disrupter and stop him. "Easier said than done," Michael thought to himself.

He had scouted the area for about thirty minutes but had seen nothing unusual. The pavements were starting to get busier as spectators began to line the streets in anticipation of the president's arrival. With the increase in footfall, Michael's job of identifying the Disrupter became increasingly difficult. Nonetheless Michael moved position frequently to ensure he was covering the whole junction. As he strained to look north up Cedar Springs Road, he heard a commotion behind him. He turned violently, every noise setting him on edge. The cause of the disturbance was not immediately apparent, but Michael thought he could make out a small amount of smoke two blocks south of his position. He turned to walk in the direction of the fracas, breaking in to a jog as he approached the junction with Olive Street. He could finally make out the cause of the smoke and as he saw it, he came to an abrupt stop. The traffic was starting to back-up beside him and he realised that it would not be long before the traffic was solid back up past the junction with Olive and then onward approaching Pearl.

This was undoubtedly the work and intention of the Disrupter. He could now clearly make out an old blue pick-up truck with its bonnet raised and white smoke bellowing from the engine. The truck appeared to have been abandoned across the two lanes heading south. The drivers of the cars behind leaning on their horns as they failed to get past the broken down blue 1955 International R120, with a continuous passage of cars on the northbound lanes.

Michael knew he would have to get the vehicle moved, and quickly. He crossed the road weaving amongst moving and stationary cars, attempting to get to the east side of the road and the approach to the broken-down truck. As he got closer, he noticed a figure cowering behind the bonnet as if inspecting the engine. Briefly he was filled with hope that this was a helpful member of the public trying in vain to get the truck started and moved out of the way, but as he got nearer to the rear of the vehicle the figure rose and Michael was once again staring in to the abyss that was the blackness of the Disrupter's eyes. This time however the Disrupter was staring right back at him. His sight locked on the figure's sinister appearance, Michael's peripheral vision blurred and anything in it disappearing away and the cacophony of sound around him falling silent in his mind. For what seemed like an age the two stood staring at each other not moving, as if in some absurd game of chicken. Michael felt his life was about to end, overcome by the potency of the evil that he was faced with and the inevitable strength of the Disrupter that he knew he could not compete with. Suddenly however, the noise of the revving engines, car horns and now increasingly large crowd came back in to focus. The crowd becoming increasingly vocal sensing that the effort they had made to interrupt their daily routine on the off chance of a brief glimpse of the president of the United States, their president, was about to be disturbed by a broken-down truck.

The crowd were beginning to turn on the Disrupter, the target of their rising frustrations. Arms flailing, fingers pointing, voices shouting in his direction. The Disrupter was suddenly faced with the wrath of the crowd and the drivers who were being prevented from going about their business.

The Disrupter turned his head back to Michael who remained in his vulnerable position. Seemingly weighing up the options available, the Disrupter recognised that the odds of defeating the member of the Circle were against him with the crowd likely to come to the aide of this young boy.

Instead the Disrupter decided to flee, hoping that the position of the truck was sufficiently obstructive to cause a delay and force the redirection of the motorcade.

Michael watched on in disbelief as the Disrupter disappeared pushing and shoving his way through the growingly inhospitable crowd. Shouts continued to ring out in his wake with abuse for leaving his truck blocking the road and causing continued disruption. As he finally lost sight of the Disrupter, Michael's attention was brought back to the challenge of getting the truck moved to ensure that traffic freed up, ready for the president's motorcade. Michael knew time was against him as he glanced back down the line of traffic continuing to back up behind him. With the crowd now congregating in greater numbers packing every available space on the pavement, there was little room, if any, to move the vehicle off the road. Equally pushing the truck toward the next junction was impracticable, the tyres had been deflated and even if he had help from those gathering around him, it would take far too long. Michael shouted to the onlooking crowd to see if there was a mechanic who could take a look at the truck in the vain hope that they might be able to get it started. There was a momentary pause before some murmurings could be heard coming from deeper in to the crowd. All of a sudden, the crowd parted as if Moses had ordered it and a young man dressed in overalls walked steadily through the walls of the crowd to where Michael was standing. "Hi, I'm a mechanic," the man said.

"Great," Michael replied. "What's your name?"

"Sam," he responded, hesitating momentarily, bewildered at being addressed by a teenager with a strange accent. "This truck belong to you?" Sam drooled in a particularly heavy Texan accent.

Michael paused. He considered whether he ought to invent a story to make his reasons for getting the truck moved more plausible, but on balance as he took a second to view the anxious crowd, he knew that it would not be necessary. "No, I'm just here to see the president," Michael attempted an American accent in an attempt to appear less out of place. "And if we don't get the truck moved, he may well just drive some other route," he continued. Michael wasn't convinced his accent had been that successful, but nonetheless the mechanic appeared willing to help out, vociferous support coming from those looking on.

+++

Michael frantically checked his watch for the seventh time in five minutes. Sam sensed the boy's anxiety and without moving from his position, hunched under the bonnet, he continued to tinker with the engine as he tried to reassure Michael. "I'm pretty confident I have it this time." He signalled to Michael to try the engine once more. Michael dutifully pumped the accelerator pedal and pulled out the choke before turning the key once more. A sequence of steps that he had been repeating for the last five minutes without success. The ignition failed to turn the engine over as it wheezed and clunked with every attempt. Each endeavour wasting precious minutes and chipping away at the remaining time before the scheduled arrival of the motorcade. The noise around him had somewhat abated as the drivers holding their positions behind him became more resigned to their predicament and eased off their horns. The crowd sensing their singular opportunity to see a president in office at close quarters fading away.

Sam peered over the top of the bonnet and looked sheepishly at Michael through the windshield. Michael knew immediately from his expression that there was very little hope of getting the truck started. His heart sank. He felt he had faced up to the Disrupter and still lost. The repercussions of his failure dawned on him and with it a deep sense of regret and guilt. He placed his head on his hands that remained tightly clenched to the steering wheel. Those around must have been perplexed at the sight of him. Surely the disappointment of missing the opportunity to see the president at close quarters could not have such a profound effect on this young man. After all, he could just move to another part of the planned route, as they were now doing.

A voice from the crowd called out, "Unlucky kid. Looks like the president won't make it this way. Best to come along and catch him at Dealey."

"If only they knew," Michael thought to himself. The crowd was slowly dispersing, mutters of the inconvenience filling the air. Michael raised his head and looked at the crowd ebbing away. It struck him that seeing the crowd disperse was an apt metaphor, given the inevitable destruction of the multiverse, for the demise of the human race. Resigning to the fact that he was out of options, his attention was drawn to a sudden glare coming from further down the road ahead of him. Instinctively turning his head to the source, a smile started to spread across his face as he recognised potential salvation. For in the distance turning out of North Harwood Street on to Cedar Springs Road was a recovery vehicle, the midday sun, which had replaced the morning's drizzle, bouncing off its windscreen. With no time to spare, Michael leapt from the truck and raced down the road towards the recovery vehicle. His heart beating faster and excitement once again rising within him, he hollered at the top of his voice. The crowd which had been dispersing turned in unison to see him running and gesticulating like a mad man. Some, impervious to the young man's antics resumed their exodus, whilst others, curious and full of fascination with his actions, stopped and stared.

The driver of the recovery vehicle was about to turn left away from the on-rushing Michael. Were this to happen, Michael knew there would be no further breaks. He had to make sure that he reached this vehicle before it turned. With once further piece of luck, the driver glanced one more time to the right before proceeding to manoeuvre his vehicle out of the junction. His eyes lingered on the road for longer than usual, presumably the lack of oncoming traffic at that time of day creating an unconscious spark of curiosity in his mind.

The slight pause provided Michael with the additional precious seconds he needed to make it closer to the vehicle's position. The driver's interest in the traffic was swiftly replaced with intrigue in the bizarre figure bearing down on him, shouting loudly in his direction, arms frantically waving. His instinct was for flight. The town had been a melting pot of cranks and fanatics for some time and the visit of the president had only brought more of these crackpots out in to the open. He shifted the gears and began to press down on the accelerator with a view to making a speedy exit, but his paternal impulses kicked in and placed his foot on the brake.

The sight of the young man in obvious distress had made him think of his own children which he estimated were of similar age. He knew he would not be able to live with himself if he didn't stop to help. He hoped someone would stop and help if his kids were in trouble. The disgruntled drivers behind him were not so sympathetic however and were making their frustrations known but, to Michael's relief, the driver of the recovery vehicle was immovable. "What's the matter kid?" he bellowed as Michael drew ever closer to his position. Michael was unable to make out what the driver was saying over the sounds of car horns and his own heavy breathing. Reaching the vehicle, out of breath and barely able to speak, in between heavy panting he conveyed the need to commandeer the man's vehicle.

Seconds passed as the man processed the request. His expression remaining blank and unresponsive. Eventually he responded, "Who's gonna drive it? You?" A broad smile breaking through across his face, showing an impressive set of white teeth, which stood out in contrast against his black face. Within the soft and friendly eyes, Michael spotted a mischievous look.

"Well I was rather hoping you would help," Michael explained. "I just need that truck up there moving." Michael pointed back from where he had come. The man stared over Michael's shoulder where he spotted the truck haemorrhaging smoke further up the road.

The prolonged delay caused a rather obnoxious man in the car behind to holler out racist abuse.

"My name is Joe," the man said choosing to ignore the repugnant calls from behind him as he held out his hand to connect with Michael.

"Please to meet you Sir," Michael responded.

Joe burst in to laughter, "Well that is the first time I've been called that." Joe leaned further out of the window and turned toward the car behind him. "This young fella has more manners than you'll ever have," he shouted. The man behind merely responded with further abuse which Joe chose to ignore. "So you want the truck moved eh?"

Michael nodded. "If that's not too much trouble."

"Hop in," Joe responded. Michael ran around to the passenger side and climbed up in to the cabin. Joe pulled out right and moved the vehicle up toward the abandoned truck.

"Why you so interested in this truck being moved anyhow? Where is the owner?" Joe pressing for some reasoning behind Michael's request.

"I need to free up the road so that the motorcade can pass through," Michael replied.

"You a member of the secret service son?" Joe chortled.

Michael smiled, but was conscious that he would have to provide a plausible explanation. His ability and confidence in creating a fantasy was improving but he wondered how he would be able to explain this situation in a way not to scare off his new friend. He decided a liberal account of the truth was the best policy. "I was just waiting with the rest of the crowd and this truck breaks down right in front of us. Driver must have been some kind of nut because he gets out and just runs off. Traffic starts to back up and I'm thinking my chance to see the president in person is going to go up in smoke. Then I see you and I think that here is my chance to get that opportunity back." Michael felt this was good enough.

"He is a fine man that Mr President. Things are changing for the better with him in the White House and King and all, and I sure as hell don't want that hangdog Nixon getting in there. I was hoping to see him myself, but I have to work."

"I really appreciate your help."

"I'm guessing you ain't from around here. First, you is much too polite and second you have some strange accent there."

Michael paused but explained he was from the outskirts but was the son of polish immigrants. He had no idea why he had chosen Poland as the origin of his fictitious ancestry, but it appeared to do the trick as Joe accepted his explanation.

"Right, here we go. I'll reverse up and we can attach the truck and tow it out of here." Joe swung the vehicle around, temporarily blocking both sides of the road, before manoeuvring back up to the front of the offending truck. Joe jumped out, followed closely by Michael. The crowd on realising hope was at hand had stopped their exit and returned to their positions close to the side of the road. Joe lent on the lever which dropped down the heavy chains attached to the winch. The large claws at the end of the chains hit the ground with a fierce clunk. Joe knew he had sufficient slack to attach them to the truck with ease. He moved himself in to position on the floor under the front of the truck to find the best point to attach the claws. A few seconds passed and Joe finally emitted a "Hmmm". It was not the sound Michael was hoping for.

"Any problem?" Michael enquired, cringing in anticipation of an unwelcome response.

"Maybe" came the reply. Michael's heart sank. "What now", he thought. He felt he couldn't catch a break. Joe shuffled his way back out from under the truck and looked at Michael standing over him. "Whoever had this truck didn't take much care of it. The tow hook is broken which is where I need to attach the line." Joe sensed Michael was fearing the worst, the expression on his face plain to see.

"Don't worry kid, I may have something in the back which can help." Joe sauntered off with the urgency of someone who had all the time in the world. Unfortunately for Michael he did not and hesitantly checked his phone for the time. It was eleven thirty-five and he calculated that he had less than twenty minutes to clear the road.

"Anything I can help with?" he asked Joe with an air of desperation.

"This should do the trick," Joe suggested, retrieving a length of pipe from the back of his vehicle. "If I can wedge this on the under carriage using what is left of the hook then I reckon we got something to hold on to." Joe seemed pleased with himself and was looking to Michael for some recognition. Unfortunately for Joe, Michael was preoccupied with the time.

143

"How long is that going to take?"

"Oh, not long, ten minutes tops," he suggested as he went about heaving the pipe towards the underside of the truck.

Michael continued to check his phone surreptitiously, intent on avoiding unwanted attention. The time was ticking by more rapidly than he would have wanted and he was beginning to break in to a sweat. Joe's estimate of ten minutes had passed, and things were now getting tight. Michael was torn between pressing Joe for some urgency and risking him giving up and taking off or letting him get on with the job and hope that it would be completed in the next minute or so. Michael decided to give it another couple of minutes.

At last Joe jumped up from below the truck and his face beamed with satisfaction. Michael was not counting any chickens, but it was looking hopeful. He checked his phone again. He had five minutes. Just five minutes to get the truck out of the way and the backed-up traffic moving. He gently encouraged Joe to get a move on. Joe willingly complied and leant on the lever to get the winch to pull the truck upwards.

The makeshift hook creaked under the strain, fighting the winch as it slowly coiled the chain around its shaft. Michael had his eyes closed and everything crossed, desperately hoping that the hook would hold. Michael was not certain, but he was convinced the metal grinding was the loudest thing he had ever heard. His senses heightened, he was pessimistic about the outcome, just waiting for the crash to come. But it never came. Instead a clunk was audible as the winch completed its cycle. "All set," Joe announced as he rounded the recovery vehicle and stepped up to the driver's seat. "You coming?"

Michael hadn't really planned for the question. His focus had been squarely on dealing with the truck and he had not contemplated what came thereafter. Joe detected his hesitation. "It's ok, you don't need to. I understand you want to wait to see Mr President, but I need to know who to get hold of to come pick the truck up." Joe was faced with a blank expression. Michael had been clear that the truck was not his and had just assumed that Joe would take it away and deal with it. He had not reckoned on having more to do with it and was now struggling to formalise an appropriate response. The honest truth was that he had no idea, but he recognised that it was unfair to leave the matter entirely to Joe, especially as he had been so helpful. Michael suggested that the truck might be stolen.

"Probably best to notify the cops," Michael suggested.

"Great," replied Joe, with a healthy dose of sarcasm, not entirely convinced by the recommendation. "Bosses are gonna love this one sitting in their yard with the cops sniffing around."

Michael gave a sympathetic look. "I really do appreciate your help with this."

"And it was a pleasure meeting you young man." Joe took a scrap of paper from the glove compartment and retrieving a pencil from behind his ear, scribbled something down. "Here, just in case the owner turns up." Joe held the paper out to Michael. Michael looked at it and noted it was a phone number. With that Joe pulled out in to the traffic, removing the blockage and alleviating the build-up of vehicles. Michael checked his phone and noted the time had ticked past twelve. According to the schedule, President Kennedy was minutes away from his location. The traffic was flowing, and Michael could see no further obstruction.

He was confident that the Disrupter would have considered his mission successful with the broken-down truck having done its job. By the time he would realise that it had not, he would have no time left to carry out an alternative plan. He consulted his phone again, this time to check the messages.

They had all been advised that should their briefs change; they would receive an alert notifying them. He saw nothing and involuntarily let out a big sigh of relief. He now needed to get back to Dealey Plaza where he would meet the others. He left his position in order to find a bus.

11 DEALEY PLAZA

Rhianna and Lucy had woken early to a knock at the door. Reluctantly they had answered, tentatively peering around the door. They were greeted with a lovely surprise. Andy, the manager from the previous evening, had arranged for the girls to receive room service. They were presented with a lovely spread and thanked their lucky stars that they had landed on their feet.

Over breakfast the girls had discussed their brief and the events which were to take place over the next few hours. Lucy had checked her phone and was pleased to see that she still had sufficient battery. Uncertain as to how exactly the phone would assist, she nonetheless felt more comfortable knowing she had it if needed. Rhianna on the other hand had spent far too much time playing around with the phone since leaving home and now the battery icon was flashing, indicating very low levels. "Not much juice," she exclaimed.

"Doesn't surprise me," Lucy responded unsympathetically.

"It's not my fault I'm popular," Rhianna retorted.

Lucy didn't rise to the bait. She knew Rhianna was trying to make a point that the only friends Lucy seemed to have were a small group of dysfunctional boys. "Well it seems all my friends are safe and well," she said as she scrolled through the mobile app which showed where her friends were currently positioned. "No messages to worry about." Lucy looked up from her phone to catch an expression on Rhianna's face which she had not seen before. For the first time she noticed a little insecurity in place of Rhianna's usual bravado and confidence. Lucy did not usually have much empathy for anyone. Her parents had been keen on discipline and academical achievement and had not placed much importance on feelings. As a result, Lucy had not allowed them to enter her consciousness to any notable degree. However here she was in that moment feeling something for Rhianna as she sat across from her. It wasn't the usual disdain, no it was much more, well, empathetic. It threw her and she did not know quite how to deal with it. She struggled to engage with girls on the same level, unable to comprehend their insistence on occupying their minds and conversation with nonsensical topics such as make-up and boys. Neither which interested Lucy much. She had however been forced to spend some time with Rhianna on this trip and to her amazement, she had rather enjoyed it. She let herself reach out. "All ok?"

Rhianna, realising she had let her guard slip immediately regained her composure, forcing a smile and drawing attention back to the job at hand. "Yeah sure. So, where do we start today?"

Lucy decided not to force the issue, partly because she was on unfamiliar ground herself and was not entirely sure how she would react to Rhianna opening up to her.

"Let's go over it once more," Lucy suggested.

Rhianna nodded in agreement, the steely look returning to her eyes.

"From memory we have two objectives. One, to ensure that the police do not intervene in the course of events which lead to the assassination, something the Disrupters will be trying hard to achieve. And two, to make sure that the man, dubbed the 'umbrella man' is where he should be as the motorcade passes. Is that right?" Lucy looked to Rhianna for confirmation. Rhianna duly obliged.

"Who is this 'Umbrella man' anyway?" Rhianna asked. "I get the whole distraction thing for the police, but no clue as to what this man with an umbrella is trying to achieve."

"No idea," Lucy offered unhelpfully. "The brief just said he was needed to signal when the final shot needs to take place, other than that," she shrugged. "Tom may know, I could text him." She turned back to her phone and began to type out a message.

"You know", Rhianna paused, struggling to find the words she needed. "I don't have friends like you do."

Lucy cringed; the conversation she had deliberately tried to avoid appeared to be taking place. "How do you mean?" she asked without looking up from her phone, hopeful that it was merely a lead in to a sly remark. Instead Rhianna was beginning to open up, much to Lucy's dismay.

"We have fun of course. But they are not like your friends. I am not sure I could rely on them if I needed them, you know."

Lucy didn't know what to say in return. Was Rhianna fishing for compliments or was she genuinely looking to make friends. Lucy decided as uncomfortable as it was that she would succumb to the empathy she had felt and play her part in offering up an olive branch. "Well you are part of us now, you know. And of course, we are all happy you are with us."

"I'm not sure Mikey is. I am sure he would be much

happier if I was not around."

"Mikey is complicated. He doesn't really share his feelings with us, but I know that he sees you as his older sister and looks up to you, even if there is not much of an age difference between you. I am sure he loves you, he may just not act like it."

Rhianna was surprised by Lucy's candour. She could not quite bring herself to believe what Lucy was saying but it struck a chord with her and she felt a warmth inside which she had suppressed for a very long time. She decided then and there that she would try to build a proper relationship with Michael. She realised that he was the closest one in the family, the only one who could truly understand her, given their similar experiences. And now she had this new connection through their adventures which she felt could bring them together, and maybe, just maybe, she may gain three other friends too. However, for now they had a job to do. She decided to lighten the mood. "Well that's totes emosh," she said.

Lucy broke in to a laugh. She knew she liked this girl really. "Ok, well let's get on with our planning. We can't let the boys get the better of us. Girl power eh?!"

"According to the brief the police will be distracted outside the book depositary, where we were yesterday lunchtime. We need to make sure that they still are," Lucy recalled.

"Agreed, but how do you think the Disrupters are going to try to change things?"

"No idea. If I were them, I would just tell the police I saw something suspicious inside the building. That's bound to get them to take a look."

"I guess, but that kind of assumes there is a policeman there to tell."

Lucy checked her notes that she had put together when she left the book depositary. "Look here. Seems like there are over twenty officers around the place but a lot of those are secret service guys riding on the motorcade. There is this one officer, Henry Smith, who is near the depository building, maybe we should focus on him," suggested Lucy.

"Ok, what time is it?" Rhianna asked, feeling lost without her phone.

"Nearly ten-thirty. We had better get a wriggle on."

+++

Lucy was tapping her fingers against the wall. She had been ready to go for about ten minutes and she was becoming increasingly frustrated with the time it was taking Rhianna to make an appearance. "Anytime now would be good," she shouted out.

"You can't rush perfection," came the reply through the bathroom door.

Rhianna emerged finally. Lucy looked her up and down as if wondering what difference the last twenty minutes had made. "Ready?" she asked rhetorically and with a hint of sarcasm. "Then let's go," she added, not letting Rhianna answer. The girls grabbed their belongings and headed out of the room.

They exited the lift to the lobby and headed toward the reception desk. They understood that the manager was not on duty but they wanted to leave a note of thanks for taking them in for the night and arranging such a wonderful breakfast. As Lucy was attempting to get the attention of the receptionist who was busy dealing with a belligerent couple, Rhianna leant casually up against the reception desk taking in the elaborate décor of the lobby. She silently observed the patrons, scrutinising their attire and casting a critical eye over the ensembles that the women had chosen to wear. She liked very little of what she saw and was grateful that she had not be born at this time. She was being particularly critical of a young lady who walked past with a garish yellow miniskirt when she became distracted

151

by a blurred image she glimpsed out of the corner of her eye. She turned her head frantically to get a better view and confirm what she thought she had seen. "Jake?" she whispered under her breath. She thought she was seeing things, but of course it was possible that their paths may cross. This hotel was not exclusively on their path, in fact it reminded her of the explanation the old man had given them at the house which seemed to her to have been an age ago but which in reality was just a couple of days before. She stepped away from the reception desk, turning to Lucy seeking some affirmation of what she felt she had seen, but Lucy was still trying to get the attention of the receptionist who was getting progressively flustered with her irate guests. Rhianna stepped further forward trying to see over the increasing numbers of guests joining the queue to get their time with the overworked and underpaid reception staff. Craning her neck, she followed what she guessed was the direction of the individual's travel. She observed the figure intermittently moving between the thick mahogany pillars but could not quite determine whether it was Jake or not, until he stopped. Rhianna suddenly enlivened with the prospect of catching up with another of their group rushed from her position, pushing through those guests patiently waiting their turn in the line. As she approached, a fearful thought hit her, she paused out of sight but with a clear view of Jake who was rooted to the spot, unmoving, staring straight ahead of him. Rhianna could not decipher what or who it was that Jake was preoccupied with but knew any wrong step on her part could potentially create problems for him, so she proceeded with caution. Moving laterally to gain a vantage point from where she could try to make out the focus of his attention, she noticed a group of men huddled around a set of lounge seats at the bottom of the spiralling staircase that went up to the rooms. She did not recognise any of the men that were gathered there. She only concluded that they were some sort of business men, with their sharp suits and shiny black shoes, smoking cigars and looking very, well business-like. Apart from one man. He had a suit, but she felt it was much more flamboyant than the others. It was lighter in colour and shiny, much more show business than the stuffy suits of his companions.

Rhianna remained in her position and continued to observe the group of men seated on the soft furnishings, huddled and whispering. She could not make out what they were saying but overheard the man with the shiny suit refer to one of the group as 'Clint'. This resulted in some consternation and a raising of voices. It appeared that this man Clint was not keen on his name being used. Rhianna glanced over toward Jake. At that moment his attention had been drawn toward the increasing volume coming from the reception desk where the irate couple were now insisting on taking their grievance up with the manager. As he turned his head back toward the group of men, he caught sight of Rhianna staring at him. At first, he seemed unable to compute seeing his school crush standing in the lobby of this grand hotel. It seemed more fantasy than reality. Seconds later, however, once clarity had been restored, he left his position and wandered over to her. "Hey, you ok?" he asked.

"Fine," she replied. "What are you doing here?"

"Following my boy," Jake said, nodding his head to the group of men.

Rhianna's gaze followed the direction of his nod. "Which one's yours?" she enquired.

"Guy with the light grey suit and receding hairline. Jack Ruby's his name. Keeping an eye on him as he has a big role to play in the next couple of days. Don't want him going missing, assuming that is that you guys don't fail before then," Jake smiled. Rhianna didn't appreciate the humour.

She was already concerned that the plan that Lucy and

she had devised may not be enough. Nonetheless she attempted a smile in return, as part of her new-found appreciation of her group of friends. Jake was not expecting this response, prepared instead for a tongue lashing as usual. When it didn't come, he was slightly perplexed. Silence now occupied the space between them, until Lucy interrupted proceedings.

"Hey Jake, how's it going?"

Jake spluttered back in to action. "Good," he responded preoccupied and maintaining eye contact with Rhianna, still bemused by her reaction.

Rhianna on the other hand was happy to let Lucy take the lead with Jake, not yet comfortable with the whole friend thing. "Did you give the note to the receptionist?" she asked.

"Sort of," she suggested. "Not entirely sure it will get to Andy though. The receptionist was a bit distracted. Still it was the thought that counts."

"Where you off to now?" Jake asked.

Lucy looked around the lobby, attempting to identify whether anyone was snooping on their conversation. "Back to Dealey Plaza," she whispered cautiously, as if their destination was highly confidential.

"OK," Jake whispered back mocking her.

"You're still an idiot, I see" she suggested.

Jake laughed and looked back to the subject of his brief. "Looks like my man is on the move again. Catch you later. Stay safe," he added as he turned and followed the man out of the hotel.

"We best get going as well," Lucy turned to Rhianna who looked a bit sheepish. Lucy did not say anything but made a mental note to warn Rhianna off getting involved with Jake on any level other than just friends.

+++

The girls walked the six blocks from the hotel to the school book depository on Elm street in approximately fifteen minutes. As they approached the book depository, they noted the large digital clock on the roof which informed them that the time was eleven forty-eight. They also noted significant changes from the previous day. The pavements were now lined with crowds, twenty or thirty people deep at some points trying to get a view of the presidential motorcade which was due in just over half an hour. People were standing on the road, police officers intermittently positioned attempting to hold the crowd back away from the traffic as it continued to pass along. There were no barriers erected which would be standard operating procedure in the modern world. The whole area was open with very few safeguards to protect the dignitaries that would pass by. It struck Lucy that there was an inevitability that those that wished to carry out heinous acts would succeed as there was very little to stop them. It was also obvious to her that the Disrupters would have very little difficulty in moving around unimpeded. They would be able to mingle in with the gathered crowds and it would be an impossible task to try and identify them. She concluded that they had been right to focus on potential disruptive opportunities rather than the Disrupters themselves. If they were lucky, they would not need to come in to contact with them. She hoped. They continued to push through the crowds, manoeuvring themselves closer to the book depository in an attempt to locate the police officer they wished to monitor.

Lucy positioned herself on the steps of the school book depository. The sun was now shining brightly, and the lateness of the year meant the sun was low in the sky. Lucy shielded her eyes as she cast them over the growing crowds in front of her, slowly scanning for signs of local enforcement officers. Rhianna was undertaking the same exercise across the road on the southwest corner of

Houston and Elm, directly opposite from the depository. She had climbed up on to a small retainer wall of a little park pool which gave her an excellent view of the surrounding streets over the heads of the waiting crowds. She was nervous, frightened to come in to contact with the Disrupters, but filled with adrenaline and satisfied that for the first time she felt she was doing something worthwhile. She spotted Lucy and attempted to catch her attention by waving, but it was clear that Lucy's view in her direction was impeded by the glare of the sun at Rhianna's back.

There was a quiet excitement permeating through the din created by the expectant onlookers. Lucy expected that to change before long. It was just past noon and there had been no sign of the Disrupters. She anticipated some activity, but it had been unnervingly uneventful. The steps which she was currently occupying were filling up as the occupants of the book depository stepped out in their lunch hour to get a quick glimpse of the visiting president. Lucy has adjusted her position to maintain a view of the road but was being squeezed in to the dark shadows in the corner.

Rhianna maintained a better view of proceedings and she caught sight of what appeared to her to be three suspicious looking characters. Dressed in overalls and safety hats they would have not looked out of place on a construction site, but here in the midst of the waiting crowds there was something unusual about them. The reason Rhianna was suspicious was because they were the only ones who appeared to have no obvious interest in the expected presidential motorcade. Whereas the expectant crowds were facing south along Houston in the direction of the motorcade route, these three were huddled on the eastern side of Houston, facing directly west. Not speaking just observing, they waited. Rhianna continued to watch closely for any signs that these men were the Disrupters she had been anticipating. They appeared to be waiting for something.

Lucy was being backed in to a corner and realised that time was passing. She knew that the Disrupters would need to make their move soon. She was concerned that from their positions they may be covering an insufficient amount of the plaza to prevent the Disrupters succeeding in their quest. Confident that Rhianna had this end of the plaza covered she decided to venture further down toward the triple underpass. She stepped out from the shadows of the stairwell and headed south-west along Elm street.

Rhianna had not seen Lucy move her position as her attention had been fixed on the three men. She was beginning to conclude that they were not Disrupters, but she could not take her eyes off them. One of the men checked his watch. Instinctively as he did so Rhianna's eyes were drawn away from the men up to the roof of the school book depository and the electronic clock. She could just about make out the time. The clock read twelve-twenty. As she moved her eyes down the building, she hoped to catch sight of Lucy on the stairs. The crowds had built up in that area and she was unable to locate her. Failing to see her friend she refocused her attention on the three men. There was a commotion approximately twenty yards from her position in between where she was and were the three men were standing. They were staring towards a group of people who were gathered together, preoccupied with a man on the floor who was having some sort of seizure. The men watched and then appeared to ready themselves to make a move before one of them held a hand out to stop the group. Police officers had moved from crowd control to investigate the disturbance. The three men evidently had no desire to come in to contact with the officers and held their position. As they did so Rhianna caught sight of another figure coming in to view. He appeared to be much keener to engage with the officers and was making his way directly toward them.

Rhianna was momentarily taken aback by the

introduction of this new character. Intuitively she was able to figure out that this figure was the Disrupter she had been expecting, moving toward the police officers potentially with a view to draw them away from the man with the seizure, convincing them to head toward the book depositary instead. She had expected something different, something sinister and foreboding. But this figure appeared rather abject. No real presence and from the lack of stature and gait, appeared fragile rather than intimidating. Nonetheless Rhianna did not want to take the risk of presuming that he did not pose a risk.

If he got to the police first, he could direct their attention to the school book depository and potentially prevent the planned assassination from taking place. Rhianna immediately leapt from her position toward the dark figure.

She had no plan in mind and as she rushed toward him, she hoped that something would come to mind and quick.

As the Disrupter stepped ever closer to the police officers, Rhianna broke in to a sprint. Her heart racing, breathing heavy, she was grateful that her one aptitude was paying dividends. She was quick across a hundred metres.

As she ran, getting close to their position, she was a few yards away from the Disrupter connecting with the police officers. She attempted to draw the attention of the police officer as she ran, recalling the name Lucy had referred to earlier she gambled this officer was the one mentioned in the notes.

"Henry," she called. The noise from the crowd was too loud and her voice disappeared in to the general din, unheard. Rhianna understood she would just need to get there first. She only had seconds before her job would get a whole lot more difficult. If the Disrupter got there first, there was no telling what would happen, but there was a certainty that no good could come of it. The Disrupter was almost there. Another few steps. She could make it. She had to make it. Everyone depended on her making it. The thought of applying herself selflessly for once, spurred her on and gave her the extra impetus she needed. The Disrupter was reaching out his hand to grab the police officer's arm and take their interest away from the man on the floor. Rhianna frantically launched herself between the Disrupter and the police officers. Knocking the Disrupter off his stride, Rhianna drew the attention of the police officers. They turned abruptly to observe this young girl fling herself in their direction. Presented with the startled expressions of the two officers, Rhianna was now faced with a dilemma. What to say. The Disrupter, seeing his efforts to intercept the police officers had been scuppered, stepped back, melting back in to the crowd. Rhianna was left with some explaining to do.

"Hey there young lady. What seems to be the problem?"

"There's a man," she spluttered, still panting from her sprint across the road. "He needs help," she continued, pointing in the direction of the man having an epileptic fit on the floor.

"Yes ma'am," responded the police officer, "We are aware. You will have to move yourself along now. This road needs to be cleared. Please step back." The police officers turned and made their way to the position of the man on the floor, moving the small gathering of onlookers aside, who were bent over him offering assistance. At this moment an ambulance with sirens blaring pulled alongside. The driver stepped out and engaged in a conversation with the officers.

Rhianna looked around, in search of the Disrupter and the three men she had observed earlier. All were gone. Her eyes traced back to the depository steps, looking for a sign of Lucy, but she had also disappeared. Rhianna did however see the three men enter the building, disappearing through the front door. What she did not see as she turned away in search of Lucy, was the female figure who followed them in.

+++

The Disrupter had barely moved from her position, holed up in a coffee shop off Jackson Street. The eyes of Tom and John firmly fixed upon her. There had been nothing eventful, no sign of her planning next steps. She had sat there with a coffee, which she did not drink. Unmoving, just staring ahead. They were not going to let her out of their sight. They had spent several hours debating what her next move might be and how they might deal with each of the possibilities. John had suggested on more than one occasion that he could easily deal with the potential threat by 'taking her out' as he put it. Tom had not been keen. As much as he had a job to complete, he was not going to be part of an unlawful killing, no matter what the consequences might be.

As each hour had passed, they concluded that she must be waiting for the assassination attempt itself, may be interrupting the target at the exact moment as the shots were to ring out.

As lunch time approached and the small coffee shop started to fill up, a figure entered and made his way over to her table. This was clearly someone who she knew but there were no obvious signs of familiarity. No warmth in the interaction. Indifferent, unemotional and detached. The encounter was reasonably brief. Whatever the message was it made no impression on her. Tom watched the other figure as he made his way to the door. A cold chill ran through Tom's body as he caught sight of his face. There was a serenity to his appearance which shrouded a malevolent intent. Tom took a moment to try and reconcile what he knew about these instruments of doom. He understood how they could be disenchanted with the human race. It was after all flawed to its core, but to want its ultimate destruction, surely there was an alternative. Tom's train of thought was broken when the Disrupter made her move. Tom and John immediately rose from their positions and followed her out of the shop. She moved without any urgency and had the appearance of someone with no care in the world. Tom could only imagine that she had a heart of ice. She was graceful in her movements and had the air of quiet determination. She was definitive in her actions and single-minded in her objective. Tom and John followed her back on to Houston, the school book depository clearly standing out at the junction with Elm ahead. The minute on the clock turning to nineteen as they ventured further up Houston in no real hurry. The pavements were now filled with onlookers. Windows lining the street open and occupied with workers taking a break from their working day and taking advantage of their raised positions in readiness for the arrival of the president.

As they approached the corner of Houston and Elm, Tom and John quickened their pace in order to stay in touch with the Disrupter who had successfully made her way through the crowds and was now standing just short of the school book depository. A commotion appeared to be taking place not far from the entrance where an ambulance was parked, the paramedics assisting with an individual lying on the floor. Tom could see the backs of a couple of police officers who were addressing someone in the street. They ended the conversation and walked over to the paramedics.

The Disrupter gazed temporarily at the scene, then abruptly took off in the direction of the book depository entrance. After a brief pause she moved quickly up the stairs past the increasing throng of onlookers, through the double doors and into the building.

Tom and John looked at each other. Tom had taken the

opportunity to fill in the gaps in John's knowledge as much as he could, and they were now both aware of what the Disrupter's intentions were. The Disrupter would attempt to prevent Oswald firing the shots from the sixth-floor window.

+++

The crowds were more dispersed further down Elm. This was the scheduled end to the parade before the president was due to travel on to a lunch at the Trade Mart and Lucy had this in mind as she wandered amongst the spectators, knowing this would be the final opportunity for the Disrupters to alter the history of the assassination attempt. She was aware of her brief and was seeking out the man who would become known as the 'umbrella man'. She was not entirely clear on his purpose, but she understood he played a significant role which would preoccupy conspiracy theorists the world over in years to come.

Lucy weaved in and out of the bystanders straining to see up the incline to the corner of Elm and Houston in anticipation of the motorcade. The weather was pleasant with the sun shining, warming her face but the chill throughout her body remained. She would rather be anywhere else than where she found herself at that moment. She had never imagined that she would be in a position of such importance. Given her background she had always imagined a rather mundane life of school followed by a career undertaking menial tasks in an office somewhere. Lucy suffered with a severe lack of self-confidence, hated her looks and very much doubted she would attract a partner.

So, whilst she yearned for kids one day, she did not consider that this was likely to be part of her future. Yet here she was, with her friends, charged with safeguarding one of the most instrumental historical events of the twentieth century. She had walked the short distance from the book depository and found herself next to a small grassy area which led up to fencing in front of the railroad tracks which the friends had passed the previous day. There were very few people on this stretch of the road so Lucy's objective of locating the man with the umbrella was reasonably straightforward. Given the early morning drizzle there were a few people dressed for those conditions including a lady with a distinctive bright red raincoat on the opposite side of the road. On her side of the road there were men with jackets, hats and overcoats but only one man was holding an umbrella. Dressed in dark trousers and a dark three-quarter length raincoat, the man held a closed umbrella in his right hand. Lucy knew this was to be her man.

What was less clear to her was how she was to prevent any Disrupter from interfering with him. There was no way of knowing how or from which direction the Disrupter would appear. Her best guess was that he would appear from out of the crowds further up Elm, but he could quite easily appear from the stone walls behind her, the underpass to her right or directly from across the street. Lucy started to become more agitated. Glancing up at the clock she noted the time was nearly upon them. It was twelve twenty-five. Five minutes to the expected assassination. Lucy's eyes were drawn back down from the roof of the book depository, pausing at the open sixth floor window, where a shadowy figure was undoubtedly preparing for the kill. Her eyes moved down to the crowd which bustled with the excitement of the president's visit, blurred by the bright yellow hue from the noon autumn sun and a soft haze of heat rising from the roads which had dried from the early morning drizzle. The scene was one of serenity which was about to be devastatingly fractured with the sounds of rifle shots which would echo through future history.

Continuing to turn her head in all directions in an attempt to spot the Disrupter early, agitation grew inside her as the minutes passed. That agitation turned to fear when out of the crowd appeared a figure what she immediately recognised as a Disrupter. Although approaching with some speed the whole episode was playing out in slow motion in Lucy's mind. The Disrupter's menacing form careering towards her, Lucy had seconds to formulate her response. Given the remaining time until the fatal moment, Lucy concluded that the Disrupter's only option was a brutal and crude plan which would involve attacking the Umbrella man, knocking him from his position so that the sequence of events for the fatal shot would be interrupted.

Lucy positioned herself between the oncoming Disrupter and the man with the umbrella. She dug her heels in and prepared herself for impact.

+++

"Why don't we take the lift?" John pointed towards the shaft at the back of the building which was used to transport the boxes of books.

"Too noisy," Tom replied. "We need to ensure no one gets spooked and abandons the job. The stairs are the better option, but we had better be quick. She has a head start on us."

They both set off up the staircase, John taking two steps at a time, taking a marginal lead. Tom caught his ankle painfully on a step and stumbled. John looked round to check on him. "Go, go," Tom shouted. John immediately turned back and raced around the corner and out of Tom's sight. Tom recovered and set off after him. He calculated John was a flight of stairs ahead of him and would be reaching the sixth floor in a matter of seconds. The pain in his leg was slowing him down a little, but he was determined to get to the sixth floor and assist John in restraining the Disrupter. He just hoped that they were not too late and Oswald was still aiming from the window ready to complete his objective. Tom finally reached the bottom of the last flight of stairs which would take him to the sixth floor, as he placed his foot on the step, he heard a large thud hit the floorboards above him. He paused momentarily. A thousand thoughts running through his mind. The adrenaline was coursing through his veins now and any pain to his leg forgotten. He quickened his pace, almost throwing himself up the final stairs in a desperate attempt to understand what had taken place. As he appeared around the corner his worst fears were realised. John was flat on his back, blood splattered over his front. Tom's instinct was to rush to his aide, but John raised an outstretched arm, his palm open towards Tom demanding he go no further. A confused look crossing his face, Tom gesticulated to John checking if he was ok. John turned his palm, closing his thumb and forefinger to suggest he was ok. The blood was evidently not his. John appeared fairly ashen despite not being injured. Whatever he had seen in the moments before Tom had reached him had clearly disturbed him. John moved carefully and slowly to Tom's position, ensuring he remained low and out of sight. As he reached Tom, he grabbed frantically at Tom's collar and whispered urgently in his ear. "You need to get out of here. It's not what we thought. The target's not here, there are others. Serious guys. Go and find the target and I am sure you will find her. The job's not done." He indicated to the blood on his shirt. "She is injured, but I am not sure how badly. Go quickly." Tom was in the process of turning when a distinct shot rang out sending a cold chill through his body. He was certain this was the beginning of the slaughter. Momentarily traumatised by the alarming sound of the gun, Tom stood still, wracked with fear. He would later try to recollect whether in those few moments he heard several shots or whether the unnerving sound of the single shot had just played over and over in his mind in that moment. John shook him to bring him back to reality, he was calm despite the circumstances, obviously more used to the sound of gunfire. "Go, now," he ordered.

+++

"Lucy! Lucy wake up," Rhianna shouted. Lucy was prostrate on the floor, Michael kneeling beside her. Around them pandemonium had set in. The crowd which had filled the air with cheering only moments before was now filling the air with screams and shouts as people took cover or raced in all directions. Lucy came round. "What happened," she asked.

"It's happened," Rhianna explained. "The Disrupter was heading straight for you. He was massive. I am surprised you are still alive. How are you feeling?"

Lucy did not much appreciate Rhianna's comment about how lucky she was to be alive, but feeling the stiffness already coming on all over her body she couldn't help but agree. The knock had taken the wind out of her and she was conscious of extreme pain around her ribs.

"We need to move, can you walk?" Michael asked, observing increasing numbers of law enforcement officers circling their position. They were just three more people littered on the grassy embankment seeking refuge from further gunfire, but it would not be long before someone took an interest in them. Members of the press who had been covering the presidential visit had also jumped in to action, their professional instinct kicking in to capture historic moments. Michael recognised that they could not risk being captured in these pictures which would attract global scrutiny for decades.

"I'm not sure," Lucy responded. "I feel pretty banged

up. I think I may have broken something. My ribs kill."

"That's not the only thing that kills," Rhianna quipped. Michael and Lucy shot her a look. "Too soon?" she added.

"We are exposed here," Michael anxiously announced. "We don't want to get caught up in what happens next. Let's head back up to the book depository and we can mingle in with the crowd up there." Michael and Rhianna lifted Lucy under each of her arms, careful not to put too much pressure on her ribs.

"How did you get here?" Lucy exclaimed finally acknowledging Michael's presence.

"I took the bus here," Michael replied with no hint of sarcasm. "Took ages as the roads were slow with traffic from the motorcade. Thought you guys might need a hand."

"Be honest, you were worried about me, weren't you," Rhianna goaded him.

"As if," he replied.

The three of them waddled up the hill back up to the book depository in search of the others.

+++

Tom knew he had very little time to locate the Disrupter and would need to be careful not to be discovered himself by the policeman that was due to enter the building in only a couple of minutes. He had planned an excuse if he was spotted but he hoped it would not come to that. He understood that the Disrupter was most likely searching for the target, who still had a vital role to play over the coming days. He wondered whether the intention of the Disrupter would now be to get Lee Harvey Oswald to evade capture. If he was not caught as planned, who knew what that might mean. One thing for sure is that it would turn everything on its head and as he understood it, would have a devastating effect on the balance of the multiverse. He was confident he would have the upper hand if he came across her, knowing that she was injured and likely hampered. She had not passed him on the stairs so her exit from the sixth floor must have come via the freight lifts. The question he had was whether she knew Lee Harvey Oswald was on the second floor where it would eventually be reported that he was spotted after the shooting. If not, she may be delayed searching the other floors and he could get there first. Tom sprang down the steps two at a time. This time making sure he didn't slip. His question was answered when he reached the fifth floor. He immediately noted, as he turned the corner, that the two lifts were both there. The floor was crammed with stacks of boxes and there was no way of knowing whether someone was manoeuvring amongst them, but given he had the stairs covered and the lifts were both there, it was safe to bet that the Disrupter was somewhere on this floor. He knew that it was critical that he moved swiftly down the floors, so he continued without looking back. He reached the third floor and was about to continue down to the second when he heard voices ahead of him. He concluded that this was officer Marion Baker confronting Lee Harvey Oswald in the lunch room. Tom decided to retrace his steps back to the third floor and hide out there to wait for the officer to pass by. He heard the steps of two men climbing the stairs and held his breath. Thankfully they passed right by on their way to the roof. Tom ventured down to the second floor. He noticed that there were a few people milling about and deducing that Oswald would have commenced his exit from the building having heard the news of the assassination, rather than wasting time scouting this floor Tom decided to continue straight down to the first floor. He reached the first floor and stunned by the commotion coming from outside the front doors which he observed from his position at the bottom of the stairs. People were swarming here and there. Tom first looked toward the back entrance by the docks which he and his friends had accessed just the day before. There was a group in deep conversation paying little attention to who was walking the floor, but no sign of Oswald. Tom decided to take a chance and move towards the front door. As he did saw he was astonished to see the target emerge from the storage room next to the south-east stairway from the first to the second floor. He appeared calm and stopped briefly to give some instructions to individuals seeking access to a phone. "A time without mobile phones," Tom thought to himself. It was a lucky break as Tom considered he could keep an eye on the target and make sure that the Disrupter did not get access to him and try to interfere in the reported history of events. Oswald passed through the inner door of the reception area before reaching the double doors of the entrance and out in to the bright sunshine of the afternoon. Tom was keen to keep close, but he was suddenly interrupted by a hand coming down firmly on his shoulder. He stiffened with fear and his heart skipped a beat. He immediately feared the prospect of being hauled off to a police station to be interrogated. There was no way that he would be able to blag his way out of this one and given how much he knew, he would be unable to convince them he was just an innocent bystander. A panic set in until a familiar voice spoke behind him. "Did you see her?"

Tom swivelled abruptly and came face to face with John. "How did you get down here so fast?"

"I'll tell you on the way," he gestured towards the exit. "For now, let's get to safety."

"We need to follow Oswald," Tom said rather too loudly in John's opinion.

"Let's go," John grabbed Tom's arm and they exited. The streets were awash with law enforcement officers and crowds in disarray. The noise was deafening as the sounds of sirens filled the air. They pushed through the hordes of people now occupying the stairs up to the entrance to the depository and followed Oswald across Houston. They followed him along Elm Street just past Griffin and boarded the same bus that he got on. Oswald appeared to be very calm, but Tom wondered why he had left the building and where he was going.

12 THE ARREST

It was clear to Tom now that Oswald had not been involved in the assassination, or certainly had not fired the shots, but where was he going when it would be expected that he stays at work. Tom's thoughts reminded him that John had yet to explain what had happened at the book depository. "So, what happened? You know, on the sixth floor. And how did you get back downstairs? You weren't behind me otherwise you would have been stopped by that police officer," Tom asked.

John made a conscious effort to keep his voice low. "One thing you need to know is that it will not do you well to speak loudly. There is clearly something bigger at play here and it's best not to show you know too much."

"But I need to know. It is important to me," Tom pushed, giving a look to John which suggested he would keep asking until he was satisfied, despite bringing unwanted attention from the other passengers on the bus.

171

John looked around him and was confident they were not being watched. "When I reached the sixth floor the Disrupter was standing there right in front of me. It was seconds before there was a muffled shot, probably benefiting from a silencer. I immediately hit the floor and she fell on top of me. We were now hidden by the stacks of boxes. She crawled over me towards the lifts and took the west freight lift down. I am pretty sure whoever shot her did not know I was there and hearing the lift descending did not investigate any further. You appeared at that exact moment."

"Did you see who was there?" Tom pressed.

John shuffled uncomfortably in his seat. "I really think you are better off not knowing. It's dangerous."

Tom didn't need to say anything further; John could see the determination in his eyes clearly conveying the message to John that it would be more dangerous for him if he did not tell him everything.

"You cannot speak about this to anyone, do you understand?"

Tom nodded.

"I didn't see everyone, but I could tell there were two or three guys on the floor. After I heard the first shot and had pushed you to leave, I looked over to the south-east corner. It was difficult to see with all those stacks of boxes, but I got clear sight of one man. I immediately recognised him from my days in the service."

Tom stared at John aghast, his mouth wide open.

"Look, I can't say for certain that he is still on government time as we lost touch when I left, but whoever he is working for, he is a professional which means this whole thing is bigger than either of us. I suggest you keep your head down."

Tom took some time to process this. "So, it is definitely a conspiracy then. They were right."

John looked puzzled. "Yeah, I would certainly say so.

With some powerful people involved. You don't successfully shoot the president without serious backing, but who are you referring to? The guys that asked you to keep an eye on this Oswald fella? What have you got yourself in to here?"

Tom realised that his story to John may be starting to unravel. He suspected that this may happen once the assassination took place but had a faint hope that he would get away with it. He couldn't risk telling John before this point as John may have wanted to prevent the assassination taking place and Tom would have been left with having to deal with him and the Disrupters.

"Look here kid, I think you owe me some more answers."

It was obvious to Tom that John would not accept any further nonsense and any attempt to create a fiction which just lead to more questions. It was likely that he would end up tying himself in knots. Tom decided to come clean, well, clean-ish.

"It is true what I said, that I was asked to keep an eye on this man, Oswald and that it was important no harm came to him. It is also true that we were chosen as a bunch of kids as less conspicuous than adults. We tend to go unnoticed where adults are likely to raise suspicions." John nodded recognising a tactic that had been standard operating procedure back in the day. "What I didn't mention is that they suspected he was part of a conspiracy to carry out the assassination."

John let out an audible whistle, which he immediately regretted. He wasn't a stranger to dangerous situations and had experience in working on black operations in the past, including assassinations in foreign countries. But he had never envisaged one taking place on home soil, against his own government. But of course, power corrupts, and it was only a matter of time. It was one of the reasons he got out in the first place. He saw a shift in the plays that he and

173

his colleagues were being asked to carry out and he was becoming less and less comfortable with the moral questions they raised. And so, it had happened, but to involve kids had never sat well with him. It shouted of cowardice, as did the way in which they carried it out. John suddenly viewed the bigger picture and the danger that they were now exposed to. He felt an urge to vomit.

"Sorry I didn't tell you before," Tom said with sincerity.

John, realising he had not been absolutely truthful himself decided to let it slide. If anything, he just wanted more answers. "So, these guys who recruited you, I assume they wanted you to warn them if there was any chance their plans would be affected?"

"That's right. We were told there would be people wishing to stop what was happening and if possible, we should make sure they weren't successful, but if they were, that we should immediately notify them."

John was disgusted that they would put the lives of innocent kids in danger to achieve their aims.

"What are your instructions now that the assassination attempt has taken place?" It was not clear to John whether the assassination had been successful. Tom was of course aware that the president had been killed and was conscious of not letting anything else slip which would cause him problems explaining away.

"We need to keep an eye on him until he is caught and arrested."

"So, he is to take the fall eh?" John realised.

"I guess so," Tom responded.

The bus had only gone a couple of blocks and was stuck in traffic. Oswald got out of his seat and moved to the door to alight. John and Tom followed him off the bus and south on Lamar. They wondered whether he realised he was being set up and was trying to get out of town. Shortly after, John and Tom were surprised when Oswald jumped in to a cab. They had no choice but to follow suit. Tom conscious at how clichéd it was nonetheless instructed the driver "follow that cab."

There was a short period of silence before Tom spoke up. "You still haven't explained how you got down from the sixth floor."

"I took the lift."

"But they weren't on the sixth, not after the Disrupter had taken the other one down," Tom stated.

"Not the freight lifts, the passenger lift in the south-east corner," John explained.

John could see the confusion on Tom's face which amused him. He decided to put Tom out of his misery.

"After the shots rang out, I remained out of sight and could hear some light shuffling going on. I was worried as they were certain to spot me if they headed for either the stairs or the freight lifts. But they didn't move toward my position. I tentatively looked up over the boxes and caught sight of them moving down in to a hole in the floor. The floor boards were then replaced behind them. I flew down the stairs to see if I could spot them exiting on the fifth floor taking great care not to be spotted as there were a few workers on this floor. Thankfully they were distracted with what was going on outside and they didn't spot me descending the stairs, but I couldn't risk spending any longer on that floor so continued down. When I got to the fourth floor, I heard footsteps coming up from the lower floors. I decided to check out the south-eastern corner of the fourth floor to see if there was any exit from above and noted the passenger lift. There was no-one on the floor, but I had to wait for the lift to arrive. Once I got in the lift, I looked around for any sign that someone had used it recently. There were no signs, but I did spot an emergency hatch in the lift ceiling. I could not reach it, but I imagine that the lift shaft went up to the boards of the sixth floor just beside the shooting position."

Tom was flabbergasted. He knew there were conspiracy

theories of course but here was a plausible explanation of how other elements may have made their escape from the building without being noticed.

The thought was left to fester in Tom's mind as the cab came to a stop. They exited the cab and Tom and John found themselves in a suburb, south of downtown Dallas.

"Where is he going? We just came from that way," Tom asked as he observed Oswald heading north on Beckley Avenue

"Looks like standard operating procedure when you suspect a tail," John suggested. "He is doubling back on himself. Let's keep back. If he is under surveillance, we don't want to be associated with him."

"You think he was involved?" Tom asked.

"He is certainly acting suspiciously," John suggested. "If he was not involved, why is he here and not at work. Where is he going and why? We know he was not part of the team that carried out the shooting, but he knows something, I can smell it."

Tom was aware that the brief he had been given had Oswald arrested at the Texas Theatre which was a few blocks south of their current position. He also knew that Oswald would be charged with the murder of police officer Tippit which was to take place not far east of them in less than fifteen minutes. The question for Tom was how he could use this information without alerting John. Intelligence that suggested someone was involved in an assassination plot was feasible but knowing that he would carry out a random killing and knowing the exact position of his subsequent arrest was a bridge to far. "I'm going to have to keep quiet on these specifics," Tom thought to himself.

As they continued to observe from a distance, a police car came in to view driving down toward the house now occupied by Oswald. The car slowed down just outside, the sound of the horn was audible before Oswald exited the house and approached the car. It appeared Oswald was about to be picked up, by the police. Tom and John looked on. Tom was starting to get concerned. What he was witnessing was not in accordance with the brief. If they took him in to custody now, he would not be connected to the Tippit murder. This could potentially be catastrophic. Tom was rooted to the spot, unable to comprehend the situation and unable to formulate a plan for resolving what had the potential for putting the multiverse at risk. All the effort the friends had put in to this point could suddenly be made redundant from an unexpected development that he had not considered and certainly had not foreseen. Before Tom could act however, the situation took another turn. It confirmed to Tom that nothing was certain. Out from the police car stepped the Disrupter. She appeared to be remonstrating with Oswald to get in to the car. Oswald in turn showed signs of unease as he backed away from the car. Clearly spooked as the Disrupter approached his position, he grabbed carelessly at his belt, fumbling for what turned out to be a .38 calibre hand gun. The one he would eventually allegedly use on Officer Tippit. Oswald was waving the weapon about frantically in the direction of the Disrupter, before he suddenly took off toward Tom and John. They remained at their position on the corner of Beckley and Davis as Oswald continued towards them. Tom noticed he was heading in the direction of the Texas Theatre where he would ultimately be arrested, but he was not heading to the scene of Tippit's murder. Tom spun round to look at John. "We need to keep him away from that woman. She could put the whole plan at risk."

John looked back at him. "Is that such a bad thing?"

Tom didn't have time to explain. "Look we just need to do something. If we don't other lives could be at risk."

John understood enough about black operations to know that there was unlikely to be a good outcome if the plan went south, so he agreed with Tom. "Come on then."

They turned towards the oncoming Oswald, the police car having turned and now following him closely behind. Oswald looked up and noticed Tom and John approaching him from the front. Although a man and his son would not ordinarily have spooked him, with the police car also following him close behind, he panicked and changed direction, heading left down David and on to Crawford Avenue. John and Tom crossed the road just behind. As John continued to follow Oswald at pace, Tom stopped at the intersection just as the police car arrived at this position. In an ill-conceived attempt to prevent the Disrupter from intercepting Oswald Tom held his hands out in front of him. The Disrupter was moving quickly and had little time to assess the situation as she came across Tom standing in her path in the middle of the road preventing her making the turn in to Davis. She instinctively pressed hard on the brakes sending a plume of smoke up from her rear tyres. She came to a stop with Tom's hands placed firmly on the bonnet of the car. Time slowed down again as Tom came face to face with the Disrupter. Their eyes met and whilst Tom was conscious not to show any fear, he was met with cold steely eyes of someone who appeared to have no soul. There was nothing behind those eyes that met his, no compassion, no empathy, no feelings at all. Tom was presented with a shell of a person. This worried Tom the most as he was standing on the path of least resistance between her and her target. She had come to a stop as an instinctive reaction to something in her way rather than as a result of any concern for him and he knew that she could, and would, quite easily drive right through him now if it suited her. Tom made a mental note not to stand in front of cars in the future. Twice in a day was two too many. He was relieved when instead she suddenly reversed her position and headed south on Beckley Avenue. If Tom thought this was a sign of her humanity, he would have been mistaken for in that moment she had merely calculated that she had lost time on Oswald, who although on foot, would have remained ahead of her. She chose to take a left turn further down Beckley to try to get ahead of him. Meanwhile Tom wallowed in his minor victory before deciding to follow Oswald and John on foot. A minute or so passed and Tom finally caught up with John who was standing at the corner of Patton and Tenth staring at an unfolding scene ahead of him. "What's happening?" Tom spoke as he gasped for breath.

"Oswald has just shot a policeman," John said rather matter-of-factly.

"What?" Tom said, still panting and not fully processing what he was witnessing. "What happened?"

"I guess he got spooked. Probably seems like the world is against him. The police officer got out of the car and approached him. Obviously saw him running and thought it suspicious. Didn't see the gun though until it was too late."

Tom finally recovering from his assertions and breathing less deeply looked around. "Where is he now?"

"Not sure, I lost him once he took off after the shooting. This place will be rammed with police soon, once they know one of theirs is down." John turned to Tom. "What happened to the woman?"

"She went the other way, but I suspect she may still be searching for him."

"Likely to give up once this place becomes police central. The world and his wife are going to be after our man," John suggested.

"Let's hope, but we should still try and find him. Which way did you see him go?"

"It looked like he took off down Patton. Let's try that way." Tom and John set off in search of their target.

Tom was aware that Oswald would be heading to the theatre. He felt he could suggest the way without looking like he knew too much. "I'm guessing he will be looking for somewhere to hide out?" he suggested.

"Agree, unless he has a planned escape route, he will need somewhere quiet and isolated to hole up," John replied.

It had been a few minutes since the shooting and the sirens of officer Tippit's colleagues were beginning to be heard. The streets surrounding the scene were in chaos and there was a real sense of heightened tension. Tom had seen the London riots of two thousand and twelve on the television and he imagined the tension described on that occasion was similar to what he was experiencing now.

"There is a cinema on Jefferson Boulevard I think," John said. "That might not be a bad place to get some cover."

Tom and John set off in the direction of the Texas Theatre where Tom knew for a fact Oswald was to be arrested. He just hoped that he had sufficiently diverted the Disrupter, to enable Oswald time to get to the theatre and they had not lost the police the opportunity to arrest him.

+++

John's assumption had been correct. On hearing the abundance of sirens heading toward the area, the Disrupter had concluded that there was very little chance in her finding Oswald. She had failed. She cursed as she drove speedily out of the area.

+++

"John, this is everyone, everyone this is John," Tom did the introductions briefly as he let himself fall on to the bed, exhausted. "Nice place," he added.

Rhianna was the first to react, "I'm Rhianna," she said as she held out her hand. Lucy followed, not to be out done by her new best friend. Michael was the last to offer up his hand. This drew Tom's attention to the obvious absentee.

"Anyone heard from Jake?" Tom asked, worried that he had not heard from him in the last twenty-four hours.

"We saw him here this morning," Lucy answered. "But nothing since."

"How was he?"

"Pretty good," Rhianna interjected. She glanced in Lucy's direction to check she was not stepping on her toes. Lucy nodded gently, reassuring Rhianna that she was fine to proceed. If nothing else Rhianna felt she had learned something about herself these past few days and Lucy for one had seen a new side to her which she liked. Perhaps Rhianna was not so bad. Lucy knew she would have some work to do to convince the others though.

"So?" Tom continued, frustrated with the pause.

Rhianna, emboldened continued to chronicle the morning's activities to Tom, concentrating on the part with Jake to provide Tom with the comfort he was seeking. Although a lot of water had passed under the bridge since then and nobody could guarantee Jake's safety at this moment, Tom had recognised and appreciated Rhianna's efforts. Tom looked to Lucy and without saying anything she understood that Tom had recognised the change in Rhianna and liked what he saw.

"How did you get the room?" Tom enquired.

Lucy took up the narrative. "Seems we made a bit of an impression on the manager. He went on shift shortly before it all kicked off in the plaza, thankfully. When we turned up after the shooting and he saw I was struggling, I think he took pity on us."

Tom hadn't realised Lucy was hurt and felt bad that he hadn't even asked how they all were, his levels of exhaustion such that his main objective had been to get his head down. "You ok?" he belatedly asked.

"Well, thanks for asking, but not really. My side really hurts. I think I may have damaged something," Lucy responded.

John took a step toward her, "Let me see." Lucy immediately recoiled.

Tom noticed her reluctance. "It's ok he's good. Knows a thing or two about injuries."

"You a doctor?" Michael asked with suspicion, over protective of his friends as usual.

"No, but I have seen enough physical injuries to have a good crack at a diagnosis," John suggested.

"Former training, I guess," Tom added cryptically.

Lucy relaxed and let him take a look as she lifted the side of her top to reveal a redness and swelling around her ribs. She squirmed as he pressed down gently on her side.

"I think it's just bruising," John suggested. "But better to get it checked out when you can. Not that they will do much even if it is broken, but you may get some pain relief." He looked around at that group before adding, "I don't expect any of you have medical insurance." The resounding silence told him everything he needed to know.

"How did it happen?" Tom piped up to break the silence.

"She was great," Rhianna gushed, a little to enthusiastically for Michael who rolled his eyes, yet to be sold on the new and shiny Rhianna.

"It was nothing," Lucy added sheepishly. "I am not sure the brief was quite right though. We were expecting the Disrupter to be targeting the man with the umbrella. But the last thing I remember was him heading for the fence behind me. I didn't have time to think about it though and knew whatever he was up to I had to stop him. So, I just got in his way. He sent me flying and the next thing I knew, Rhianna and Michael were helping me up and I was in pain."

"It was crazy," Rhianna continued. "I followed the motorcade just after it turned the corner by the book depository. It sounded like fireworks were going off, but I guess that was the gun being fired. I started running to try and find Lucy and saw this guy batter in to her down the hill. They were both sprawled out on the grass. Then he scrambles to his feet and heads toward the fence when the next shots rang out. Then it just got messy. People were running in all directions, screaming and shouting. Sirens started going off. I lost sight of the Disrupter in the melee and went to check Lucy was ok."

"That's when I turned up," Michael added.

"The main thing is we seem to have been successful in stopping the Disrupters. There is only one way they can win now and that is if Oswald is able to tell his story to the world."

John had to this point remained fairly silent, but what he was hearing left him no choice but to voice his concerns, "Who are you kids?"

The group fell silent as everyone in the room stopped and faced John. Lucy, Rhianna and Michael then looked from John to Tom in search of guidance. Tom realised he had let his guard down in the relative comfort of the hotel room and was suddenly presented with a dilemma. "You are all obviously more involved in this than you let on. So, what's the story?" John implored.

The friends continued to look at each other, hoping that one of them could come up with a plausible explanation which wouldn't make them look like bunch of nutters.

Finally, Tom decided that he was too tired to try another set of lies, and anyway he had kind of lost track of where he was with all his other lies. "We are part of a group," he spluttered, unconvincingly. "A group which tries to keep the universe in balance."

John's expression was unmoving. Tom became increasingly twitchy as he searched for the words to describe their situation. "The group had information about what went on today and knew what was going to take place. Our job was to make sure it happened as it was supposed to." Tom felt pleased with himself that he had given some kind of explanation which would not immediately land him in jail or worse in a psychiatric unit.

John was not satisfied though, "Who are the other guys? The one's you are trying to stop?"

"They are, er, the bad guys?" Tom suggested feebly.

"I still don't get why anyone will send a bunch of kids to do this work. You're not even American," he exclaimed. Tom was relieved that this was his main point of concern.

"As I mentioned they felt it best to use people out of town."

John understood this. He had worked with many nationalities in the past on operations which required the option of deniability for those in positions of authority. Mostly the people on the ground were expendable, which was another bonus for the chiefs who didn't want to get their hands dirty. "Well, assuming I believe all this, you lot are in big trouble. There is a reason no president has been assassinated in the last sixty-two years and that is that it is very difficult to do it and get away with it. To be successful requires tight management of the communication channels on a very strict need to know basis, with only a very few number of people knowing the whole picture, usually top officials in government or the military. Anyone with knowledge, not in this tight group, would have to be silenced. In this case, that is you."

The words landed hard on the friends. They had accepted the dangers posed by the Disrupters, but had concluded that the risk was manageable, if their focus remained on their mission. Governments and the military however, were another matter.

Tom sensed the anxiousness of the group. "We are only going to be around for a couple more days. Not long enough for them to find us."

John's face said it all. "That's just naïve," he said to add insult to injury. "If you guys are on their radar, which I can

184

only imagine that you are, then they will have you under surveillance. Which means they know you are here and watching, waiting for the right time."

Tom was not convinced they were on anyone's radar other than the Disrupters, but to argue would have raised further questions in John's mind.

"My guess is that there is reason this manager was so helpful," John addressed the girls directly. "Trust no-one," he added ominously. Lucy and Rhianna looked to each other. They had assumed the manager was just being helpful and that he had felt sorry for them. Could he be secretly working against them.

Michael made a suggestion. "I think we are safe until the last bit is done."

"Jake." The friends spoke in unison.

"When is that supposed to take place? Lucy asked.

"Less than two days from now." Tom caught sight of John shaking his head as if in disbelief but decided to ignore it. "I suggest we stay here until then and then we go and find Jake and make sure we are all together when the time comes."

John sighed. He was torn between his primary desire for self-preservation and what he considered to be a misguided sense of duty to help these kids. He looked around the room and sensed that these kids would not be dissuaded from their current course of action and if they were insistent on self-destruction there was nothing he could do to stop them. "Look guys. I'm sorry but I think you are all nuts. You have done well to get this far but my suggestion would be to get the hell out of here. This is too dangerous, and you are messing with some serious people here. For my part, I can't help any further."

"We could really use your help still," Tom pleaded.

"I'm sorry. It's just too much of a risk." John grabbed his jacket and left.

The room was left in silence for a while as they took in

what had happened.

Feeling the room was on edge after John's speech, Tom decided to give a pep talk to raise their spirits. "Look guys, we started this alone, so there is no reason we can't finish it alone. It would have been nice to have an extra pair of hands but quite frankly we can do this on our own."

The others nodded in agreement, not entirely convinced, but aware they had few other options. "So, tell us what happened with Oswald," Lucy asked.

Tom recapped on what had taken place up to the point that John and he had found themselves situated outside the Texas theatre.

"There was no sign of the Disrupter. To be fair the place was swimming with police by this time. I wouldn't be surprised if she felt there was no chance of getting hold of him and legged it. A lot of people started to gather at the front next to where we were. I am not sure where they came from. People were whispering all sorts of rubbish and I just guess they came to have a look. I heard one person say that they heard that the president's killer was inside. No idea how they might have heard that given it had happened less than two hours before, but as I said, lots of rumours."

"What happened next," Lucy asked impatiently.

"Few minutes later about a dozen people burst through the front door. In the middle of them was Oswald. He looked worse for wear to be honest, like he had been roughed up a bit. He was shouting how he hadn't killed anyone. This started the whispers again as if by denying it he was obviously guilty of it. Poor guy. Had no chance. They dumped him in the back of a car and drove off. Things settled down after that and everyone moved off, discussing what they had seen as they went. Guess it will be something they tell their kids and grandkids for the rest of their lives. 'I was there the moment Oswald got arrested'," Tom was suddenly overcome with a deep sense of sorrow. They had done what they knew to be the right thing, but he could not help feeling rather sad for this man Oswald. He may well have been involved at some point and may well have deserved what he got, but he would never be able to make his case and the world would never know the truth. It was rather depressing, he thought as he lay back and closed his eyes for the first time in what seemed to be a long while but which was in fact, just a few hours.

13 THE CAROUSEL CLUB

"He got what was coming if you ask me."

"Well no-one is asking you."

"Just sayin' surprise is it didn't happen earlier. His God damn brother will be next, you watch."

"Just shut it. No-one wants to hear what you gotta say. Now zip it."

Willie resumed his position which was half way seated on a bar stool, his arm resting on the bar, hand cushioning a crystal glass filled with brown liquor. The place was empty, but the stench of recycled air and cigarette smoke still filled the room. The lights were low as usual hiding the obvious dinginess of the club and giving the place on this day more than any ever a rather ominous feel. What lights there were bounced off the garish décor half-heartedly, creating strange lines of shadows across the empty seats and raised platform which would normally act as the stage for dancers to perform on, but which would that night, and the nights that followed, remain empty. It was a popular haunt and the drinks and conversation would undoubtedly be flowing in the weeks and months that followed, when the main topic would no longer be the assassination of the president. But for now, everyone had their opinion, and everyone would have something to say about it.

Jack walked in to the room. Uncharacteristically dishevelled, his suit crumpled, hair out of place and tie loosely hung around his neck, giving the impression that he had not slept well, if at all, for days. It was immediately apparent to those seated there that things weren't the same. His friends and those close to him knew better than to get in the way when his predisposition for violence raised its ugly head. Others were happy to stir things up. Jada was one of those and she delighted in seeing him in this frame of mind and relished in the opportunity to wind him up. Her appearance itself would have wound Jack up under normal circumstances. Standing tall in her mink coat and high heels, her orange hair piled high on her head, bringing a hint of colour to an otherwise drab environment.

"Good evening Jack," she said sarcastically.

Jack unusually did not rise to the bait. He was preoccupied and had no time nor the inclination to engage in a verbal battle with her. Jada had expected a foul-mouthed torrent of abuse and found it strange that he didn't respond. She looked over to Willie for guidance but found him with his head down, eyes fixed on the glass in his hand, body slumped over the bar. She turned instead to Tony who was seated in one of the chairs alongside the stage. Tony was equally unmoving. "Anyone?" she said invitingly, hoping for some explanation for the peculiar atmosphere. "What is going on today?"

"Leave it Jada," Tony spoke up. Attempting to avoid the inevitable battle of wills that would ensue between Jada and his boss and good friend. Tony was no wilting flower, standing over six feet tall and holding eighteen stone in his bear-like frame, but he was a gentle giant and would rather avoid confrontation wherever possible. He had also seen Jack brush with the law on numerous occasions in the past and was acutely aware that his temper could land him in trouble. He assumed the responsibility of ensuring that there wouldn't be another such episode, one which he suspected, if it did happen, would have far greater consequences.

"Hey kid," Jack called out to the kid seated in the shadows of the corner of the room. "Grab me a coffee from Joe's will ya." He retrieved a fold of notes from his pocket and stretched out to the boy who had come from the shadows in to the light. "Get yourself something while you are at it." Jake reached out for the money. Jack held on to the notes as Jake tried to take them, as he did so he gave him a quick wink, "no running off with my dough." Jake smiled in response. He had grown quite fond of his surrogate father in the short space of time he had been in his presence. Jack had found Jake loitering around the front of the club. Assuming he was a street kid looking to steal from his clientele he had decided to take him in rather than risk reputational damage to his club. Jack had pride in the Carousel Club and whilst it may have been regarded by some as a sleazy drinking establishment for men to ogle scantily dressed women, Jack was insistent that he was running a decent place. He had even gone to the trouble of forcefully escorting unwanted customers from the joint when he considered they were not of the right calibre. Sometimes too forcibly. He would rather entertain the police and newspaper men who he considered were much better for business. It was reported that Jack was desperate to be a big man in town. He was reasonably well connected on both sides of the law but rumoured not to be universally liked. It was understood that he reckoned that if he could get the club exclusive, this would give him good standing in the community and the popularity and acceptance that he craved.

"What's going down boss?" Willie asked, sensing a warming to the frosty vibe that had accompanied Jack in to the room.

"Nothing Willie, nothing," the response was short but courteous.

"We still opening tonight?" Willie asked sensing distraction.

Jack looked up. Willie noted that the usual bravado was missing. "Of course not. They have killed our president," Jack was starting to get riled again. He had appeared to take the assassination badly and had spent the previous evening ranting. Those around him had been convinced that he had become delusional, spouting all sorts of theories, none of which had made much sense. "We are not going to let some communist sympathisers get the better of us. We will mourn out of respect for our beloved president."

Jake re-entered the room holding three cups. He passed the first to Jack holding out the change. "Keep it kid," Jack said, taking the hot coffee from him. The second cup went to Tony who stood and took it from Jake giving him a hearty slap on the back which nearly sent Jake sprawling. Jake kept the third and was grateful for the hot cup of tea. It wasn't like home, Americans couldn't make tea he concluded, but it was good enough.

Jake had spent the last twenty-four hours accompanying this man and had found it hard to believe that his brief could be correct. Could this man really do what he was supposed to? Jake knew he had it in him of course, he had heard stories of how explosively violent he could be. But to kill someone. He doubted very much that this man would resort to this. It was apparent he loved animals and kids. The walls of the club were adorned with pictures of Jack with his pets and he had been really good to him since he had welcomed him to stay at the club safe from the elements and the cold nights.

191

"Right, let's tidy this place up," he announced, speaking to no-one in particular. Willie and Tony moved at the orders, whilst Jada remained sitting, observing, wondering. She knew there was more going on than Jack was letting on. He had been no patriot before now, yet here he was spouting this rubbish. She knew she couldn't rely on these other two bozzos to recognise the signs, but she wasn't just some dumb dancer. She was determined to find out what was going on.

+++

Jake had been keeping his head down, helping out around the place with the cleaning in return for a warm place for the night. He had seen many people come and go. A diverse array of people from those crassly decked out in elaborate regalia, smelling of crime and money to the bland and officious with their cheap suits and slick-backed hair. The police were also regular visitors. It appeared that Jack had his fingers in many pies. He was inclined to exaggeration and was often overheard bragging about his connections with various groups, whether they be the chief of police, FBI, CIA or even the local organised crime gangs. How much of this was reality and how much was bravado was difficult to establish, but he certainly had a lot of visitors.

Jake was wiping down the chairs when the latest callers knocked at the door. Tony looked up and gestured towards him. "Go see who that is," he directed him. Jake wandered off and opened the door. He immediately regretted doing so. Jake had hoped that after successive failures, the Disrupters may have given up with their mission, but his hopes were in vain. The creature before him had steely intent in his eyes. Jake was temporarily stricken with fear. He had never been one for melodrama and regarded himself as fairly robust when it came to facing up to his fears, but there was something deeply evil in what he saw before him which sent shivers down his spine. His momentary pause had raised the alarm in Tony's mind. He made his way toward Jake. "Who is it?" he called out. As he did so, the Disrupter looked beyond Jake in to the club and saw the imposing figure of Tony standing there in the shadows. The Disrupter fancied his chances but the risk of failure at this late stage would unquestionably end any chance of them achieving their aim. He knew he had other opportunities and so walked away. Jake closed the door. "Who the hell was that?" Tony asked.

"No idea," Jake lied.

"I have a bad feeling. Something just don't sit right," Tony rubbed the stubble on his chin.

Jack sat at his desk in a tiny back room at the back of the club. He ran his fingers through what was left of his hair. He could swear he had more before this whole sorry episode began. He suspected he would have even less by the time it was done. He was trying to make sense of things, playing everything over in his mind. The visit from the Feds the evening before, his doctor's report, his connection to the man who had just been charged with the assassination of the president of the United States of America. "Just some small matters", he thought. "Was he trying to convince himself that the course of action he was led to believe was his patriotic duty was the right one? Were they right, would he really be regarded as a hero? The sound of it certainly appealed. He had worked for years to get respect and status in this town and he was finally being presented with an opportunity to get both. But at what cost? According to his doctor it would be relatively short lived, but the chance of a legacy. His name to live on as a key figure in history." He puffed out his cheeks and exhaled slowly. It seemed to be an easy decision. He would need to put things in order first. He grabbed a pen from his desk drawer and began to write a list.

+++

Jack stared at himself in the mirror. His appearance from earlier in the day had been replaced with that of a slick, well-dressed host. Hair greased back, sharp suit and tie and the smile which exuded confidence and affability. He was the master of ceremonies and just like the stage performers he paid to keep the punters entertained, he insisted on putting everything in to his appearance, even if the bar would remain closed to patrons for now. He straightened his tie for the last time before heading out the room.

As he walked through the open the door he was met by the imposing figure of Jada. She had a smile which was ready for mischief. Fully made-up, her high eyebrows raised, suggested she was ready for answers. She could have appeared on the big screen, her presence immediately felt when she entered any room. But she hadn't had the breaks, and so instead she made her way in life by performing, and exposing more than her parents would have wished, on Jack Ruby's stage for the paying customers. She was a star in those circles and very popular. But to Jack, she could be a pain.

"I don't want to talk money now," he said, brushing past her on the way to the bar. She grabbed his arm, stopping him in his tracks. He looked at her, their faces inches apart.

"I know you are up to something Jack. Those guys may not have a clue," she gestured towards the bar. "But don't think you can keep me in the dark."

"I don't know what you are talking about. Your job is to dance and keep the clientele happy, so just stay out of my way."

She released the grip on his arm and he straightened his jacket before walking on towards the bar. She turned and walked in to his office in search of something to hold against him. As she rifled through his desk, she came across a .38-caliber Colt Cobra revolver. She had been around guns all her life and so it didn't faze her, but she wondered why it was in his possession. He had not carried a gun as long as she had known him. In fact, he had often sworn against them. She chose to ignore it and continued the search for something else of value. There was nothing significant, certainly no cash which might go some way to reimbursing her for the money she felt he owed her since working at the club. She closed the last drawer in the desk and sat back in the chair. Sitting on the desk was a coffee cup, its contents still half full and an ash tray with several cigarette stubs. Next to the telephone was scraps of paper with various notes scrawled on them. She didn't know why, but she was suddenly drawn to them. Most were of very little interest, but she did find one scrap of paper with "DCJ Basement 10am" scribbled on it. In itself not very revealing but the lack of details suggested something suspicious to her. 'Who or what was DCJ?' she thought to herself. She realised that she had stayed too long and if she didn't get out of that office soon, she could expect Jack to come and find her. She slinked out of the open door and passed Jack coming back the other way. He had company. Serious looking men. Not law enforcement officers, not on this occasion. She had had her fair share of brushes with the law so was well placed to identify them. These guys were much more business-like. She looked back towards Jack's office and her eyes met those of Jack's as he closed the door behind his visitors. Those eyes did not have the anger of previous confrontations. This time she felt there was a sadness behind the eyes. This confused her more than the comings and goings. She turned and made her way back to the bar. All the time Jake was observing in the shadows. He was sure that there would be an attempt to stop Jack before tomorrow and he was on high alert, scrutinising everyone and anyone who came through the door. After the episode with the Disrupter coming to the door, Jake was on careful watch for any reappearance. He knew that so far his friends had been successful and he didn't want to be the one that let them down, again.

He was having these thoughts when he heard raised voices coming from the office. Something was wrong and the visitors were making sure Jack was fully aware of their displeasure. The shouting continued. Jake took steps closer to the office to try and catch what they were discussing.

Whatever had happened had clearly put their plans at risk and Jack was being told in no uncertain terms that he would take the fall if it did not get back on track. As Jake stepped further forward, the door suddenly and unexpectedly lurched open. Standing there with a furious disposition was Jack. "Where is she?" he bellowed.

Jake shook with terror. He was finally witnessing first-hand the height of Jack's ferocious temper. He thanked his lucky stars that he was not at the end of this fit of rage. However, he did find himself standing in the way and decided the best course of action was to head out to the bar in search of Jada. Jake did not have a complete picture of what was happening, of who these people were in his office, or what they were discussing, but he suspected that there was a good chance it was related to Jack's forthcoming role in the events to follow.

Jake reached the entrance to the bar just as Jada was heading out the front door. "Tony, grab her," he yelled. Tony instinctively raced towards the front door. Past experience had taught him that hesitation cost dearly and it was now ingrained in him to act first and ask questions later. There was a momentary pause before Tony returned through the front door, dragging Jada behind him by the lapels of her mink coat. She was loudly protesting in vain hope that some passer-by might take pity upon her. Tony closed the door behind them and with it any hope she had of a knight in shining armour coming to her rescue.

Tony took Jada by the shoulders and sat her down on a chair.

"Give me the gun," Jack ordered, his face as close as he could bear to that of Jada's. She bore a defiant look and refused to give it up.

"You owe me," she replied.

"You'll get your money, just give me the gun."

This had been the first time that Jack had submitted so easily which came as some surprise to Jada, who in turn decided to make the most of the situation. "All of it. And extra for the inconvenience."

Jack was in no mood for games or for being blackmailed. He knew he could quite easily force her to give up the gun, but he also knew Jada and he knew she could stir up a lot of trouble for him at a time when he needed to keep his nose clean. After all he had a job to do and it would be disastrous to miss the opportunity of universal popularity if he missed that appointment.

"Fine," he agreed reluctantly. Tony raised an eyebrow. He had known Jack for a long time and not once had he seen him acquiesce so readily.

"Tony, release her." Tony let go of her shoulders and Jada stood and adjusted herself. Then she delved in to her under garments to retrieve the weapon.

"Classy," Jack commented as he took back the gun. "I'll wire you the money, now get out of my sight."

Jada accepted Jack was a lot of things, but he would not welch on a promise. She decided then and there however to get out of town and out of his reach should he decide she needed to be taught a lesson.

Jake sat back down on his chair in the corner of the room. Following Jack back to his office seemed a reckless thing to do given the mood he was in. Whilst he was tucked up in the club, Jake was confident that nothing untoward would happen. He was more concerned about

197

the events that would come the following day. He needed to be on full alert to make sure Jack got where he needed to be at the right time.

+++

It was several minutes more before the visitors left. As they did so, Jake caught a better sight of them and recognised them from the meeting at the Adolphus Hotel which took place before the assassination. Jake was pretty sure that whoever they were, they were responsible for ensuring Jack silenced Lee Harvey Oswald. The only reason to do that was to ensure their connection to the assassination never saw the light of day. Jake understood why these events had to take place as history would report it, but he wondered whether it would be better to let a different course run. He was still not convinced about this whole 'end of the world as we know it' story. It would certainly be better for Jack if the Disrupters successfully prevented him from firing the gun.

"Who were they Tony?"

Tony looked up from his newspaper. "Don't you read the papers, son?"

"Been busy," Jake quipped in response.

Tony smiled. "Those guys there, they own most of the oil companies in this town. Got a bit of money between them they do."

"And what have they got to do with Jack?"

"Business, it's always business," Tony said, resuming his reading of the paper.

Not even Tony knew what that business entailed on this occasion.

"Is the club opening tomorrow?" Jake asked.

"Doesn't look that way kid. Jack's real cut-up about the shooting. Don't suppose we'll open until next week. Jack said out of respect."

Willie who had been busy wiping down the bar and sweeping the floors spoke up. "Can't see why, not after what he did to our boys in Cuba."

"Don't start all that again," Tony rolled his eyes in exasperation.

"What happened?" Jake asked, immediately regretting it when Tony shot him an annoyed look.

"Bay of Pigs kid," Willie offered. "Our boys were left high and dry out there because he didn't have the guts to go in full and hard."

"Bay of Pigs?" Jake questioned, not aware of the landing site on the south coast of Cuba used for what turned out to be the botched invasion of the country led by the US Central Intelligence Agency.

Ignoring Jake's question, Tony angrily addressed Willie. "You don't know what you are talking about. It wasn't his fault that the bombers couldn't hit a barn door with a shovel."

"But he did call off the second strike and let our brothers land on those God damned beaches only to be shot up by the Cuban army. They didn't stand a chance."

"Brothers? You're not even Cuban," Tony shouted.

"We're all brothers in the fight against the commies," Willie responded.

Jake watched the volley of abuse heading back and forth between them, keeping his nose out of the argument he appeared to have inadvertently caused.

Tony shook his head. He had taken part in the same argument several times over the previous few days and had never won. "There's no talking to you," he conceded.

It was just as well as Jack appeared from the back office shortly thereafter. He had his coat and hat on and announced he was heading out. "Lock up for me Tony, I won't be back tonight."

Jake went to follow but Jack interrupted him. "Not this time kid."

"I'm keen to learn the business sir," he thought the pleasantries might sway his decision.

"Maybe tomorrow," and with that, he left.

Jake knew he had no choice but to follow, but the job would be a whole lot more difficult keeping out of sight. He waited for Tony and Willie to be occupied and slipped out the front door in to the darkness of the night in pursuit of his target. Thankfully for him, Jake was lighter on his feet than Jack and he was able to work his way ahead of him unnoticed before they arrived at Nichols garage where Jack parked his car. Jake slipped in to the back seat of the unlocked car and waited the few seconds before Jack arrived.

Jake made himself as small as possible, hunkering down in the footwell of the back seats. It was particularly uncomfortable but luckily for Jake, it was only a five-minute journey. Jack had decided to pay a visit to the Pago Club and pulled the car up outside its entrance. Jake opted to remain where he was, assessing the risk of an imminent attack on Jack in a busy club as remote. It transpired that Jack evidently didn't want the company as within thirty minutes he was back in the car and making the fifteen or so minute journey home. Jake had been to the apartment before, so he was familiar with the layout and knew he could gain access without Jack. He let him go ahead of him and waited until the coast was clear before following him in to the building. Everything looked calm and peaceful and Jake headed toward the laundry room to get his head down for the night.

He knew Jack had not been sleeping much so expected to get only a brief night's sleep. By staying in the laundry room, he would hear any movement in the apartments above and ensure he did not miss Jack when he left in the morning for his fateful mission.

14 THE LAST STEP

Jake woke with a start. He had slept restlessly with the pile of laundry providing an insufficient substitute for a bed. He had judged correctly that movement above him would wake him. He moved gingerly, aching from the uncomfortable night and approached the door to the laundry room. He pulled the handle, but the door did not move. He pulled again, this time a little harder assuming it was stuck, maybe having expanded from the humid conditions created by dank clothing and electric dryers within the room over time. No luck. Jake started to feel slightly uneasy. He pulled again and again at the door, agitation starting to rise within him. The door had no intention of moving. Jake looked around for signs of a lock but there was none. The door had clearly been tampered with from the outside to keep him in. There was no other plausible explanation. He heard more sounds from above and knew he had to find another way out if he was to stand a chance of seeing his mission through. He looked around the room for inspiration. The only light coming from the strip lighting attached to the ceiling which flickered uncontrollably, emitting a grating hum as it did so.

The laundry room was positioned in the basement so there was no access to any windows. The only feasible exit point was a vent which appeared to lead out from the laundry room up to street level. He just had to find a way to remove four screws and the metal cover and overcome his fear of small spaces. He searched for something to assist him with this task, trying not to focus on the trepidation that would inevitably overcome him when faced with the escape route.

As he did so he could hear further movement above. He castigated himself for allowing himself to be caught out like this. He was not sure how long he had but assumed it would not be long before Jack would leave, unless of course the Disrupter had already got to him. Jake felt his heart skip a beat and stepped up the urgency in his search for a screw driver or similar implement. He noted a metal box alongside one of the machines and on further inspection he was delighted to find various screwdrivers. He picked the one most suitable for the job and attacked the vent with full vigour. Three of the screws came out easily but disastrously the fourth broke off in its casing and as it did the screwdriver slipped, the sharp end scraping along the metal casing before inserting itself in to Jake's hand. Jake yelled and dropped the screwdriver, immediately clutching his hand which had started to emit blood from the open wound. Jake grabbed somebody's discarded laundry in which to wrap his hand to stem the bleeding. With no time to lose he picked up the screwdriver in his good hand and started to leverage the metal cover from its position. The stubborn screw was not making it easy and Jake resorted to pulling frantically with both hands at the screwdriver as it poked out from behind the cover. With an almighty wrench on the screwdriver the casing suddenly gave way and Jake fell backwards, landing awkwardly on his back side and letting out an audible gasp.

Meanwhile the cover crashed to the ground with a cavernous din. "If the residents were not awake before, they certainly were now," Jake decided. The removal of the cover was not to be the biggest challenge however. Jake picked himself up from the floor and stared long and hard in to the dark entrance of the vent. He guessed that the route to the exit was not far but he had not anticipated how frightened he would be to enter the black space in front of him. Jake started to sweat, his blood pressure increasing, his heart beating louder and faster. Jake knew he was facing his biggest fear and he was desperately trying to deal with the rising anxiety attack. He had never really got over the episode that had caused him to develop such a phobia and living in denial and failing to face his fears had now come back to haunt him. Of course, everyone would forgive him, given the circumstances and the trauma he had survived, but this was of no help to him now.

Jake stared at the black hole for what seemed to him to be absolutely ages. In reality it was less than a minute. His attention diverted suddenly by banging at the door. He realised that the noise of the falling cover must have alerted residents to his plight, and he ran over toward the door, before swiftly coming to a halt in the realisation that on the other side of the door could be the Disrupter.

There were further bangs on the door. With each one, Jake flinched, nervously creeping back and seeking solace towards the rear of the room. Suddenly the banging stopped and the door began to open. Jake composed himself and prepared to meet his adversary. The door swung inwards, and figures emerged from the shadows in to the light of the room. Moments later, he was face to face with them.

Standing in front of him were his best friends Tom and Michael.

"What the hell are you doing here?" Jake's relief palpable.

"The hanging around just waiting was too much. We thought you might want some help," Tom looked around the room. "And it looks like we were just in time!" he sniggered.

Jake didn't see the funny side but was delighted to see his friends. "How are the girls?" he asked.

"You mean Rhianna?" Tom was in a mischievous mood.

"And Lucy," Jake blushed.

"They are fine. Safely hiding out at the hotel," Michael responded.

"Cool," Jake looked up as a noise emanated from above.

"We need to get back to business," he checked his phone and noted the time. "According to my brief Jack will be on the move shortly and we need to make sure we stay with him." He looked at his friends, "I am glad you are here, although I am not sure how I am going to explain this to Jack."

"We'll think of something," Tom suggested.

"OK, well let's get upstairs. I have a bad feeling about being locked in here. I think the Disrupter is here."

The boys made their way out of the laundry room and took the stairs up to the apartments. They were half way up the flight of stairs when they heard footsteps coming toward them. The boys shared a look and intuitively decided to head back down to the ground floor. Worst case scenario was that it was the Disrupter coming toward them. If that were the case, then they did not want to be boxed in the stairwell. Best case was that it was Jack and they would meet him out the front and try and explain their presence at his home.

The boys didn't have to wait long, their hearts racing. Jack exited the building in front of them. He stopped, a confused expression on his face, surprised to be met by three young boys, one of which he recognised.

"Jake?"

"Hi Jack," Jake replied.

"What are you doin' here? And who are these guys?"

Jake paused, his head whirring in an attempt to come up with a credible answer.

"Good morning Mr Ruby," Tom interjected, extending his hand out. "Jake here mentioned you may be able to give us a lift down town.

Jack hesitantly shook Tom's hand. "Sorry kids, I gotta lot to do today and don't have time to babysit you guys."

"Really we are just looking for a lift, you can drop us anywhere."

"Sorry guys, I must run."

The boys felt they had pushed it as far as they could. They were grateful that Jack had not asked further questions, evidently he was distracted by other priorities.

Jack walked past them to his car. The boys remained, watching as Jack entered the car and attempted to start it up. The engine failed to start. Jack attempted the key several times and appeared to be getting more exasperated with each turn.

"Looks like something's wrong," Jake suggested.

The boys stepped forward closer to Jack's car. More attempts with the same result. They observed Jack, his temper rising, punching the steering wheel.

"You probably should know, Jack can be a little, er, feisty!" Jake announced.

"We can see that," Tom said.

"We need to get him going otherwise he is going to miss his appointment," Michael declared.

"What do you suggest? Giving him a push?" Jake responded sarcastically.

"No, I think I have an idea," he said as he delved in to his pockets. "How long have we got?"

Jake checked his phone again. "About an hour, assuming he still makes the stops he is expected to."

"Should be enough time. As long as I can get hold of him."

"Who?" Tom asked.

"Guy that helped me out with the truck. Where is there a phone?"

Jake looked on rather perplexed. "Truck, phone, wait what?"

"Don't worry just get some coins for the phone for me," Michael requested.

Jake turned to Jack who was by now pummelling the steering wheel with his full force. Jake wasn't looking forward to interrupting him. He knocked at the window. Jack turned to face him, anger in his eyes. He rolled down the window and shouted, "What the hell is it kid?"

Jake mumbled a response. "I think we can help. Do you have any coins for the phone?"

"What?" Jack replied increasingly irritated by the distractions.

"Coins. We can call for some help. For the car," Jake blurted somewhat incoherently.

"Fine," came the response. "Here," Jack passed some coins through the window.

Jake took the coins and re-joined his friends. "All yours," he said to Michael handing them over.

"Phone?" Michael said incensed.

"Oh, through there," Jake pointed back towards the apartments. "There is a payphone in the entrance."

Michael turned clutching the scrap of paper and entered the building.

+++

Michael returned several minutes later. Jack had in the meantime left his car and was pacing up and down the road, pushing his fingers through his hair and muttering to himself.

"So, my guy is on his way. Says he will be about five minutes as he is already this side of town." Michael announced.

"Great, do you want to let him know?" Tom nodded in the direction of Jack.

Jake turned and saw Jack continuing to pace, getting increasingly agitated.

"Guess so," Jake reluctantly agreed. He walked over slowly, giving himself time to prepare for Jack's mood.

"Jack, we have a mechanic on his way, should be five minutes," he delivered the news much quicker than he had walked.

Jack stopped in his tracks, looking at Jake in amazement. "How did you organise that kid?"

Jake smiled nervously. "Lucky I guess," he said.

+++

The truck, the boys and Jack had so desperately been waiting for to arrive, pulled up to the building. Joe was hanging out of the window, the familiar broad smile back on his face. "Anyone call for a hero?", he shouted, chuckling at his own humour.

Michael approached.

"What is it with you and broken-down vehicles?" Joe asked.

"Guess I must be some kind of magnet," Michael responded half-heartedly.

Joe opened the truck door and jumped down. "This the car here? And you the driver?" he addressed Jack who came over to speak.

"Yeah, this is mine. I'm in a real hurry. Any chance you can get it going?"

"Well, let me take a look," he paused. "You a paying customer?" he looked back to Michael and winked.

"Yeah I got cash, I just need it done quick," Jack responded impatiently.

Joe took the hint and approached the white two-door 1960 Oldsmobile. He opened the bonnet and took a step back whilst inhaling a large gasp of air. "My advice is for everyone to get the hell out of here," he yelled.

It was obvious that something was really wrong, yet no-one moved. Even Joe remained standing, staring at the open bonnet and the engine block of the car before him, despite his protestations.

Jack moved tentatively around the car to Joe's position. The sight had less of an impression on him but he remained motionless and speechless. In the seconds that passed, not a sound came from either man. The silence was broken when Jake went to make a step toward the vehicle.

Joe raised an arm towards Jake, his eyes remaining fixed on the engine. "Don't come any nearer."

"What is it?" Jake asked.

"Something that is likely to take you straight to your maker if this thing goes off," Joe cryptically answered.

Jake recklessly as ever ignored the warnings and in a fit of curiosity joined Joe and Jack at the car.

"Is that dynamite?" Jake asked, having never come close to it before.

"Yep," Joe confirmed. "Easy enough to pick up, not so easy to hook up to the car battery it seems. Sir, you are lucky you are still here to see this."

"I, er, I don't understand," Jack uncharacteristically spluttered.

"Looks like whoever did this, didn't connect the battery properly otherwise this thing would have exploded when you turned the ignition."

209

"How do we remove it? Jack enquired.

Joe turned to look at him. "We? This ain't nothing to do with me. I'm a mechanic, you need bomb disposal."

"I don't have time and besides I don't need the Feds crawling over me, not today."

"This is too much risk for me." Joe started to back away.

Jack grabbed at his arm. "I have money."

"And I have a wife and kids to feed. Ain't no use to them me blowing myself up," Joe insisted.

"How about five hundred dollars?" Jack offered.

Everyone turned to Jack at the offer. Joe in particular was aghast. He stood open-mouthed, unsure if he had heard correctly. "Five hundred bucks?" he queried.

"Yes, if you can help remove it now," Jack promised.

This was more money than Joe earnt in a month. The question was whether it was worth the risk. The problem was that he could not tell how badly the device had been put together. It looked professional enough, though he was no expert. Likelihood was that whoever had put it there had been disturbed and rushed the final installation. Joe reluctantly decided to take a closer look before he agreed to help remove it. He slowly approached the car and took a look from all available angles.

"Can it be done?" Jack asked.

Joe gave him a look which suggested he was out of his depth. "I can see a loose wire and expect this has come loose as you have attempted to start the engine."

"I expect the ferocious banging on the steering wheel may have helped as well," Jake whispered to Tom. Tom looked at Jake, amazed at his attempt at humour at such a time. Jake noticed and quickly withdrew his smirk.

"OK, I'll give it a go, but you kids make sure you move well out of the way," Joe said. "I must be mad," he muttered under his breath.

Joe was pretty confident that the device needed a power source so if he could make sure that there was no connection to the engine, the device would be neutralised. Just as long as he did not inadvertently make a connection between the engine block and the device, he would be fine. He retrieved his tool box from the truck and began to work on removing the device from the car.

It was still early enough for the sun not to have reached full strength and as a consequence the temperature was chilly. But a sweat was forming on Joe's brow as he bent over the bonnet of the vehicle looking down at the engine block and the four sticks of dynamite taped to it. There were two wires which hung free. Joe had deduced that these were the offending wires that prevented the device from discharging.

He was not going to take any chances however and he continued to look around to make sure nothing would give the device an excuse to explode. He reached down and gently pushed at the dynamite to see how secure it was. The dynamite barely moved. Joe cursed as he grasped the extent of the ordeal he was faced with. He shifted his position and noticed a small gap between the tape securing the dynamite, and the engine block itself. He determined that this was the best approach and reached for his wire clippers which he would use to cut through the tape at this position. The sweat began to make its way down to Joe's eyes as the tension increased. Clippers in hand, Joe wiped his brow with his sleeve before extending his hand towards the side of the dynamite, careful not to knock them. Although the engine had not started, undoubtedly the engine turning over would have caused some heat and movement and he did not want to cause any further disturbance which might set it off. Slowly the clippers moved in to place. Joe worked steadily and assuredly at the tape, making small incisions one at a time. The tension in his arm was beginning to cause lactic acid to course through his veins. His heart was beating faster, his eyes twitching as sweat ran in to them. He was close to breaking through the tape. "Get a move on," Jack shouted from a safe distance away. Joe's hand involuntarily jolted at the sound, the clippers grazing the engine block, the sound of metal on metal generating a cringing screeching which set Joe's nerves further on edge.

"For F..." Joe stopped himself from uttering the profanity. "Can we keep quiet out there?" he shouted, admonishing Jack and reminding those looking on of the seriousness of the circumstances.

Silence was restored as Joe set out to release the last of the tape, gently cradling the sticks of dynamite in his hand so that they didn't fall when the tape finally released. 'Snip' the last of the cuts completed and the dynamite instantly loosened. Holding the sticks in one hand Joe used his other hand to remove the tape from the engine block. Taking his time, the lactic acid and adrenaline in his veins having a field day, Joe slowly removed all the tape and carefully pulled toward him. He paused for a few seconds, allowing the blood to resume normal service through his arms. Cramp was beginning to set in, but Joe held the device tightly, hugging it like a baby. Sufficiently away from the car he stood cautiously and looked over at the group who were cowering behind some concrete bollards. "I got it," he announced. There was a ripple of applause before Jack made his way over to him.

"Best discard that safely," Jack sagely advised before stuffing the cash in Joe's pocket and returning to his vehicle. The car started first time and Jack silently thanked God, before hollering to the kids, "You coming then?"
Michael looked over his shoulder out of the rear window and saw the forlorn figure of Joe left standing, clutching the device he had minutes earlier extricated from the vehicle Michael was now sitting in. Michael nodded and hoped

that Joe understood how grateful he and his friends were for the help he had been able to provide.

Jack drove the car toward downtown Dallas.

+++

"Fellas, I gotta wire some cash, so I'll drop you here," Jack announced as they parked up at the Allright parking lot at the corner of Main and Pearl Streets.

"That's great, thanks Mr Ruby," Jake replied.

They exited the car. Jack locked up and headed off in the direction of Main Street, giving a nod to the boys as he left.

"Plan?" Michael said curtly.

"I think we should split up. I can follow Jack and maybe you guys can head off to the police station to make sure the coast is clear," Jake suggested.

"Agreed," Tom confirmed. "You better get going in case you lose him."

"See you later," Jake said before turning and heading off in pursuit of Jack.

Jake quickly regained sight of Jack as he headed along Main. He remained at a discrete distance so as to avoid Jack spotting him and raising any uncomfortable questions. He knew Jack's destination and needed to make sure he got there. He was hopeful that the Disrupter was relying on the explosive device doing the trick and therefore there would be no further attempts on his life, but his head told him that they were unlikely to give up that easily. He had been keeping an eye out for any suspicious looking individuals following them since they left Jack's apartment and had been comforted that he had seen nothing obvious, but he continued to have an uneasy feeling, so remained on full alert.

Jake watched Jack enter the Western union building. Jake continued to walk past, glancing through the window as he did so, watchful for any sign of a Disrupter. He saw only the staff working at the counters and was confident that it was safe to leave Jack to his business inside whilst he remained outside, eyes locked on the entrance. As the seconds passed his mind began to wander and he became increasingly concerned about how all this might end. His job was to make sure it ended how history told it, but there were so many ways it could go a different way and Jake knew it would all be his fault. He was not sure if he could deal with being responsible for the end of civilisation as he knew it.

He contemplated further, "what if he was able to prevent any disruption, but in so doing something ill-fated happened to one of his friends. He certainly would not be able to live with that." Jake caught himself and decided it was not helpful to have his mind wander like this. He talked to himself to get a grip and concentrate on the matter at hand.

He must have done this audibly however as a couple of ladies walking close by stared at him as they passed. Jake smiled at them hoping to diffuse the situation. They shook their heads and moved on.

It was not long before Jack reappeared. Jake had checked his phone and noted the time was eleven seventeen. Just five minutes until Jack would pull the gun on an unsuspecting Oswald, killing him and ending their adventure. He had enjoyed the experience but if the truth be known he was looking forward to getting back home and out of the reach of the danger that they had found themselves in. He was also quite keen to get to see Rhianna again. He felt she had warmed to him a little when they last met and wondered whether there might be something between them. He was ever hopeful. For the moment he had a job to do and continued to follow Jack. He judged the time to the police station from their current position was a walk of a minute or so. This would bring him to the police station bang on time.

+++

A siren blurted out which startled Tom and Michael. They had positioned themselves across the road to the police station and should not have been surprised to hear the siren as the police vehicles exited the underground parking on to Commerce Street, but their senses were on high alert and any sudden sound or movement had them jittery. They watched the ramp that led down to the basement of the police station attentively. If the Disrupter was to make an appearance, they judged that this would be the entry point. They understood that Jack would use this as his way in and it made sense that anyone else trying to sneak in discretely would use the same way. At the moment however the entrance was blocked by an armoured police car. "Something is not quite right," Tom observed. "I'm pretty sure there is no way in past that truck."

"Are you sure this is the right building?" Michael asked inquisitively.

Tom turned to give him a look which intimated the absurdness of the question. "No, there are lots of buildings with police vehicles going in and out," he suggested sarcastically. "Of course this is the right building." He turned back to look at the ramp. "Perhaps the truck will move on shortly."

"It will have to be very shortly, there are only a few minutes left."

"Where are Jack and Jake, surely they should be here by now?" Tom started to get concerned.

"I can't see them? Check Jake's location on your phone," Michael instructed.

Tom pulled out his phone and selected the app that he had used earlier to locate Jake's position when he was locked in the laundry room. After a few seconds the signal appeared. "He's close. What road is this?". Tom asked.

"Michael noted the street sign. "Commerce Street," he responded.

Tom turned once again to Michael looking anxious. "We are on the wrong street. They are the other side of the building," he announced. They stared at each other, immediately recognising that their error may have left Jake walking in to an ambush. The took off, sprinting down Commerce and then up Harwood to re-join Main. As they turned the corner, they saw Jake up ahead enter the ramp entrance to the police station.

Tom and Michael's instincts had been right. Their error had meant the Disrupter had managed an unimpeded entrance to the station. Dressed in a black suit and conveying a sense of authority, the Disrupter entered the building from Main street, down the ramp that both Jack and Jake would also shortly take. Clutching a white piece of paper which he was hoping would enable him to complete his mission. He made his way past the office to the Jail elevator and made his way up to the third floor. The atmosphere was chaotic on the floor with uniformed officers as well as plain clothes officers rushing around and journalists firing questions in all directions, desperately seeking answers. The Disrupter stopped one such officer and waved the piece of paper in his face. "Here to collect prisoner Oswald for transfer to a secure facility", he said. The police officer was taken aback by the forthright nature of this man and stuttered.

"You'll need to speak to Captain Fritz. He's leading the investigation. He's in his office over there."
The Disrupter stepped towards the office and wrapped on the door. He made out a number of individuals within the room, standing and pacing around an individual seated at the desk. It was several moments before a figure approached to open the door. "Yes," the man spoke.

"I have instructions to transfer the suspect to the county jail," the Disrupter announced.

The man turned around and spoke to the men inside the room, "Looks like the transport has arrived."

A voice came back, "No chance. We've already agreed we'll take him over. Tell him to go away."

The man turned back to the Disrupter. "Chief says no," and with that he closed the door. The Disrupter was frustrated but had understood that it was a long shot. There was too much attention around for him simply to walk off with the prize possession. He would have to think of some other way to ensure Oswald remained fit and healthy.

It was eleven-nineteen when Jack entered the underground car park to the police station, Jake hot on his tails. There were so many journalists and police officers around that no-one took a blind bit of notice of a smartly dressed gentleman walking down the ramp in to the car parking area, followed by an odd-looking young man. All the focus was on the imminent parade of the man charged with the assassination of the president. Jack could have entered naked and no-one would have batted an eyelid. Here was an historic moment, and everyone present was determined they would not miss a thing. The police had played their part in announcing the time of arrival of the suspect so that the journalists could get a front row seat.

Jack waited. Jake hid behind a concrete pillar, keeping a close eye on Jack, hoping that there would be no further disturbance to the sequence of events that had been clearly recorded in the history books. Eleven-twenty. Only one more minute to go. Jake began to sweat, despite the cold and damp conditions of the carpark. His hands were shaking with expectation. He had not witnessed a shooting before and here he was, about to witness one of the most famous shootings in history. He observed Jack who was as calm as he had seen him over the previous couple of days.

The agitation that had accompanied him appeared to have disappeared. His eyes were focused on the corridor which led off to the lifts. Quietly waiting for his prey. Seconds before the time to act was due, Jack twitched. His calm appearance replaced with a steely-eyed determination. Jake's eyes were drawn to the procession of individuals appearing from the back. It was then that his worst fears were realised.

Jake saw his adversary coming around the corner, walking directly towards Jack. He could tell this was the Disrupter, despite the similarity of his appearance to the other officers, black suit, cream Stetson. The intense eyes bearing down on Jack gave it away, seemingly preoccupied with the single-minded intention of taking Jack out of the equation. No-one else saw what Jake saw as they were all focused on the activity behind him. Jake knew he had to act. Somehow, he would need to get to Jack and secure him. Jake moved towards Jack at the same time as the Disrupter approached from the other side. Jack did not see the Disrupter however as his focus was on the individual behind him, the figure of Oswald, handcuffed and escorted by two law enforcement officers.

The moment came. Jake jumped at the Disrupter who was within inches of getting a hand on Jack. The collision knocked the Disrupter aside and Jake fell on him, letting out a cry with pain as he landed awkwardly, banging his head on the floor. The sound of his cries drowned out by the sounds of a car horn emitting several loud honks. At the same time Jack was leaning in to fulfil his destiny as the shot rang out.

The officers surrounding Oswald jumping to action grabbing at Jack, trying to retrieve the gun that he had just discharged.

Tom and Michael arrived to utter carnage. There was an unusual atmosphere as the events of the previous seconds sank in to the collective consciousness of those present.

Jack was being manhandled and speedily escorted out of the car park up to the holding rooms. Not far from him, Oswald lay prostrate, his guardians standing over him, attempting to keep the crowds back having failed to protect him. The mood changed to one of panic as scuffles continued, all the time, the journalist's cameras continued to roll, capturing the unfortunate event for the records.

"Jake!" Tom shouted as he spotted his friend laid out alone on the floor. There was sufficient confusion in the car park that no-one other than the boys had observed Jake lying there, blood oozing from his head. Tom and Michael raced over and bent down over his lifeless body, amateurishly checking him for vital signs. "Here, let me," came a voice from behind them, gently pushing through to get to Jake.

"John?" Tom blurted, confused at the sudden reappearance. "What are you doing here?" he asked.

"I suspected you kids would be hanging around Oswald. I couldn't leave you hanging while this thing played out."

John examined Jake to feel for a pulse and was pleased to find one. "He is going to be fine, but we need to get him to a hospital."

John proceeded to pick Jake up and carry him out of the car park, Tom and Michael following closely behind. They passed out of the car park without incident. The chaotic scenes providing a perfect camouflage. Once outside they moved to a parked car. John placed Jake in the front passenger seat and instructed the boys to get in the back. He then drove them all to Parkland hospital.

+++

Tom, Michael and John sat alongside each other at the emergency room, staring at a group who had congregated around a small black and white television set. They could not make out the pictures but the sound of the newscaster reverberated around the waiting room. "Oswald, the man charged with the assassination of President Kennedy has been shot."

"Looks like that's it then," Tom said, turning to Michael.

"Once Jake's up we need to get back home. I'm exhausted."

15 THE HUNTED

His fist hit the wood with a venomous crack, those present were under no illusion of the ferocity of his anger at the failed mission. No words were exchanged amongst them. This was not a time for excuses or explanations. Those who had made it back would have to face the wrath of their leader. Those who had provided assurances of success would be specifically targeted. The members cowered in fear of the retribution which was coming their way and which was expected to be particularly violent in its delivery. They braced themselves for the inevitable. But it never came. He slumped back in to his seat and the silence that followed was as disconcerting as any reprimand they could have received.

It was several minutes before there was any change. Finally, he spoke. "We have failed. We have failed the future. We were not strong enough. We were not committed enough." One of the Disrupters adjusted his position as if preparing to defend himself. Noting the expression on the leader's face however he reassessed his position and decided it safer to remain quiet.

"Kids," the leader continued. "A small group of kids were allowed to get the better of us and stop us from achieving our aim. We can't do anything about that now. We must hope we have another opportunity soon." His tone and manner remained calm, but it was clear to see the anger in him. The pulsating veins, the clenched fists, the edge to his voice. He desperately wanted to hold them all to account for their abject failure, but he knew and understood that he had further need of them and keeping them onside was the primary objective. "But there is something you must do. We cannot be embarrassed by these kids. We are a laughing stock and the Golden Circle must suffer some pain if we are to limit the damage to our reputation. You must go back and deal with the kids." Those present shifted uncomfortably in their seats. They had been more than willing to sign up to anything that was asked of them in dealing with guilty men and women involved in the assassination, but they considered the kids as innocent bystanders. Pawns in a wider game of course, but enough to be killed? This did not sit well with them. They would need convincing.

As if sensing their reluctance, the leader continued. "If you are in any doubt, may I remind you of the state of the Earth. A direct consequence of the actions and omissions of a human race. Depravity, neglect, greed, ignorance, selfishness. Just some of the charges that lie at the feet of generations who have led us to the ruination of a once glorious planet. These kids may belong to a generation who tried to make a change, but even their penchant for technology, convenience and materialism has contributed to the desolation that we now have to survive. It could have been all so different, and so it can, if we succeed in ridding the planet of this vile parasitic race. Just take a look outside

222

and this should give you all the incentive you need to finish the job. You should know that your colleagues have faced similar dilemmas to what you face now, and they chose the right path. They had the resolve to do what was right, what was best for the future. Now it is your turn."

There were a few murmurings, but the harsh reality was that there was no other option and they knew it. If it meant that any future opportunities had a greater chance of success, they would need to address the obstacles now.

The leader left them to ponder for a few seconds before giving them their final instructions. "If you fail again, don't bother coming back." And with that, he left the room.

+++

"It's not like there is anything in there to damage," Tom suggested cheekily. Jake laughed and then winced.

"Don't," he said. "It hurts when I laugh."

"You were lucky," John suggested. "With all those guns flying around it could have been a lot worse."

"I don't remember much to be honest," Jake said thoughtfully. "I saw the Disrupter approaching Jack and just ran and leapt at him."

"It was just moments before Ruby got his shot off," John clarified. "It all happened so fast and with the car entering in to the garage at the same time beeping its horn there was a lot of confusion."

"Looks like your special moment was pretty much lost then," Tom goaded his best friend.

"Well I think you did great," Rhianna jumped in.

Jake blushed, which did not go unnoticed as the rest of the group whooped in unison.

The joviality was broken with the sound of a mobile ping. Tom reached down to retrieve his phone from his pocket and opened up the message application. It was the Circle confirming the mission had been accomplished and passing on congratulations. Tom relayed the message to his friends but as he did so there was a noticeable change in his demeanour. "Listen," he barked over the din as the friends were congratulating each other on a job well done. "It's not over," he said.

"What do you mean?" Michael asked.

"We are not out of the woods yet. Seems the Disrupters were a little put out and now they are after us."

The room fell silent as the friends comprehended what they had just been told. It was one thing to be protecting a target, it was another to be the target.

"We need to get out of here," Jake shouted overcome with panic. The call to arms sent the friends in to a frenzy, grabbing what items they had, frantically slipping on shoes and heading for the door.

"Stop," Tom shouted. "We don't know where they are. We could be rushing right in to their hands. We are relatively safe here so let's think about it first."

The group paused and reflected. They knew Tom was right, but the fear was starting to trump their common sense.

"Tom's right. You need a plan," John spoke up. He was not sure his input would be welcome, but time was not on their side and their safety was paramount. "Where do you need to get to? If we need to get you out of town then we should look at the train or bus."

Tom realised that John was not yet fully appraised of their situation. He was not clear on how he could suggest that they needed to get to a place at a specific time in order to travel forward in time. He concluded he may well just lose the support. "Less is more," he thought.

He consulted his phone again. "We need to get back to the park by midnight," he announced.

"Trinity?" John enquired.

The friends all stared at him with suspicion. "How had he known? There were many parks to choose from in the city," they thought.

John immediately realised he had let something slip. He cursed himself for the lapse in concentration. Normally an attribute he could rely on had let him down on this occasion.

He tried to convince himself that it was down to this not being usual circumstances, but it did nothing to console him.

John decided it was time to come clean. "Hey look, I'm not just a random do-gooder. I am ex-military, now independent security consultant. I was hired to follow you guys."

A gasp went around the room, followed shortly thereafter by all eyes on Tom. "Did you know?" Lucy asked accusingly.

Tom cowered slightly under the pressure of the stares from his friends. "Some of it," he reluctantly acknowledged.

"Why didn't you tell us?" Michael blurted, offended that he had not been trusted with the information.

"I didn't know he had been following us, or working for someone else, I just knew he was in the business," Tom responded defensively. "Anyone, what matters is that he has been helping us, so I don't see it makes any difference now."

"You don't think it makes a difference?" Rhianna chirped incredulously. "He could be reporting back where we are. There could be a knock at that door any minute."

The group instinctively turned to face the door. There followed a period of silence as Tom reflected on his omission and the group wondered whether their time was up. The silence was dramatically broken by a wrap at the door. The group all jumped backwards, suddenly filled with fear and apprehension. This was it. Having successfully achieved their mission, it was all going to end in a lonely hotel room. They looked at each other seeking comfort at what they expected to be their final moments. The visitor knocked again, this time more urgently. Nobody moved or said anything. Maybe, just maybe they could pretend no-one was in the room. Their unexpected guest may be deceived in thinking they had already departed. A third louder knock. It was apparent that the visitor was not giving up. This was it.

John looked around the room before speaking in a soft tone. "I am not sure if someone was coming to do you harm, they would wait politely on the other side of the door."

As the thought sunk in, the friends relaxed a little. "Well should we answer it then?" Lucy asked.

"I guess so," Tom replied but did not move.

"Oh, for goodness sake," Rhianna huffed and approached the door.

She opened the door, peering around its edge as she did so. To her relief, and the relief of the group she was faced with the member of the Golden Circle who had met them at the School Book Depository.

"Evening," the man said rather too cheerfully as he entered the room.

"Easy for you to say," Jake suggested. "You haven't got evil dark lords chasing after you." The man looked at Jake with a sense of confusion. The Star Wars reference was lost on him, given it would not show in the cinemas for another fourteen years.

"Here are your clothes," the man said, brandishing a box of their belongings. "Don't want you travelling back to the future with old clothes on."

"Funny, kinda got used to these new ones," Jake said, holding up his 2018 World Cup t-shirt and comparing it to his current attire. "I'll miss them."

"You're more than welcome to keep them," the man said.

"Great," Jake responded. All the while John was looking on somewhat perplexed.

The member of the Circle spoke. "You received the message, yes?"

Tom confirmed that they had.

"Good. Our understanding is that the Disrupters are not yet certain of your position, but they are around and will be searching across the downtown area. You have until midnight tonight to get to the extraction point. Don't be late or the window will shut and with it your chances of getting home anytime soon."

Tom became aware of John's presence in the room and became increasingly uncomfortable. He expected the questions to come thick and fast once the man from the Circle had departed. The man picked up his hat from the bed and placed it back on his head before making his way toward the door. He paused and turned back to the room. "Remember, don't be late." And with this he exited the room and their lives.

Tom avoided eye contact with John, knowing that the third degree was about to follow.

"So, do I need to ask?" John enquired.

"It's complicated," Tom responded as the rest of the friends stood motionless, grateful that it wasn't them fielding the question.

"I'm not sure we have time," Tom suggested.

"It would appear that is exactly what you have," John said accusingly, growing uptight with the stone walling.

"I'm not sure you would believe me if I told you. I hardly believe it myself," Tom answered.

"Try me," John demanded.

Tom gave an abridged version of events which had led him and his friends to be in the city of Dallas in nineteen sixty-three. He was not entirely sure that he had adequately explained the multiverse theory that had been described to him but in the circumstances, it was the best he could do.

When Tom had finished, his friends cringed with how it must have sounded. Remarkably, John did not overreact, in fact, there was barely a reaction at all. Tom incorrectly assumed he was in shock, but it was not the case at all. After several confusing seconds John calmly said, "I knew it. Those guys in tech must have finally found the secret."

The friends looked at each other as though they were the ones grappling with the concept of time travel. Understandably they had been expecting a rather different response.

"Aliens, right?" John quizzed them. The friends looked even more confused. "You know from Roswell," John acknowledged the blank faces. "There was this story about a weather balloon crashing in New Mexico back in forty-seven. Got the locals right stirred up as they were convinced it was some kind of alien flying machine. Anyways, the air force pretty much explained it away and nothing came of it. I don't know why, but the story stuck in my mind. Wasn't until after I joined the special forces in fifty-two that I started to wonder whether there might be some truth to the rumours. I saw some crazy stuff during my time.

"As far as I know, there are no aliens involved," Tom suggested.

"Although you could probably say we are," Jake mused, causing the rest of them to immediately throw their hands up in the air and start berating Jake for his untimely sense of humour.

"It's a joke, it's just a joke," Jake protested. Lucy gave a firm punch to his stomach as a reminder that now was not the time for joking. Jake doubled-up, recoiling from the contact with his injuries sustained in the garage. Lucy, realising, immediately apologised and went to his aide. Rhianna jumped to him at the same time and suddenly Jake had two attractive girls ably assisting him. "I could get used to this," he wheezed.

Tom looked on before rolling his eyes and turning his attention back to John. "Look, I can't tell you anymore than we know, and to be honest I don't understand most of it. All I know is that we have to get to the park by midnight otherwise we can say goodbye to getting home. And all that appears to be standing in our way is a group of assassins."

John appreciated the seriousness of their predicament. He was less sceptical of the time travelling element of their story given his experiences with the black operations he had participated in. Stories had often been told of advances in technology, mostly advanced weaponry, but there had always been an obsession with teleportation and time travel, ever since they had cracked travel in space only a couple of years earlier. The possibilities this had presented were considered to be immeasurable and as a consequence the available budget for development was uncapped. There was a palpable excitement across the country in the space race with the Soviet Union. The US had lost that particular race, but it was apparent that they did not intend on losing the next one. John wondered whether they had beaten the Russians in developing time travel capabilities. "Who are you working for?" John asked. Tom hesitated. He understood the need for secrecy, and he wasn't about to give them up.

"Just a private group," he responded vaguely.

"Who is financing them? Is it us or the Russians?" John pressed.

Tom looked confused. He did not appreciate the fierce rivalry between the US and the Soviet Union, despite what he had read when briefing for this mission. He wondered how John would react to the news that the Soviet Union would not exist in the future and that China would become a dominant super-power.

"Not sure, but I don't think it is financed by any government," he suggested.

John returned to his own thoughts and there followed a period of silence as the friends exchanged looks.

Tom once again broke the silence. "SO, can you help?" He asked rather too strenuously. John appeared disgruntled with Tom's tone, but he gave a nod which indicated his willingness to assist.

"Great," Tom added, "Let's put a plan together."

The group huddled around and agreed on a plan of action to get them safely from the hotel to the exit point. They decided that the best course of action would be to split up. They had considered all getting in to John's car but the possibility of being stopped with all of them trapped in the car was too great. All six of them squeezed in to his car would be pretty conspicuous. Divide and conquer was agreed upon, but they were cognisant that in order to make it back, they would need everyone to make it to the park. If anyone was missing, they would not be able to complete the circle.

They judged that it was about a thirty-minute walk from the hotel to Trinity Overlook Park and their 'ride' home, if they took the direct route. Some of them would need to take a more circuitous path. They did not want to be out in the open for much longer than was necessary so agreed that they would stagger their departures. John suggested taking the car and driving around to see if he could spot any Disrupters. He felt that it could also act as a distraction to put them off the scent and draw them away from the destination. "I think that is a good idea, but it may work better if you have one of us with you. Give them something to go after," Tom suggested. He looked at Jake. "I think given your condition; you should go with John."

"No way. I'm fine, I don't need special treatment, I'll take the risk like the rest of you," Jake responded.

"Makes sense," Lucy added. "It's not like he could sprint if they suddenly appear."

"I agree," Rhianna added.

"That's settled then, Jake you go with John," Tom confirmed.

"Hello, I am here, you know" Jake protested. "I think I know myself and how I feel better than you lot."

"Look we need someone to go with John and you are still in a bad way, no matter what you say. We can't take the risk with you being caught by the Disrupters because you can't move," Tom was adamant.

"Thanks for your confidence," Jake mumbled, disgruntled with the lack of support from his friends.

"For the rest of us, who is going with who?" Lucy asked.

"I suggest one of the boys goes with each of the girls," John said.

Lucy turned and addressed him angrily, "And why is that? You think they need protecting?"

John was taken aback by her vociferous response. "I just meant-,"

Lucy cut him off. "Yes, I know exactly what you meant. We are not in need of a babysitter."

Tom smiled to himself, having been on the sharp end of Lucy's tongue on more than one occasion.

"I'll go with Rhianna," Michael suggested. "Not sure I would live it down if either one of us didn't return."

"Ok, so you and me Lucy," Tom said looking at Lucy, hoping to placate her.

It did nothing to alleviate her mood, but at least she no longer set her sights on John. John for his part decided to avoid eye contact. He had come up against some serious people in his time, but none had instilled fear in him like Lucy had just done.

"I suggest Jake you take the pieces of the circle with you. Worst case, if some of us don't make it at the allotted time then whoever has made it, they complete the circle and get home," Tom said.

The group fell silent, not wishing to accept that their fate might be to remain in 1963, or worst still death. There were however no protestations.

"Just make sure you all get there," Jake added.

Tom checked the time. "It's getting on for eight now. I suggest we get a few hours rest before we need to get ready to go. We can take it in turns keeping an eye out of anyone wants to get some sleep."

It sounded like a great idea, but none of the friends expected to get any sleep.

+++

Darkness had descended on Dallas, Texas matching the continued mood of the city. Still reeling from the events of the previous days and in the knowledge that the city would forthwith be known as that place where the president was killed, the city was unusually still. However, that stillness was suddenly disturbed by the arrival of numerous Disrupters.

The sky dark under the cloak of night, suddenly swirled with black, ominous clouds. Intermittent flashes of lightening adding to the already tense atmosphere. At several points across a sixty-block downtown area, black-cloaked figures appeared with little fanfare but with an aura of malevolent intent. Their objective was clear, to hunt down and terminate five children.

+++

As expected, no-one in the room was sleeping, but the ping of the phone stirred the group in to action once more. Tom checked the message and announced that the Disrupters had arrived, "It's time."

232

They gathered their belongings and huddled together like a sports team ready to take on their fiercest rivals, showing both unity and defiance. Tom spoke again in an assured tone, rallying the group, aiming to instil confidence and determination in them for their endeavour. "We can do this," he said. "Be vigilant. We must all get to the rendezvous by midnight or we will be stuck here until God knows when.   But most importantly stay safe, it is more important that we all get out alive."

"Yep, nobody gets left behind", Jake added enthusiastically, overcome by Tom's passionate call to arms.

"Really?" Lucy chirped unimpressed, "You want to use that cliché?"

Jake sheepishly withdrew.

"Come on, we are all in this together. Let's smash this," Tom concluded.

"Jake, let's get going," John instructed.

Jake grabbed his bag, heavily laden with the pieces of the circle, and hobbled behind John to the door. "See you there, mate," Tom called after him.

Jake turned, looking back on his friends for what could be the last time. "Yeah, defo," he said unconvincingly. At this the friends rushed in for one last hug.

John and Jake cautiously made their way to the underground car park where they were met by a disinterested old man on duty. He bellowed to a young colleague to retrieve John's car. Moments later it appeared, and the young man handed over the keys. Everyone was greeted with suspicion, but the wide smile on the young man's face which accompanied a hearty, "Have a great night," was a strong indication that he was not to be feared.

"We hope so," John replied.

John turned to Jake and suggested he sit in the back where he could hunker down behind the driver's seat. "No sense in taking too many chances," he said.

Jake was more than happy to avoid as much risk as possible and climbed on to the back seat. John got in to the driver's seat and drove up the ramp and out in to the cold, dark night. He would use all his training and experience to try and spot the Disrupters whilst keeping his cargo safe. He turned right out of the carpark heading east along Commerce street, in the opposite direction to Trinity Park. If they were to be spotted, he wasn't going to make it easy for them to make out where the kids needed to get to.

It was with great relief that there was no sign of a Disrupter in the immediate vicinity of the hotel. He knew of course that this could change rapidly but he conveyed his observation to Jake who was hidden behind him. Jake took his phone and typed a quick message which he sent to his friends, "All clear," it read.

"So far, so good," John added.

"Don't speak too soon," Jake responded, nervously.

John's plan was to continue to criss-cross the blocks between the hotel and Trinity Overlook Park. In a couple of blocks, he changed direction, making his way on to Main street and heading west.

+++

Once John and Jake had left, the rest of the group sat down to work out the routes they were going to take. Whilst they had no reason to believe John was not now fully on their side, they could not be sure what information he had already passed on to the Disrupters, including their route from the park to Dealey Plaza when they arrived. They decided that the best bet would be to avoid that option.

"If we stay south of Commerce it takes us here," Michael pointed to the map on the phone. "It looks fairly open so we can see if anyone is coming. We can cross the river at the turnpike and then take our way up Beckley Avenue and come in to the park from the other side."

Tom considered the suggestion for a few seconds. "Sounds good. We could go even further down Houston Street. We can then trace the outside of the park up to the extraction point."

"The problem is that that will take you longer, which means you will be out in the open for longer," Michael highlighted.

"True, but I just don't think they will expect us to be that far out of downtown." He turned to Lucy. "Well, buddy, what do you think? You up for that?"

Lucy looked at him, nodding. "I trust you," she said.

"Right," Tom asserted, "We will cross immediately out the hotel and head south down Akard Street, down Canton Street which crosses with Houston here," Tom showing Lucy on the map.

"I suggest you guys take a right and then down Field Street and then on to Young Street. This should take you down to Reunion Park and access to the turnpike."

"Agreed," Michael and Rhianna said in unison.

It was then that they received the message from Jake.

Tom reflected on the message. "All clear," he announced. "We should get going Lucy."

Lucy dutifully got her stuff together and hugged Michael and Rihanna. "See you in an hour."

Tom hugged them also before the two of them left the room.

+++

The Disrupters flowed around the downtown area passing through the streets like blood through arteries. They had only a rough idea of where their targets were. The information had given them a one square mile block around main street. Even with their resources it was going

235

to be a tough ask to locate the children in time. They were going to need some luck, something they had been desperately devoid of during the whole mission. They were at least thankful for the time of day. It allowed them to pass relatively unnoticed whilst at the same time the quiet streets enabled them to clearly identify who was roaming them.

+++

John and Jake had been driving up and down the streets for ten minutes when they spotted the first Disrupter. They had just turned off Main heading down Lamar when they saw the shadowy figure walking towards Commerce. Jake was immediately on to the phone to warn his friends.

+++

Ping. Every time it sounded the friends collectively jumped. Tom checked the message and was relieved to report to Lucy that it was nothing to worry about, they were far from the position being reported and were travelling away. For Rhianna and Michael however, it was more of a concern. Assuming the Disrupter continued down Lamar, they could well meet at the cross section with Young. They had not left the hotel yet and were considering changing the route as a consequence of this news. "There are no guarantees the Disrupter will continue along that road and there is no guarantee that we will arrive at that junction at the same time. Plus, for all we know we change route and then we come across another one. No, I say we stick with our plan," Michael said.

Rhianna decided not to say anything. Michael was making perfect sense and anything she said would most likely just raise doubts that they didn't need right now.

"I think we should make a move," he added. They took a deep breath and set out on their way.

Tom was calculating that the Disrupters would be no further south than Young Street. He reminded Lucy to remain on full alert until such time as they passed that checkpoint. Lucy did not have to be reminded and made sure Tom was aware of that fact. Tom apologised. The tension was palpable, and they were all feeling the pressure. Lucy understood and accepted his apology. With their concentration now absolutely acute, Tom and Lucy came to the junction with Young. As they stepped out from the cover of the buildings on the corner, they luckily observed the Disrupter before being seen. They immediately jumped back, their backs pressed tightly against the wall, ensuring that no part of their bodies could be seen from the Disrupter's vantage point.

Tom whispered to Lucy, "Did you see which direction they were headed?"

Lucy, starting to breath very heavily did not respond.

"Lucy," Tom whispered again, this time more strongly. "Did you see, which way they were going?"

Again, there was no response from Lucy, she appeared to be going in to shock, her body beginning to shake, gripped with fear.

Tom decided to risk a quick peek around the corner. He approached carefully to the edge of the wall. As he edged closer, he heard his own breathing and his heart pounding in his head. There was no other obvious sound and every move he made appeared to be amplified. He was just about to move his head in to position to see down the road and a hand suddenly and unexpectedly grabbed his shoulder pulling him back. Tom close to heart failure was staring Lucy in the eyes.

She had recovered from her temporary paralysis and whispered into his ear. "He was heading our way. We need to double back."

Tom knew they had no time to discuss and they both ran back up the road. They reached the previous junction and turned the corner, continuing to look out for any further Disrupters. There was no-one about and they considered the best bet was to continue around the block and come back to Young further down the road behind the Disrupter they had just seen. They proceeded, watchfully. A minute or two later they were back at a junction with Young. On this occasion Tom was not prevented from peering around the corner. As his eyes turned the corner, he saw at a distance the back of the Disrupter heading further down the road. He turned to face Lucy to tell her, but before he could utter a word he saw over the top of her head, a couple of blocks away, another dark shadowy figure appeared. Not wasting any time Tom grabbed Lucy's hand and pulled her as they began to run as hard as they could south of their position. Neither of them dared to turn to look, instead they were intent on getting as far away as they could, desperately hopeful that they had remained undiscovered. They ran in silence for what seemed like an eternity. Their lungs busting for air, lactic acid forcing its way in to their legs. The adrenaline pushing them further, harder and faster. Eventually, they found themselves amongst trees and were able to stop to take a breather as they looked around to see if there was anybody following them.

All was eerily quiet. They waited, not wishing to make a noise until they were satisfied that they had escaped the danger. Several seconds past and they started to breathe more easily as it became apparent that they had successfully avoided detection. Relief however was quickly replaced with anxiety as Tom realised that the second Disrupter had been heading directly towards the hotel. Knowing that Michael and Rhianna had staggered their exit to leave some minutes after Tom and Lucy, he calculated that they could be walking straight in to the Disrupter's path. Tom dropped his bag and frantically grabbed at his pockets for his phone. Lucy stared at him wondering what had happened. She was still gasping for breath. "What is it?" she wheezed.

"It's Mike and Rhianna," he stuttered. "I need to warn them." And with this his thumbs punched at the phone's display wildly, attempting to get a message through as quickly as possible, trusting that auto-correct would not make the message unintelligible. He watched anxiously as the message seemed to take an age to send. Finally, it went and Tom let out an audible sigh. He hoped the message got there in time.

+++

Michael pressed his finger to his lips. Rhianna was clearly uncomfortable, her facial expression appeared tortured as she was battling with the pain and the imperative to remain absolutely silent. Michael slowly reached out to provide her with some comfort, knowing that any false move could result in their capture. Other than the hum of an air conditioning unit positioned a few metres above their heads, there was very little noise to assist them in concealing their whereabouts. The dumpster, which was providing cover was sufficient for them not to be seen but that would provide very little help if an errant sound gave away their location.

They both stiffened as they picked up the slow footsteps coming from the direction of the pavement at the end of the street, not far from the hideout they had constructed for themselves. As the footsteps stopped, so time stood still for the two of them. Michael shut his eyes, yearning for the moment to pass. He was cursing himself for not being more vigilant when they had exited the front of the hotel. It was not until they had reached the corner that he had seen the Disrupter walking directly toward them. In desperation to avoid detection, he had taken hold of Rhianna and hurled her around the corner. She had lost balance in the effort and fallen hard against the side of the building before ricocheting off and landing awkwardly on the pavement. With no time to assess her injuries Michael had then dragged her behind the dumpster situated in a small alcove at the side of the hotel. It provided a decent hiding place, assuming the Disrupter had not seen them and assuming the Disrupter continued along Commerce rather than changing direction to walk directly past them. The wait was tortuous. Michael internally pleaded for the Disrupter to carry on his journey.

Rhianna was bursting to let out a cry in response to the pain she was suffering. Quietly they waited. Then their wish came true, the footsteps recommenced and began to fade as the Disrupter moved away from them. Suddenly the silence was broken with a ping. Michael's eyes met with Rhianna's and the fear was plain to see. They froze. Questions rushing through their heads haphazardly. "Did the Disrupter hear? Was he far enough away? Should they move? Should they hold out? Would the sound have given away their position?"

The questions in their minds continued as their worst fears were confirmed, the footsteps were increasing in volume and coming straight towards them. With Rhianna's injuries they knew running was not an option, they would surely be caught. They had no choice but to wait it out and hope for a miracle. The footsteps got closer and closer. They stopped next to their position. Michael's heart felt like it was about to explode out of his chest. The wait was agonising.

The dumpster behind which they were hiding shifted, they gasped uncontrollably expecting the Disrupter to come into view. Instead the lid of the dumpster opened. Maybe all was not lost. They gave each other a confused look as it sounded as if someone was depositing rubbish bags in to the dumpster. The lid shut again with a loud bang. As it did so, Rhianna let out a small yelp. Immediately clasping her hand over her mouth. "Hello?" came a voice. The dumpster was manoeuvred in front of them and a face came in to view. "Rhianna?" the voice said. Rhianna looked up and removed her hand from her mouth, "Andy?" she replied.

The General Manager of the hotel was stood in front of them, looking bewildered. "What are you doing here?"

Rhianna did not have the presence of mind to invent an appropriate excuse so decided to give a version of the truth,

"We thought we were being followed by someone and got spooked so decided to hide in here."

"What happened to you?" Andy asked noticing blood running down Rhianna's arm. She followed Andy's eyes down to her arm. Only then did she notice the pain once more and the sight of blood made her slightly queasy. "Let's get inside and we can patch you up."

"I'm not sure we have time, we are supposed to be meeting our friends," Michael said.

"At this time of night?" Andy questioned. Not waiting for an answer, he continued. "Well, you can't go anywhere like that. I am sure your friends will wait."

Thinking on his feet Michael explained that they were catching a lift out of town and did not want to make their driver wait.

Andy looked at him suspiciously but left it at that. "I'll do you a deal. You let me take a look at these cuts and then I'll drive you over to your friends."

Rhianna shot Michael a look with a broad smile on her face. They both looked back to Andy and nodded in agreement. "That's very generous of you, thank you," Michael replied.

"My pleasure," Andy said and then helped Rhianna to her feet. She winced as the full effect of her injures took hold.

241

"Can you walk?" Andy asked.

"I think so," Rhianna responded. "I think it is just my arm."

The three of them wandered back into the hotel, Michael looking around to ensure there were no other Disrupters lying in wait.

+++

Ping, went the phone. Another message, this time from Michael. Tom read it aloud to Lucy. "Guys, we are fine. Getting a lift to the meeting point. Will explain later. Might want to put phones on silent!". Tom looked at Lucy with a confused expression. "Not sure what that is all about. But at least they are safe."

"So, let me get this right. We are now the only one's walking!" Lucy said. "I knew I should have gone with Rhianna," she added cheekily. "Girls are much more resourceful."

Tom smiled, welcoming the short moment of light relief.

They proceeded along their agreed route. Despite their close shave with the Disrupters they were making good time. They remained wary but it seemed as though Tom's prediction that the Disrupters would be focusing on the centre of the downtown area was proving to be correct. There had been no sightings in the last twenty minutes. They were close to approaching Houston Street where the planned to cross over the river to the south of the park.

"So, you seem to be getting on well with Rhianna," Tom spoke, in an attempt to make light conversation.

Lucy looked at him. "Well there is nothing like death and time travel to bring people together," she said giggling at how that had sounded.

Tom laughed. "I know what you mean." Pausing he added, "What do you think it will be like when we get back?"

"You mean between me and Rhianna?" Lucy asked.

"That as well, but I mean, for all of us." Tom clarified.

"I have no idea. At the moment I am just looking forward to getting back and having a nice long bath, maybe getting a Maccy D's and not worrying about being chased by creatures in black robes."

"Fair enough," he said. Lucy then lost Tom to his own thoughts. She had known him long enough to recognise the signs and had learnt that it was best to leave him to it at those times. They spent the next few minutes walking in silence.

Tom reflected on how the last few days was going to impact on his life back home. He knew it would not be the same ever again. Whether it would better he did not know, but definitely not the same and he didn't think it could be worse. One thing for sure was that he had finally found purpose.

"Tom, I think we might have a problem," Lucy announced, interrupting Tom's thoughts. "I can't see how we get up there." Lucy pointed to the flyover ahead of them. "That is the road we need right?"

Tom conferred with his phone before confirming. They both looked around to see if there was a way up to the road, but there did not appear to be any obvious access. "Looks like we would have to head north, back toward downtown to see if there is access to the road. I am not sure I fancy that, and I am not sure we will have the time."

"What other option do we have?" Lucy asked slightly agitated.

Tom consulted his phone again. "I think we carry on and take the turnpike across. This keeps us south and in plenty of time. Plus, as Michael and Rhianna are not taking this route anymore, we won't bump in to them."

"What time is it?" Lucy asked.

Tom checked. "Eleven thirty-eight. I reckon it will take us about fifteen minutes to get there, which leaves us five minutes or so to reassemble the circle and get the hell out of here."

Lucy admired Tom's confidence, but she had lingering doubts and suspected that it would not be as plain sailing as he was making out. Only time would tell.

+++

Michael was starting to get jittery. He had checked the phone several times out of sight of the lady who was applying some bandages to Rhianna's arm. "We really must be going," he said. Andy who was standing by shuffling some papers behind the reception desk asked the lady how long she would be. "Nearly done," she replied, in a tone which suggested that patching up young girls from the street was not in her job description.

"Ok I will go and get the car. I'll meet you outside," Andy told them before disappearing through a door behind reception.

"If we don't get a wriggle on, we are in danger of missing the window," Michael said.

Rhianna nodded but her attention was on her arm which was now heavily bandaged covering a nasty laceration. "I hope this doesn't get infected," she said. "You don't think I could lose my arm, do you?" An anxious expression crossed her face as she looked up at Michael.

"Don't be so melodramatic," he scolded. "It's just a scratch."

"It's alright for you to say, you didn't get thrown across the street," she retorted.

"Maybe next time I'll leave you to the –," Michael paused as he realised he was about to say something out of place. "Rats," he finished.

Rhianna looked at him in surprise. "Rats?" she queried before they both burst out in laughter.

"All done," the lady said.

"Thank you," Rhianna replied.

Michael and Rhianna got up to leave.

"And watch out for those rats," the lady called after them as they walked away.

Rhianna and Michael smiled back at her as they exited the front door. "Was that a strange expression on the lady's face?" Michael thought to himself. He shook his head deciding he was being paranoid, but it did remind him that they were not safe yet and as they exited, he was on high alert.

Michael was right to be cautious because, unknown to them, the Disrupter had seen them enter the hotel. Rather than follow them in, he had decided to contact the rest of the group to advise them of developments. On conveying the news, it had become clear that the friends had successfully evaded the rest of the Disrupters and the decision had been taken to regroup at the hotel and wait for the kids to exit. They sat in a car a block down from the hotel. Lying in wait.

Andy was waiting in the car outside as they exited. The Disrupters spotted them and one went to get out of the car but was stopped by the driver. "Let's see if they lead us to the others. We can get the whole group," he suggested. Andy started the car and they began the drive to their destination, the Disrupters in tow.

16 THE ESCAPE

John and Jake had been driving around for just short of an hour. They had spotted a couple of Disrupters within that time and had let the friends know. They remained hopeful that they were all safe and on track to meet at the rendezvous on time. "I'll drop you close to the extraction point and continue to drive round to make sure the coast is clear," John announced.

"It should just be a couple minutes' walk. Do you think you can manage that?" John asked.

Jake answered in the affirmative from his position in the footwell of the car. Moments later, he was out of the car, swinging his bag over his shoulder which was now considerably heavier with all the pieces of the circle stored within it. "Thanks for all your help," Jake said, realising that he would probably never see John again, all being well.

John shook Jake's hand and wished him well before driving off.

Jake checked the time. It was eleven fifty-five. Jake anticipated that the next five minutes would be the longest of his life. He made his may east from his position to that of the extraction point, highlighted on his map by a blinking cross, all the time looking around him to check for errant Disrupters.

+++

Tom and Lucy had picked up the pace in the last few minutes, worried that they were falling behind. They hit the park broadly at the time Jake had been dropped off and were now racing to the same point. Excitement growing at being so close to getting home they moved fast through the park which was caped in darkness. They could not see very far in front of them but followed the path which would take them close to the extraction point. As they drew closer, they spotted a dark figure up ahead. He appeared to be moving slowly hunched over as he went. Tom held out an arm and slowed Lucy down. "Wait," he said. "I think there is someone up ahead."

"Where?" Lucy asked, straining her eyes to see in the gloomy conditions.

"Just there," Tom pointed, "Moving between those trees."

Lucy saw the movement.

"Is it one of us?" Lucy asked, hopeful that it wasn't a Disrupter foiling their escape at the last hurdle.

"Let's just go easy," Tom suggested.

Quietly but briskly they proceeded. They were within fifty feet when they were relieved to see that it was Jake. They ran harder. Lucy shouted to Jake, overcome with excitement of seeing him. Jake swung round and seeing two dark figures approaching him at speed let out a high-pitched yelp. "It's ok, it's just us," Lucy called. Jake relaxed as he saw them come in to focus.

"Thank God," he said. "You nearly gave me a heart attack."

Panting Tom asked, "Where's John?"

"He said he would continue to drive around the area and make sure that all was clear. I am not sure we will see him again."

Tom was visibly upset that he hadn't had the chance to say goodbye and thank him for his efforts.

Lucy saw the angst on his face and tried to reassure him. "I think he knew how much you appreciated what he had done for us."

"I did thank him," Jake added.

Tom, acknowledging that there was nothing he could do about it and noting they only had minutes left before the window opened, suggested they start assembling the circle in readiness.

"Have you heard from Rhianna? And Michael?" Jake quickly added.

"Last I heard they were on their way," Tom said.

"Getting a lift. Lazy," Lucy commented, only half begrudgingly.

Jake looked around for any sign of them. There were very few cars on the roads at that time of the night, so it was easy to make out the headlights of a car driving in their direction along the slip road. The car stopped and Jake could just about make out two figures silhouetted by the headlights of the car, making their way toward them. "I think it is them," Jake declared. Tom and Lucy looked up. Their smiles instantly replaced by grimaces as they saw a second car screeching to a halt behind them. From it several figures emerged which appeared now to be moving fast in their direction. The lights of the two cars behind them were creating even larger silhouettes of what was undoubtedly Disrupters, intent on their destruction. Tom froze, immediately reminded of the nightmares he had experienced back home with the dancing shadows.

"Quick," Jake shouted to Michael and Rhianna, who were now busting a gut to get to them before the Disrupters caught them.

Tom calculated there were seconds between them. "We are not going to have enough time," he murmured.

"Come on," Jake and Lucy now shouted in unison. Michael and Rhianna would be with them in seconds, but the Disrupters were not far behind.

Tom held the final piece of the circle in his hands, ready to complete the circle as soon as the remaining friends reached them. Everything else he understood was out of his hands. He hoped the circle would do its magic in time for them to escape. The Disrupters continued to pursue at speed and were bounding down on their position. They continued to be an ominous black swirl as the headlights far behind flickered between them. Tom was close to thinking all hope was lost when suddenly another set of headlights came in to focus from the north. Tom turned his head to see a car bouncing uncontrollably over the uneven surface of the park. The engine was revving at full speed and the noise was deafening in the stillness of the night.

With the Disrupters almost within reach and focused on capturing the friends, they had not seen the car approaching at speed. The first knowledge they had of it was when it careered in to them sending them flying in all directions. Tom looked on at the carnage as the car came to a stop near to their position and a figure emerged from the car. Tom saw immediately that it was John.

Rhianna and Michael speedily joined them, grabbing at the circle and Lucy, noting Tom's distraction fixed the last piece in to place. The winds that they experienced the last time they had completed the circle again started to rise around them as the circle began its transformation. Tom nodded to John as he stood there watching in disbelief. He nodded back, saluting Tom, acknowledging Tom's gesture of thanks. Tom instantly became horrified as a looming dark figure rose up from behind John, crashing down on top of him. Tom's immediate reaction was to let go of the circle and begin to rise to rush to John's aide. The winds continued to swirl around them, picking up speed. Lucy looked round at Tom and grabbed his hand. Tom turned to Lucy, attempting to remove his hand from her grip. "We have to help him," he yelled over the sound of the rushing wind.

"We don't have time," Lucy loudly pleaded with him. "If the window closes, we will be stuck here."

Tom looked back to John bravely fending off the Disrupters, who were now attacking him in numbers. Tom realised there was nothing he could do and going to his aide would only put his own friends at risk. He looked reluctantly back to Lucy.

"Hurry, Tom please," she whispered gently in his ear as she saw tears well up in his eyes.

Tom returned his grip on the circle. A bright light emitted from the circle and as suddenly as they had arrived, they were gone.

17 HOME

Light grey shadows flitted gently across the ceiling almost melodic, soothing Tom as he lay there reliving the adventure. The open window letting in both an early morning summer breeze as well as the familiar cacophony of sound from everyday life. "As if nothing had happened," he thought to himself. Which of course it hadn't as far as everyone outside their group of friends was concerned. Life went on as usual. People went about their daily lives, waking, working, enjoying life for the most part, ignorant of the dangers that threatened their entire existence. Tom's thoughts turned to the final moments of their time in another time. He wondered what happened to John and whether there was anything he could have done. His rational mind told him not, but his heart was still beating him up over it. He wondered whether there was any way of finding out what happened to him, however painful it would be to know the truth, he needed to know to give himself closure. He doubted there would be a great deal of press coverage and he didn't have a surname to research. He had misgivings that John was even his real first name. It seemed an impossible task. But then again Tom was used to impossible now.

He rose and prepared himself for the day ahead. A less eventful one he conjectured. He went downstairs, not entirely sure what to expect. It reminded him of the conversation he had had with Lucy on the way to the extraction point. He entered the kitchen but there was no-one there. In fact, there was no-one anywhere. He was home alone. "Maybe nothing will change," he chuckled to himself. For the first time this did not seem to bother him. Whether it was because in his heart of hearts he didn't believe it, or because he had greater things to concern him now, he did not know. Maybe it didn't matter. His priorities had changed, that was clear. He moved to the lounge where the television was on, a repeat of Blue Planet II was being broadcast. He stood there glued to the television and the softly spoken David Attenborough. The episode was illustrating the impact of human activity on marine life. Albatross parents unwittingly feeding their offspring plastic; dolphins exposing their new-born to contaminated milk; a whale with a bucket caught in its mouth, the stories went on and the pictures depicted the devastation caused by the carelessness of the human race. As Tom watched images of oceans filled with plastic, he couldn't help but wonder whether they had done the right thing. Was this what he and his friends had risked their lives to protect? A human race which was determined to destroy the planet on which it existed. Tom was suddenly full of conflict and emotional turmoil. Scenes like these raised feelings of hatred for humanity within him which he had not experienced before.

The episode concluded with a speech, "The future of all life now depends on us," was the message. It was as if the rallying call was being communicated directly to him. He knew now that it was not just about survival but about change for the better. It was not the past that needed to change, but the future and it was his job, and the job of his friends and like-minded individuals across the world to foster and cultivate that change for the sake of the planet.

Just then he heard a key in the front door, before it opened, and someone entered. "Oh, you're up," his mother exclaimed. "I thought I would let you have a lie in, given your adventures. You must have been exhausted; you fell asleep as soon as you got back. Kevin had to carry you up. Are you hungry? Bought lots of food, not sure what you fancied. Can do a full English if you like, or cereal. How about some hot croissants?"

Things had changed.

His mother waddled off to the kitchen laden with shopping bags. Tom followed closely behind. He noted that she had her own canvas bags, not the plastic bags he had just seen swimming in the oceans. "Have you always used those?" Tom pointed at the bags. His mother looked at him and then to the television, through the door to the lounge.

"Yes love. We all need to do our bit for the environment," she winked at him, acknowledging that some had a greater role to play. "Crêpes?"

Tom nodded, not yet comfortable with the new relationship.

"What are your plans today?", she enquired.

"Not sure yet," Tom responded. He was not being evasive; he was genuinely not sure what he was doing.

"I bumped in to Jake's mum at the shop," she announced as she whisked a batter mix in an oversized bowl. "Said Jake was bouncing off the walls when he came back. Couldn't make much sense of it mind you. He was still in a bit of pain though and she thinks she is going to run him by the doctors when he wakes, just as a precaution. You're not hurt are you?" She temporarily halted the whisking and turned to him for affirmation of his well-being.

"No, no, fine," he responded without making eye contact.

She continued to look at him, wondering if he would ever open up to her. She was desperate to form a bond with him but knew she would have to give it time. She resumed the whisking. "Guess you will meet up later," she advocated.

Tom remained pensive as he ate his breakfast. "How do I get hold of George?" he said.

His mother was a little startled by the question. "You still have your phone?" she asked.

"Yep," Tom responded.

"Just send a message. It will get through. Much easier these days. I remember back in the day it was all done by word of mouth," his mother continued to natter about the good old days, but Tom's attention had moved on and her voice was now just background noise as Tom tapped away on his phone. He wasn't entirely sure what to say. In the end he decided to keep it brief. "George, would be good to chat. Let me know when you are free."

"Thanks for breakfast Mum," Tom announced before leaving the table and returning to his room. His mother watched him go, a warmness in her heart and a smile across her face. "Small steps," she thought as she dried a glass with a tea towel.

+++

Rhianna and Michael had spent some of the morning at the NHS walk-in centre. More out of precaution, but Rhianna was adamant she wanted a second opinion. Her arm had continued to cause her discomfort and the thought of having a scar on her arm spoiling her perfect skin made her cringe. "Somethings never change'" Michael had thought. He had gone along with it, but his real agenda had been to ensure she got a tetanus shot. He didn't mention it to her before going, assuming she would take it badly and he couldn't be doing with her histrionics. The nurse at the centre was not happy with the arm and said that they would need to go to accident and emergency at the local hospital to get an x-ray. It turned out that there was a hairline fracture.

Rhianna was devastated. Not because of the injury but because she had nothing to accessorise a plaster cast. On the positive note the doctor had been able to reassure her that the wound would not result in any long-term scarring and that within time it would completely heal. There was no sign of infection.

Lucy had spent the morning catching up with her family. It was nice that she had somebody else to talk to about her experience, although as usual, she had to compete with her younger twin siblings to get her parent's attention. She was conscious that her story sounded so impossible that she questioned whether it had been a reality at all. After all, there was no evidence and Lucy was a stickler for hard evidence.

Her parents took it all in however and whilst they were an easy sell having apparently lived with the Circle in their lives for decades, she was still getting her head around it. She was eager to get back with her friends to go through what happened and make some sense of it all.

Jake had indeed been to the doctor once he had finally crawled out of his pit and of course polished off a hearty breakfast. The prognosis was severe bruising and possible ligament damage but with appropriate physiotherapy there should be a full recovery. To be on the safe side he was provided with a single crutch to assist him and take some of the pressure off the leg.

It was late afternoon by the time all the friends got together again. Tom had commented how it looked like a doctor's reception room when he joined them. He was, however, pleased to see them all safe and smiling.

They spent the next hour or so recounting their own stories of the previous days' excitement. The stories getting more and more exaggerated the more they were retold. Details became blurred, heroics inflated, danger overstated. However, the group was keen to keep each one of them honest and no-one was allowed to embellish their version of events without severe ribbing from the rest of the group.

They were enjoying their moment and being back together in a safe environment. There was much more positivity around the group. It was if there had been a lifting of the heavy burden of their past lives, of the mental and in some cases physical pain of their early childhoods. As Tom looked around the group, he saw sincere smiles and laughter and for the first time really believed what he saw was not put on for show or masked inner turmoil. It made him think of his own childhood again and his parents. He had a sense that George held some of the answers to the questions he still had. It reminded him to check his phone to see if there had been any messages.

"Anything important?" Jake was peering over Tom's shoulder.

Tom edged away suddenly conscious that he was still not ready to share everything with the group. "Nothing," he abruptly responded.

"Alright, easy tiger," Jake joked.

"Sorry, still a bit jumpy," Tom added, realising he had reacted badly.

"No worries mate," Jake said, putting his arm around his best friend. Tom always felt uncomfortable with physical contact but had grown accustomed to Jake's tactile nature. He also understood where it came from and knew if he rejected it, it would have a damaging effect on Jake. Always over protective of his friend, he couldn't be responsible for that.

Tom needed to make his excuses, however. He had received a response and George was available to speak. He was not keen to discuss with the wider group at this stage but decided to confide in Jake to help him provide a cover story. He was prepared to take the risk that he would keep it secret from the others for now.

"Where are you off to?" Lucy asked as Tom got up to leave.

"Just got to pick up some bits for Mum. Won't be long," Tom explained.

Lucy was unconvinced. "We'll come with you," she suggested.

"Really? I can't keep hobbling around on this leg?" Jake chipped in. "He's a big boy now, I am sure he can cope on his own. Pick me up some biscuits," he demanded.

"I won't be long. Will be quicker on my own. You guys stay here and I'll bring stuff back with me. Any orders? Other than biscuits?" he asked.

Lucy agreed to let it go, but she made a promise to herself to quiz Tom later.

The friends put their orders in and Tom left, leaving them discussing how they took for granted their favourite sweets and drinks and how they would have missed them if they had got stuck in the US in the nineteen sixties.

+++

Tom had received a message to meet back at the old house and was standing on the corner of the road where they had stood as a group of friends the morning before they had left for Dallas. It seemed like a long time ago as he stared at the old house where it had all started.

Tom jumped suddenly as a hand came down on his shoulder.

"Whoa, only me." Tom turned to see George standing there, holding his hands up in apparent surrender. "Didn't mean to frighten you."

"Not frightened," Tom said defensively. "Just wasn't expecting it. Thought you would be in the house."

George smiled. "If you say so," he joked. "Needed to take a break. Fancy a coffee?"

"I'm not really a coffee drinker," Tom answered.

"I'm sure we can find something you will like," George insisted. "Let's walk and talk."

George then led Tom along the road to the local coffee shop which was fairly empty and would be easier to have a conversation. George nodded to the proprietor as he entered. "Usual for me please Greg," George called out.

"And for the young 'un?" Greg replied.

Tom looked around and noted a drinks chiller. He looked through the products on sale, selecting his beverage of choice. He felt there was something unusual about it but could not immediately ascertain what it was. He asked for a Coke. He continued to stare at the chiller trying to work out what was unusual. Then all of a sudden in dawned on him. There were no plastic bottles. Tom looked at George and then back to Greg. He wondered how many local people were part of the Golden Circle.

"Let's sit there," George said, pointing to a table in the corner.

Tom and George proceeded to the table and sat down.

"So, what can I help you with, Tom?" George asked.

Tom was taken aback by George's directness and apparent disinterest in the adventures they had just been on.

"Don't you want to hear about how it went?"

"Of course," George replied. "I just thought you had more pressing matters to discuss."

Tom thought for a moment and wondered whether he was subconsciously delaying asking the questions he had prepared on the way over. Before he could ask the first of those questions, Greg came over with the drinks. As you placed them on the table he turned to Tom, "Well done sonny. Nice job." And with that he turned and left to see to some other customers who had entered.

George noted the confused look on Tom's face. "I told you there were lots of us now. And we are all aware of the success you and your friends have had and the great job that you did for us all. But if you would like to talk through it, I am happy to listen."

Tom realised that whilst it had been a unique experience for him and his friends, George must have seen it all before on more than one occasion.

"I need to know more about my parents," Tom blurted. It had not been the way he had planned to raise the topic, but he was suddenly overcome with the need for answers.

George had expected the question ever since he had mentioned to Tom that he had known his parents.

"What do you want to know?" George asked in a vain attempt to delay the inevitable.

"How well did you know them?" Tom asked.

George paused, contemplating the best way to disclose what he knew. He knew enough of Tom to recognise that he could handle the truth. He was level-headed and bright, but what he was about to tell him could come as quick a shock. George decided that it was time.

"As well as any parent could."

The words hung in the air like fog on a damp and hazy morning. Tom stopped drinking from the can and slowly placed it back on the table. The cogs in his mind spinning, the information slowly processing and the message becoming clear as the fog began to lift. Tom looked up from the can and stared directly in to George's eyes. "Are you saying -," Tom stopped himself, not prepared to say the words in case they proved to be incorrect.

"Yes Tom, I am your grandfather."

+++

Tom had not spoken for several minutes. George had allowed the news to sink in and had dared not break the silence. Only Greg had made any attempt to converse, offering free buns. George had given him a look which suggested now was not the right time, but accepted the buns nonetheless. He was particularly fond of the one with the cherry on top. Tom, for his part, had too many questions and he was desperately trying to put them in some kind of sensible order within his head before directing them at George. Or should he say, "Gramps."

He finally spoke. "So, where have you been?"

"A tricky one to start," George light-heartedly began, only to realise the enormity of the news for Tom and that the conversation warranted a more serious approach. "Well I have been around. Watching over you if you like. I agreed that I would always do that, as long as I lived of course, if anything ever happened to your parents."

"But why didn't I know I had family?" Tom asked.

"We thought it best."

"We, who is we?" Tom demanded, annoyed that faceless individuals had been making decisions about his life.

"The senior members of the Circle, and your adoptive parents. It was felt that placing you with a normal family was the best course of action until the time was right. I thought it best to keep a distance until you had a chance to accept your fate. If it helps, I have never been far away. I have followed your life and seen you grown in to a well-grounded young man. It has given me immense pride. You are a credit to your adoptive family."

This riled Tom. "What do you mean, a credit to them. They have done nothing for me. I have basically been a glorified tenant in their home," his voice rising, attracting attention from the few other patrons.

"I understand," George tried to placate his grandson.

"Understand? You can't possibly understand," and with this Tom eyes began to moisten. He knew he was close to tears as the painful memories of abandonment hit home.

"You are probably not aware of the sacrifices they have made, so that you were kept safe. Of the pain that they have suffered in order to ensure that no unwanted interest came your way. Sometimes it is necessary to be cruel to be kind. Your adoptive mother continually pleaded with the Circle to allow her to tell you the truth; to be there to comfort you. It was always declined. Your anonymity had to be respected and protected at all costs."

Tom shook his head, not believing what he was hearing. He couldn't, he wouldn't believe it. He had lost his parents and his childhood all because a group of stuffy old man and women had decided that it was for the best. "The best for who?" he thought.

George decided Tom was best left with his own thoughts for a few minutes and announced that he was going to use the toilet.

Tom sat there, staring at the can on the table in front of him. The condensation dripping down the side, mirroring the tears that he felt sliding down his face. Tom reflected on the rollercoaster of emotions that he had experienced in the last few days and was continuing to experience.

The bell on the door chimed as further customers entered. Tom looked round and had an urge to run out the door and far away. He resisted the urge however, deciding instead to remain and search for more answers.

"How is he taking it?" Greg asked George as he returned from the toilet.

"As well as can be expected. It's a lot to take in."

"Poor lad. Must be a bit of a shock, finding out about his parents," Greg added.

"Oh, we haven't got to that bit yet," George confessed. "Just told him about me so far."

261

"Oh blimey," Greg exclaimed. "I'll get the next round of drinks ready."

George wandered back to the table and sat down. Tom did not raise his head but continued staring at the coke can. George took a deep breath. "There is something else you need to know," he started. Tom looked up, his eyes red and full of expectation for the next round of revelations. "It's about your parents." Tom's eyes widened in anticipation.

"They are not dead, just missing." George paused to give Tom a moment to process the news.

Tom didn't move. He didn't say anything. He just cried.

+++

Lucy approached Jake, leaving Michael and Rhianna to have another sibling rivalry discussion. "So, where has Tom really gone?" she asked.

"What do you mean?" Jake feigning ignorance.

"You know what I mean. I didn't believe that rubbish story about getting shopping for his Mum. You told me his mum had been to the shops this morning and that your mum had spoken to her."

Jake realised he had been rumbled and was now desperate to come up with a plausible explanation. The time it was taking was evidence enough for Lucy. "See, so come on, what's going on?" she demanded.

"Look I don't know for sure, honest," he said dishonestly. "But I think he has just gone to find out what happens now."

Lucy remained unconvinced, sensing that the redness appearing in Jake's face meant that he knew more than he was letting on. "And?" she persisted.

"And what? That's it," he spluttered.

"No, there is more to this. Spit it out, now," she insisted even more vehemently.

"Ok, ok. Keep it down," Jake peered over to Michael and Rhianna who were deep in conversation about who had made the most contribution to the success of the mission.

"He doesn't want everyone to know. He thinks there may be able to find out something about his parents," Jake whispered.

"How?" Lucy said, rather too loudly for Jake's liking.

"Shhhh," he hissed, looking around again. "He has gone to see George. Apparently, George mentioned he had known his parents. Tom thinks there may be more to it."

Lucy was surprised. "You don't think he is getting his hopes up do you? He's always had a problem with his adoption, not being able to settle in to it as well as the rest of us. You don't think he believes they are still alive, do you?"

"No idea. I think he believes they are dead; I just think he wants to know more about them," Jake said trying to convince himself as well as Lucy.

"I think we should go and find him," Lucy went to stand up but Jake put his hand on her shoulder.

"I think it is best to leave him to it. He knows where we are if he needs to talk."

+++

Tom needed to talk, but no words would come out of his mouth. George looked on, wondering how long he should leave it before he spoke again.

"I don't understand," Tom said shaking his head, struggling to comprehend what he had just been told. "I mean, I had always wondered but why was I always told they were dead?"

George composed himself for the inevitable barrage of questions. "It was easier. Until we knew you could understand the work of the Circle, there was no way you would grasp the possibility that your parents may be stuck somewhere in another time and place."

"You could have told me when you told me you knew them," Tom said.

"It was too big a risk. We needed your focus on the job at hand," George explained. "It's what your parents would have wanted. They would not have wanted you to risk your life worrying about them."

Tom reflected on this for a moment. His feelings conflicted and his mind was all over the place. He recognised that the news would have distracted him, but he was angry to have been misled all these years. Angry at his adoptive parents, angry at this man in front of him who he had known for just a few days but turned out to be his blood family.

Angry at the world for taking his parents away from him. But as he pondered further, his anger was slowly being dissipated, for now there was real hope. Hope of finding his real parents.

"So, where are they? My parents? What happened to them?", Tom fired off more questions.

"It's easier to explain now that you have experienced the work of the Circle first hand, but you should be prepared that not everything is clear to us," George began. "Like you, your parents were part of a small group of friends which travelled as part of the Circle to protect humanity. There was a risk that we had identified in Illinois, that's in the United States that needed addressing. Ideally once individuals have families of their own, we discourage them from continuing to travel but your parents understood the significance of this particular episode and they insisted on going. On this particular occasion however, they failed to return. We hoped that they had just missed the window and started to work on trying to identify when another window might open. This always depends on a number of things being in parallel at the same time, so it is possible to calculate but there are no guarantees. We have to look at historic events, the alignment of the planets and constellations, times, dates-"

Tom interrupted, "I get it, go on."

George irked, but tolerating Tom's rudeness, resumed his narrative. "There was always the possibility that they were dead. Not until we developed the technology to track DNA through the multiverse did we have any idea that they were still alive."

"Well can't you communicate with them?" Tom asked anxiously.

"Unfortunately, we are still working on that," George reluctantly admitted. "We can't currently communicate cross-universe or through time."

Tom's head dropped as the realisation hit him that as quickly as hope had risen that he may be reunited with his parents, so that hope was being dashed.

"Look, we are always working hard to find them. Technology is always moving on and we never give up, but you must understand that at the moment there is not much we can do. If we find a window to the same time and place, then we will immediately send a team to extract them. I'm sorry Tom that I don't have better news for you."

"I need some time," Tom announced rising from his seat. He left the coffee shop.

+++

Tom wandered the streets for the next hour, the information whirling around in his brain. He knew there was nothing he could do and wondered whether it would have been better to never know. As far as he was concerned it was as if they were dead to him. But he couldn't help but hold on to the small possibility that he may see them again, no matter how remote that possibility was.

He continued with these thoughts until he returned to his friends.

"So where is the grub?" Jake reminded Tom with a wink.

Tom looked down at his empty hands. "Oh, err I forgot," he murmured.

Rhianna was not impressed and made sure he knew. "Well you go off for hours and we have to wait here hungry. We could have gone ourselves but-"

Tom cut her off in her stride yelling, "It's not all about you, you know."

Shocked, Rhianna stood open mouthed at the outburst. Tom had always been the placid one. Collectively the friends knew immediately that something was not right.

Lucy moved, putting her arm around Tom. "What is it?" she asked.

Tom stayed quiet for a few moments before making eye contact. Lucy immediately noticed the redness around his eyes. "What is it?" she repeated, concern entering her voice.

"It's my parents," Tom responded, breaking down in more tears.

The group gathered together around Tom and all hugged.

EPILOGUE

Jack Ruby was found guilty of the murder of Lee Harvey Oswald and was sentenced to death. He was granted an appeal and a new trial, but before this could take place, he became ill and died in his prison cell on January 3, 1967.

No-one was ever convicted for the assassination of John F. Kennedy. The official Warren Commission report of 1964 concluded that neither Oswald nor Ruby were part of a larger conspiracy, either domestic or international, to assassinate President Kennedy. However, conspiracy theories persisted and in 1978 the House Select Committee on Assassinations concluded in a preliminary report that Kennedy was "probably assassinated as a result of a conspiracy" that may have involved multiple shooters and organised crime. The committee's findings and those of the

Warren Commission continue to be widely debated and disputed. All, however, are silent on the role played by five children from the UK.

The friends met every day over the next few weeks. Enjoying each other's company, recounting stories, sharing jokes and getting up to the occasional mischief. Rhianna was spending more time with the group than her own friends which Michael gave the impression he was unhappy about but secretly appreciated. Lucy enjoyed having another girl in the group, although she was not quite ready to lose her tomboy appearance despite Rhianna's best efforts to influence her clothing and make-up. Jake was delighted to see more of Rhianna and was more than happy to accept the ribbing from the rest of the group. Tom was recovering from the devastating news of his parents and was slowly coming to terms with it. He had spent a fair amount of time with his 'new' family and most of his anger had gone. He continued to have hope.

ABOUT THE AUTHOR

Rich Kerner considers himself more of a compliance officer
than writer as he enjoys his first foray into the literary
world. Father of two, husband of one, were it not for the
passage of time and a lack of natural talent, Rich would
have been Liverpool's number 9 or England's leg spinning
all-rounder. An interest in history and conspiracy theories
has driven him to write this book, which he hopes will be
the first of a series.

Printed in Poland
by Amazon Fulfillment
Poland Sp. z o.o., Wrocław